A FATAL LEGACY

Charlotte Vassell studied history at the University of Liverpool and completed a Master's in art history at SOAS, University of London, before training as an actor at Drama Studio London.

The Other Half, the first instalment of her DI Caius Beauchamp series was published in 2023. Charlotte won the Edgar Allen Poe Award for Best Novel in 2025 for *The In Crowd*, the second volume in the series.

Also by Charlotte Vassell

THE OTHER HALF
THE IN CROWD
A DEADLY INHERITANCE

A FATAL LEGACY

CHARLOTTE VASSELL

faber

First published in 2026
by Faber & Faber Ltd
The Bindery, 51 Hatton Garden
London EC1N 8HN

Typeset by Typo•glyphix, Burton-on-Trent DE14 3HE
Printed and bound by CPI Group (UK) Ltd, Croydon CR0 4YY

A CIP record for this book
is available from the British Library

ISBN 978–0–571–39049–6

Printed and bound in the UK on FSC® certified paper in line with our continuing
commitment to ethical business practices, sustainability and the environment.
For further information see faber.co.uk/environmental-policy

Our authorised representative in the EU for product safety is
Easy Access System Europe, Mustamäe tee 50, 10621 Tallinn, Estonia
gpsr.requests@easproject.com

2 4 6 8 10 9 7 5 3 1

All shall be well, and all shall be well,
and all manner of thing shall be well.

Julian of Norwich

Characters

DI Caius Beauchamp and family

An Irish-Jamaican detective in the Met, CAIUS is a foodie with a mortal fear of scurvy. He lives in a family-owned flat in North London with his girlfriend Callie where he loves nothing better than curling up with a good book. Feeling duty-bound, Caius joined the Met after the unsolved disappearance of his sister Lydia and is surprised he's still there. He is the son of pragmatic Jamaican-British builder MARCUS BEAUCHAMP and BRIDGET BEAUCHAMP who is from an Irish family but raised in London. Last year, some complicated inheritance Tetris meant that Caius's late grandfather, the Jamaican son of a second son, inherited a baronetcy from the single worst man Caius had ever come across, Rupert Hampton, formerly Sir Rupert Beauchamp. Caius is working through his feelings over his family's change in fortune. He broke his wrist a couple of months ago and is itching to have the cast removed.

Calliope (Callie) Foster

CALLIE, a semi-posh English rose with a whimsical streak, is a milliner by trade. She recently discovered that she is the illegitimate daughter of the disgraced MP and fast-fashion tycoon Peter Simpson. Callie met Caius on the front row of a fringe theatre when an actor threw up on an audience member, who was then discovered to be already deceased. She moved into Caius's rather cramped bachelor pad last year.

DS Matthew Cheung
MATT is a thoughtful detective and Caius's wingman. They are genuine friends and seek out niche craft ales together.

DC Amy Noakes
AMY is a quick-witted and intuitive detective constable, with a talent for rugby tackling creeps. She lives with her girlfriend Fi and their furbabies.

The Rt Hon. Lord Arthur Hampton Member of Parliament for South Rutland
The 17th Duke of Shropshire, Arthur Hampton, is a former Cabinet member who keeps an exceedingly low profile, despite his role as political kingmaker.

A FATAL LEGACY

A FRIDAY IN MAY

1

The Horatio Combe Institute, Priory Square, Camden

Digby Combe-Watson is sprawled out on the antique rug apocryphally gifted to his great-great-great-grandfather in 1849 by an appreciative Naser al-Din, the then Shah of Iran, while he followed in the marauding footsteps of Alexander the Great across Central Asia and made merry with the ruins of Persepolis. For what the Shah was so grateful no one knew and it was glossed over with a knowing nod during infrequent tours. It had in fact been purchased down Portobello Road to hide an ugly port stain on the floorboard in 1927, but this fact was now lost to the vagaries of time. Besides, the rug made a great jumping-off point for Digby to talk about the six as-yet-untranslated cuneiform tablets the museum had on the second floor.

Digby can't feel his toes. Oh dear. It's all happening so quickly.

Digby was taken by surprise. He'd thought better of himself. He'd thought too much, frankly, and Digby hadn't ever stopped to consider that this little tête-à-tête wasn't the best idea. He was a man, after all, and cardinal rules like meet in a public place applied to only women. He hadn't realised that he was in danger. Why would he? Why would a man like him ever be in danger? Who could ever want to possibly harm a soft-bodied intellectual like him? A gentle soul who had only cared about the pursuit of knowledge, and of the preservation and re-evaluation of history, and was only now humbly reaching out for something more for himself.

Digby can't feel his legs. The coldness, the frozen hand of death, is moving up his body inch by mortal inch.

Digby fleetingly glances around, hoping desperately that this was an accident and that help is on the way, but he knows this was done to him on purpose, that it had been planned. He catches a cold steely eye lazily gazing back at him, and he knows that help isn't coming and he is about to die surrounded here by the morbidity of his odious ancestor. Horatio Combe's shrine to his obsessions. The relics of an exhilarating life led galivanting all over the empire collecting whatever and whoever took his fancy, whereas he has spent his short life paying homage to those seedy adventures from a decrepit town house in NW1.

Digby's throat is beginning to close. He turns his head as he struggles to breathe. The shrunken heads watch from their cabinet as his heart stops.

SATURDAY

2

The Horatio Combe Institute, Priory Square, Camden

The magnolia trees in the centre of the square were blooming. Curved petals tinged with pink grasping at the sky like desperate fingers trying to touch the clouds. Their heady scent pervaded the air. A plume of dust went up from across the way as debris was chucked into a skip parked outside one of the town houses. Another renovation. Another kitchen extension. Another basement being dug out.

'You have two minutes to say whatever you want,' Caius said. Yesterday his girlfriend Callie had filmed a live segment for the BBC's RHS Chelsea Flower Show coverage with Monty Don. Her pathetic ex Max happened to be there on a corporate jolly and had barged in, slurred a half-arsed proposal and then started a fight with Caius who, despite having a cast on his wrist, dealt with him swiftly. All of this had been caught on camera and was now doing the rounds on the internet. Caius started the timer on his phone. 'And then it won't be mentioned again.'

'I'll go first,' Amy said quickly, jumping in ahead of Matt. 'Firstly, you looked stellar.'

'Great shirt, mate,' Matt said.

'Thanks. My mum came too and she kept calling me "your man from Havana".' Caius tried to do his best poker face but he was pleased with the praise. He'd dressed up for the occasion and had been wearing a short-sleeved, deep-aquamarine Sea Island cotton shirt, a pair of toffee biscuit-coloured linen trousers and a pair of soft suede coffee loafers that he had to clean when he got home after he'd chucked Max into a flowerbed.

'Secondly, Monty Don, what a man,' Amy said, reverentially.

'A consummate professional,' Matt said, nodding. 'I hope the BBC pays him well. I don't mind him getting six figures.'

'Thirdly, are you aware that you've become a meme?' Amy said.

'What do you mean?' Caius asked.

'You know, they use an image and write funny text on it. It goes viral. Your face becomes internet famous and used for social and cultural clout.'

'Amy, I'm thirty-five not eighty-five,' Caius said, staring at the sky. 'What sort of memes?'

Amy took her phone out. She'd been saving the funnier ones. 'It's you corralling Callie's ex. My favourites so far are of the "not today, Satan" variety but there's a collective swoon going on amongst the gays and the girlies.'

'Right.' Caius hoped the internet would move on quickly. 'Anything else you've got to say?'

'Callie OK?' Matt asked.

'Dick move from her ex,' Amy said.

'Callie's fine, now. There was a bit of a kerfuffle after.'

'A kerfuffle?' Matt asked.

'Once the cameras stopped my mum had to hold her back from Max. She'd taken her shoe off and was going to hit him. Mum calmed her down by saying they were too pretty to risk damaging.'

'At least Max didn't challenge you to a duel,' Amy said.

'I'd have been happy to be your second,' Matt said.

'Good to know for next time. Callie's dad's solicitor is going to send Max a cease and desist letter.' Caius shuffled about uncomfortably. 'I feel like I ruined her big moment.'

'It was her ex not you. He jumped in front of the camera,' Matt said.

The alarm on Caius's phone went off. 'Time's up. We're going to never mention the incident again.' He ducked under the police tape, nodding to the uniformed officer standing out front. 'Right, male, mid-thirties. His name is Digby Combe-Watson and he was the owner-curator of this little museum of horrors.' He gestured up to the house.

'The Horatio Combe Institute,' Matt said, reading the sign outside the town house. The building looked shabby. The paint was beginning to peel off around the wooden window frames. 'Never heard of it.'

'It's an anthropological nightmare,' Caius said, leading them up the stairs. 'Horatio Combe was one of those Victorian adventurer types. Liked collecting artefacts, and taxidermy of exotic creatures. There's a mangy-looking kangaroo at the top of the stairs. Uniform are already canvassing the square in case anyone saw anything.'

They entered the musty hallway. A wooden collection box was nailed to the wall: '10 shillings entrance fee' was written in gold paint on the front. Amy checked inside. It was empty. Wearing gloves, she picked up a guide to the house and its contents from the small table next to the box.

'He's in here,' Caius said, leading them into the parlour. Forensics were busy crawling over the room.

Barry, the team's favourite medical examiner, was zipping up the body bag. 'Morning, morning, morning.'

'What did for him?' Caius asked, with an Ealing comedy affectation.

'Hemlock,' Barry said.

'Really?' Matt asked, peering at the corpse. 'That's such an old-school way to go. Like Socrates. Old symposium.'

'How can you tell?' Caius asked, shaking his head at Matt's poor joke.

'I can smell it,' Barry said, pointing to the salad bowl in the middle of the table that was being bagged up by forensics. 'Hemlock is a member of the carrot family and it's easy to confuse its leaves with carrot tops, parsley or dill. It stinks though. It's a bit like a mouse infestation or rotting parsnips. Musty. I go foraging on the weekends and know to avoid it.'

'Foraging.' Caius nodded. He could picture Barry scampering through the hedgerows looking for blackberries. It was probably quite relaxing. 'If you could smell the hemlock, why couldn't he?'

'Mr Combe-Watson had an open pack of tissues in one pocket and a packet of menthol cough sweets in the other,' Barry said.

'He was probably used to the smell of mouse pee,' Amy said, wrinkling her nose.

'I'll run the requisite tests, but I don't think there'll be any surprises,' Barry said, and with that the body was removed by two forensic technicians. 'By the looks of him he died in the early evening. I'd say somewhere between 7 and 9 p.m.'

'Dinner time. The table was set for two,' Caius said, looking at the arrangements – a small vase of flowers in the middle, candlesticks that had been left to burn leaving nothing but globular streams of now-cooled wax down the brass candlestick holders, a jug of water in which any trace of ice had dissolved and an open bottle of red wine that had been breathing all night. 'The same salad on both plates.'

'The other person filled up on bread,' Amy said, noting that there was a roll on Digby's side plate and just crumbs on his guest's. 'It's a fancy one too with poppy seeds in a swirl.'

'Is this a romantic set-up? It looks like it should be and yet I've got the heebies,' Matt said. He wandered over to a cabinet of what he thought were doll heads. 'What the hell are those?'

'Those are,' Amy said, flicking through the guide she'd picked up as she'd entered the Institute. 'Those are mokomokai. Oh boy.'

'What are mokomokai?' Caius asked.

'It says here that they're shrunken human heads from New Zealand.'

'How did old Horatio get those?' Caius asked, turning away from them and back to the table. 'Matt, you think this wasn't romantic?'

'It was candlelit,' Matt said, looking about the room. 'Although I can't see a light switch in here so that may have been a necessity.'

'Digby didn't live here.' Caius grimaced. How anyone could have possibly ever lived here amongst all this was a mystery. 'The whole house is his great-whatever-grandad's stuff. It might not have been a date. A work thing, maybe? A trustee for the museum? A donor?'

'It's not the most romantic setting.' Matt stared down at the battered rug on the floor.

'Who found him?' Amy asked.

'Willow Bell, she's a history student at King's College and interns on Saturdays,' Caius said, checking his notes. 'Came in to do her shift and found him like this. The front door to the museum was unusually left open and she just walked straight in. She's on her way to the station for a cup of tea and a formal interview. I'm going to head over in a minute.'

'No security?' Matt asked, scouting the room for the usual systems but not finding any.

'Nope,' Caius said. 'No cameras, or alarms, nothing. Just a lock with a key.'

'Anything worth nicking?' Amy asked. Everything looked tatty to her.

'That's the question, isn't it? I suppose if there was anything with a high value here then their insurers would've made them take precautions. Their security measures are non-existent,' Caius said, receiving the guide from Amy. 'There's two floors of exhibits and the attic contains Horatio Combe's library.'

Caius led them through a doorway into a small back room, not much more than a glorified broom cupboard, that appeared to be Digby's office. On his desk was a box of Lemsip, a congealed rotisserie chicken on a plate and two slices of Basque cheesecake. A forensic technician was busy taking them away for testing. 'Amy, once forensics are finished in here, I need you to have a look through his papers.'

'Sure.'

Caius turned to the forensic technician. 'Sorry to interrupt, has the victim's phone been found?'

'Not yet, sir,' the masked figure replied, carting away the chicken and cheesecake.

'Just call me Caius.'

Amy started poking around Digby's office.

'Matt,' Caius said, leading him back into the main room. 'Get a feel for the building's layout. I think it's likely Digby's killer came in and out through the open front door but try and work out if there are any other options. I'm going to—'

Caius stopped abruptly, stared in confusion at Matt and then moved towards the window where the commotion was coming from.

'Is that a haka?' Matt asked as he followed after him. He didn't think there was any rugby on that day.

Caius and Matt left the house to find a group of three Māoris with placards protesting outside.

Caius showed them his badge. 'May I ask what you are protesting?'

'The Horatio Combe Institute has refused multiple requests from our government to return human remains unethically kept here to Aoteara,' said one of the group.

'The mokomokai,' Matt said.

'Yes,' said a second.

The group introduced themselves as Kahurangi, Tākuta and Rawiri.

'Do you protest here every day?' Caius asked.

'No. We have jobs so . . .' said Rawiri.

'Just on Saturday mornings. I take my son to his swimming class in the afternoon,' said Kahurangi. 'I'm busy in the week. I'm a nurse in a GP practice in Kingston.'

'And you guys?' Matt asked the others.

'I work in a bank in the City full-time,' said Rawiri.

'I lecture in physics at UCL,' said Tākuta.

Caius turned to Matt and then back to the protestors. 'Did you have any dealings with the Institute's staff much?'

'That sickly-looking man?' asked Rawiri.

Caius showed them Digby's picture taken from the Institute's website. 'This guy.'

'He finally got you lot to come out then,' said Rawiri.

'What do you mean?' Caius asked.

'A couple of months ago he threatened to call the police on us because we were upsetting his visitors,' said Kahurangi.

'What visitors? We've been here every Saturday morning for the last three months, and not a soul,' said Tākuta.

'Only that nice girl who winks at us when she goes on her break,' said Rawiri.

'She signed our petition.' Tākuta handed it over to Caius.

'Sorry,' he said, handing it back. 'Would you all mind answering a few of my colleague here's questions?'

'Why?' Kahurangi asked.

'Digby Combe-Watson is dead.'

★　★　★

'The protestors alibied each other. They were talking strategy in the Covent Garden Wagamama,' Matt said, finding Caius in the hallway. He'd entered the property from the alleyway behind. 'They'd decided on a letter-writing campaign. Apparently, the mokomokai were preserved as a way to honour their ancestors by showcasing their tattoos which have specific meanings attached to them. They were kept in special ceremonial spaces, but once the British arrived they started buying them as curiosities and it all gets a bit grim.'

'What did you think of the protestors?'

'They were pretty chill. No real motive.'

Caius nodded.

'Digby's keys for the building, and presumably his house, were in a drawer in his desk. Forensics have been at them already,' Matt said, holding up a clear plastic bag. 'No car keys, but there is a very battered-looking bike splayed across the path in the overgrown back garden. I guess he comes in along the alleyway down the back and dumps his wheels. The back door and the gate were both unlocked.'

'What's the alleyway like?' Caius asked, taking the keys from Matt.

'Everyone keeps their bins there,' Matt said, remembering the smell of rotting bin juice. One bin was overflowing with ripe nappies maturing in the heat. 'You could get in and out unnoticed.'

'Any cameras?'

'Not that I could see,' Matt said, shaking his head. 'I did see a couple of houses that had them but none of them were watching the alley. They were in the gardens pointing towards the gates. They'd need planning permission to film a public right of way.'

'There's a chance that Digby's dinner guest came and left round the back then.'

'The alleyway leads onto the main road. There's a playground opposite, so no visual on the entrance.'

'Let's see what forensics find and bear it in mind.' Caius looked at the table. 'Date or business?'

'Gut says business; it's too creepy in here. Unless he's chasing after the goths. I mean, it is Camden, after all.'

'Do goths still exist?'

'I don't know. I can't remember the last time I saw one. Teenagers all look the same these days.'

'Everyone seems to wear all-black clothing but they don't care about The Cure.'

'I hope there are still goths out there. What are teenagers with a lot of emotions supposed to do otherwise? They need a safe outlet for all their little sad weird feelings.'

Caius looked at him.

'What?' Matt shuffled around on the spot, suddenly a teenager under scrutiny again. 'I wasn't a goth. I was a scene kid. I was too cool to even be an emo, and I doubt my mum would've let me.'

'My first girlfriend when I was fifteen was an emo. She dumped me for a guy called Dan who plastered his hair to one side of his head. I walked past him in King's Cross a few years ago and he was balding but he still had the same haircut. It was a geriatric emo comb-over.'

'Rawr.'

'I nearly got a tattoo of a moustache on my finger in 2006.' Caius looked at the keys in his hand. 'Digby's place is in Dollis Hill. We need to get over there today.'

Amy came down the stairs. 'Do you ever play that game when you're in a museum where you have to pick one thing you'd nick if you could get away with it? The only rule being that you have to be able to carry it home on your own.'

'Ah, so how the British Museum got most of its collection then,' Matt said.

'You couldn't get the Parthenon marbles on the tube,' Caius said.

'Have you tried already?' Matt asked.

Caius turned to Amy. 'And what would you take from here?'

'Nothing. Nada. Zilch. The glass eyes on the kangaroo on the mezzanine are crooked and the poor beast is cross-eyed.' Amy shook her head. 'I've gone through the whole visitor guide. You have to assume the items included as collection highlights are important or valuable,' she said, fanning herself with the booklet. The room was airless. 'Everything mentioned in it is still here. Nothing obvious has been taken.'

'Amy, did you find a collection catalogue of some kind in Digby's office?' Caius asked, staring around the room.

'There's a ledger in the attic "library".'

'Great, go through it and just check that everything's here, not just the highlights. I'll assign a uniformed officer to help.' He glanced around at the junk in front of him, then he noticed a door under the stairs. 'Amy, have you been down here yet?' Caius walked over and twisted the handle. It wouldn't budge.

'I didn't try it. Someone's painted the door shut,' Amy said.

'It's a town house. The kitchen and the pantry should be down there.' Caius looked at the paintwork along the door. It looked like someone had tried it and judging by the flecks of paint on the floor, recently too. 'Matt, ask forensics to give the door a proper once over.'

Caius took the keys to the Institute out of his pocket. He went down the steps to the square and again down through the iron gate, then down the basement steps. A heavy brass key fit the lock but again he couldn't get the door to budge.

'The door's been painted shut here too.' Caius called up the stairs to Amy. He traipsed back up the stone steps and up to street level. 'If we can't get in then the killer couldn't either.'

'To Dollis Hill?' Matt asked, unlocking his police car.

'Station first,' Caius said, turning quickly towards the car and straight into a young woman. She fell backwards and he caught her. He used his dodgy arm. It twinged a little – hopefully from underusage and not from further damage. He froze as he held her, as if he had been caught in the act. 'God, I'm so sorry.'

'No, it's all right,' she said, catching her breath. Caius was still holding her. She was the second most beautiful woman he'd seen that day. He released her gently.

'Sorry, again.' He swallowed hard as he took a good look at her but turned away quickly, determined to forget that he'd had his hands round her waist. 'So sorry.'

'Have we met before?' she asked as she straightened herself up, flicking imaginary dust off her shoulder and rearranging her shirt. She was flaxen-haired, although it was tied up into a messy bun at the back of her head and a plain black baseball cap was pulled close over her eyes. Nothing about her drew your casual attention. Her clothes were baggy and dull-coloured. But a spark, a curious flame in her eyes that peeked out from under the cap burnt bright.

'No sorry, I just have one of those faces.' Caius felt awkward. He assumed she recognised him from the damn memes of his stupid performance at Chelsea.

'No, we've met. I'm sure we have.'

'I don't think so . . .'

'I guess you really must have one of those faces.' She went as if to say something else but was suddenly compelled into silence. She shook herself out of her stupor. 'Are you police?'

'Yes. DI Caius Beauchamp.' He straightened himself up. 'There's been a death.'

'Oh, I see. How terrible.'

'Do you live, um, locally?'

'I do. I don't know anything about it though I'm afraid.'

'Right.' Caius felt colour rush up to his cheeks.

The flaxen-haired woman stared at Caius for a moment, smiled coyly and then moved on. She turned and looked over her shoulder as Caius watched her. He blushed.

'Excuse me.' A woman carrying a small dog stood in between him and the girl as she disappeared into the ether. 'What's happened? I've seen all the vans parked all over the square this morning.'

'There's been a death.'

'Oh my goodness. This has always been such a safe area.'

'Do you live on the square?'

'I live next door to the museum thingy.' She glanced, possibly with disapproval, at the building.

Caius looked at the woman who was holding a coffee cup with a little frog or something stamped onto it. She had ashy highlighted hair that she'd pulled back into a tight pony tail. Her face was perfectly smooth and unnaturally unmoving. He thought she was probably concerned. She was wearing a matching mauve bralette and leggings workout set. 'My colleague here would love to ask you a few questions, Miss . . .'

'Mrs, bless you, Mrs Bourne. Did you hear that, Halloumi. The handsome police officer thought Mummy was eighteen.'

Caius glanced up at Amy. 'DC Noakes here will ask you a few questions about yesterday evening.'

'Hi there,' Amy said, getting out her notebook as she came down the steps towards Mrs Bourne.

'Excuse me.' Caius joined Matt in the car.

The flaxen-haired young woman Caius had discourteously collided with peeked out from behind one of the magnolia trees in the garden in the square. She watched him leave, hoping he'd return.

3

The Police Station

Caius put a plate of digestive biscuits down in front of poor Willow Bell, the Institute's intern who had found the body. She was a small, neat young woman wearing a ruby-red cardigan covered in brooches of all sorts – shields, flowers, gemstones – over an oversized white shirt and a pair of baggy black jeans. Willow picked up a biscuit, held it with both hands and nibbled it like a mouse. Her dark hair was cropped into a sharp, angular bob and she wore no obvious make-up other than bright red lipstick. Caius stated their names for the recording.

'Please describe this morning for me, Willow,' Caius said.

'Sure,' she said, placing the partially nibbled biscuit down. 'I turned up at the Institute at 8.45 a.m. like I normally do. The door was left open, which was a bit odd, and I just walked in.'

'Was the door not normally open?'

'No. I usually had to ring the bell and wait to be let in. Mr Combe-Watson was very particular about that. I rang and I rang but Mr Combe-Watson didn't come to the door.' She tucked her hair behind her ear. 'Then I noticed it was slightly ajar anyway so I walked in. I turned into the first room and there he was on the floor.'

'Were you aware of anyone else in the house?'

'Like a presence?' she asked, touching the tarot card pendant on her necklace. 'There's something eerie about that building.'

'No, like a living person.'

'No,' she said, slightly deflated. 'I don't think anyone else was there. Or at least I didn't hear or see anyone.'

'When was the last time you saw Digby alive?'

'Yesterday, actually. I popped in in the early afternoon. I'd accidentally left a book I needed to complete an essay there last week.' She leaned in conspiratorially. 'If it's quiet I get on and do my reading for uni.'

'How did he seem?'

'Pretty cheerful, actually. I hadn't seen him look that content in a while. It's comforting to think that the day he died was a good one.'

'What time was this?'

'About 3 p.m., I guess. Hang on.' Willow took out her phone and scrolled for a moment before showing Caius what she'd found. 'My phone says I tapped back into Chalk Farm at 3.24 p.m. It's ten minutes' walk so 3.15 p.m., I guess.'

Caius nodded. That would be easy to verify. 'Did you notice anything unusual?'

'No, I don't think so. It was a flying visit.'

'Did you see anyone loitering outside?'

'No.'

'Were you aware of Digby having any personal problems? Any fallings out with family or friends? The neighbours?'

'No, sorry. He wasn't chatty like that anyway, but that just doesn't chime with what I knew about his personality. Mr Combe-Watson was a very studious man. He was a historian. Quite a serious "chap". He didn't have dramatic fallings out with anyone.'

'Did he insist you called him Mr Combe-Watson and not Digby?' Caius was curious about this old-fashioned habit.

'Oh yeah,' Willow said, fighting the habitual urge to roll her eyes. He was dead, after all.

'What exactly do you do at the Institute? What are your responsibilities there.'

'I volunteer, no, I intern, on Saturdays.' She leaned in. 'I say I'm the intern rather than a volunteer, because it'll sound better on my CV when I graduate in July.'

'And what does interning entail?'

'I was supposed to do tours of the museum. Sorry, Institute. I'm not supposed to call it a museum, it's an institute for the further study of something or another. Not that they get many visitors, just the odd weirdo.'

'Supposed to? I take it you don't do tours often. What do you do now?'

'I guess, I'm Mr Combe-Watson's research assistant.'

'Right.' Caius could see her changing her LinkedIn profile in her head now there was no one to verify that with.

'What did you do as his research assistant?'

'A lot of admin tasks,' Willow said off-handedly.

'Like?' Caius noticed that she was reluctant to elaborate. He assumed it was because she thought she was better than such lowly work.

'The filing. He did everything on paper. I was updating the little booklet that would be handed out to visitors. I did the odd thing on the website while at home for him too. Pretty boring.'

'Did you do any actual research?' Caius realised once that had left his mouth that it came across ruder than he meant it to, but as she was clearly going to upgrade her title to research assistant he thought he should ask. He tried to pull it back – he smiled and everything. 'That just seems like a waste of a promising museum professional's talent.'

'Well, I urgh, I was typing up Horatio Combe's journals,' Willow volunteered, but then looked like she regretted it. She started talking quickly. 'There are all these volumes of the damn things. They're all handwritten. Spidery writing. It takes forever because it's so hard to read. Horatio Combe would be in prison for vandalism if he was alive today. He was a womaniser too. I transcribed a diary entry last month where he blithely described chiselling a bit of a Roman villa off in Pompei, pocketing it and then visiting his favourite Neapolitan brothel. It's on the first floor in case you wanted to see it. He wasn't a good person by any stretch and a very poor storyteller, for that matter.'

'Why were you typing it up?' Caius thought the journals sounded like a liability to the Institute's reputation.

'Because I was asked to.' She shrugged.

Caius wouldn't bother asking why if he was working for free either. 'What was Mr Combe-Watson like as a boss? How did he treat you?'

'Mr Combe-Watson treated me fine. He was tight though. Very tight. He'd only pay my travel expenses. I'd seen him eat yoghurt that had been expired for a month.' Willow wrinkled her nose at the thought of gone-off milk being too off. 'Oddly, though, he was fussy. I always thought it was funny for those two characteristics to be joined in one person like that. He was very pernickety. Liked things to be exactly how he wanted them. Not that he always told you how he wanted things. I had to develop telepathy. He was antiquated, if you know what I mean. Being surrounded by all that stuff all the time had seeped into him and made him part of the past. That moustache for starters. Digby wasn't even that old. Yeah, he was born in the 1980s but that's not too old to have an email address. When I said I was looking for an internship, my mum made me write to all the little museums in London and send my CV in – she wouldn't accept that that wasn't how it worked any more and I did it to get her off my back. He was the only one who bit. He wrote to offer me the position. The whole thing was arranged by letter.'

'Didn't he call you at least?'

'Nope. Actually, I don't think I ever saw him with a phone. All his amusement came from magazines.' Willow looked up at Caius and bit her lip. 'Digby liked reading things like *Private Eye, The Cutter* or the *London Review of Books*. Very highbrow.'

'At one time did you call him Digby?' Caius noticed she'd reverted to his first name briefly.

'When I first started, he was all "call me Digby". We went to the pub after a Saturday shift and I mentioned my boyfriend at the time and that was it – Mr Combe-Watson forever on.'

'I see.'

'I guess he was lonely. Lonely and trapped. I won't miss that place. It has a funny energy.' She touched her tarot card necklace again. 'Sad though. Poor Digby.'

'Did Digby have a partner?' Willow's description made it sound unlikely.

'I don't know. He wasn't the sort to tell you much about himself.'

'So, he didn't mention going on a date? Or meeting anyone recently?'

'Nope.' Willow flushed a little. Caius wasn't sure what to make of her. She was both fond of and irritated by Digby. Maybe she'd spent their acquaintance thinking of him as a bit of a comic figure and was now struggling with the reality of the tragedy he'd become.

'I heard you signed the petition to return the mokomokai.'

'I did.' Willow nodded proudly. 'I don't get why Digby, Mr Combe-Watson, still kept them. He could've got some good PR by returning them and maybe someone would actually come and visit and he'd sell a postcard here and there. Culturally sensitive artefacts like that shouldn't be in museums. It's really disrespectful.'

4

Digby Combe-Watson's Studio, Dollis Hill

Digby's place had once been a substantial Edwardian family home but had since been partitioned off into separate dwellings. His studio would likely have been the dining room. It now had a view of a halved garden. His space consisted of one large room with a bed at one end near the window, a table in the middle and a kitchenette down the far side. A square cube that was the shower protruded into the room.

'Way more modern than I was expecting,' Matt said, taking in the whitewashed walls and bare wooden floorboards. The curtains were navy blue and the bedding was white and blue striped. The furniture was solid, Scandinavian-esque and terribly practical. No aggressively clunky old English sideboards here.

'Makes sense,' Caius said, opening Digby's sock drawer. 'If I had to see that cross-eyed taxidermy kangaroo every day I'd want to live in an immaculate little minimalist box too. It smells like beeswax. I bet he polished the place with a toothbrush every week.'

'Digby's still a bit old-school though,' Matt said, taking the case off the typewriter perched on the edge of the table.

'Willow said he doesn't have an email. Did everything by post.' Caius took in the art on the walls. 'Modern. Abstract. 1960s? Antibiotics but no mobile phone.'

'One of those live slow types.' Matt looked through the pockets of Digby's jackets hanging up on a clothes rack. There wasn't enough room for an actual wardrobe. He found a receipt for the greengrocer's by the station dated the day before he died. He put it into an evidence bag.

'Yeah. I'm wondering. There's an old TV that wouldn't be able to stream on top of the drawers and a radio in the kitchenette but no laptop.'

'That's probably quite pleasant. I bet he had an attention span that lasts longer than fifteen seconds.'

'There are no memes in Digby's world.'

'Mate, it'll be over in a week. Someone will put a tutu on a corgi.' Matt wasn't sure that was true.

'I'm just not going to look at them.'

'That's all right, Amy is.'

Caius wandered over to the fridge. Inspecting a postcard of a Goan beach clinging to the front of it, he took it down. 'Darling, meant to write when in Blighty but had mad rush for visa. Let's talk about the Institute when I get back on 27th. Mum x.' Caius turned to a half-height bookcase near the bed. A wooden box with a rose carved into the side had caught his eye. He opened it. It contained a month's worth of frequent correspondence.

'"Dearest Darling Digby,"' he read out to Matt. '"That all sounds like a tremendous plan. I cannot wait. Yours eternally, Isolde."'

'It was a date then,' Matt said, looking again at the receipt from the greengrocer's.

'He sets the date up, does it at the museum because it looks sort of impressive and then they kill him?'

'Accidental contamination?' Matt asked, showing Caius the receipt he'd found. 'What if the hemlock leaves made it into the bagged salad he bought from the greengrocer's by mistake. It says organic on the receipt. Maybe they added a bit of the hedgerow not realising.'

'Isolde, his date, panics and flees rather than ring an ambulance.' Caius glanced down at the letter in his hand. 'It's not impossible, but then this letter feels quite lovey-dovey. Would you run? They've been corresponding for a little while. He's not a total stranger. You'd think they'd have enough sense to at least call an ambulance.'

'Isolde could be married? She doesn't want to get caught on a date.'

'Or maybe she's broken her curfew? He hit on Willow the intern; she's twenty, twenty-one. Maybe nineteen when she started.'

'What's her address?' Matt asked.

'It's a PO Box,' Caius said.

'An affair for sure. I wonder how they met? Not like he's on the apps.'

'Digby's definitely not the *Hinge* type.' Caius took the other letters out of the box. A cut-out from a magazine was at the back. '"North London romantic seeks connection with fellow old soul. 37, good-ish looking, sometimes amusing, culture vulture." He posted a lonely-hearts ad.'

'How quaint.'

'The poor guy had kept the ad. A memento of their romance.'

'A memento mori now.'

5

The Police Station

'Poisoned salad, eh?' asked the Chief Superintendent, shaking his head. 'You couldn't make that up.'

'We've contacted the Food Standards Agency who are in touch with the supplier that distributes to the greengrocer's we're certain Digby Combe-Watson bought it from,' Caius said, adjusting his posture. 'They've done an emergency recall. It's possible that the bag had some hemlock leaves in it.'

'And they say eating your greens is good for you.' The Chief Superintendent chortled at his own joke.

'Indeed, sir.' Caius laughed a little too hard to be believable. 'We're trying to locate his date. They go by Isolde.'

'Like the opera.'

'Opera?' He hadn't expected the Chief Superintendent to be a fan of the genre. He was lift-worthy smooth jazz personified.

'Wagner did a version. Tristan and Isolde. It's a very old story and a very long opera. Four hours.'

'I see,' Caius said. He would put Classic FM on sometimes while he pottered about the flat cleaning but he couldn't tell his Handel from his Bach.

'How are you doing?' The Chief Superintendent leaned in and spoke quietly. 'You must be pretty disappointed that your special unit has been disbanded. A bit of a shock when that happened so suddenly. Your team had had some real success in a short space of time, but, what with your champion Arthur Hampton leaving the Cabinet and the appointment of a new Home Secretary keen on further budget cuts, its closure was inevitable really. Those cold cases and the double train murder, all within a year. It was very impressive.'

'Thank you.' Caius watched a solitary magpie fly past the window. He resisted the urge to salute it. 'It is what it is, sir. Just happy to be out there serving the community.'

'That's the spirit.' He himself had been disappointed. It had brought a little prestige to the station. The Chief Superintendent nodded at Caius decisively and left the room.

★　★　★

'What sort of tea?' Matt asked.

'Peppermint,' Caius said as the kettle boiled.

'Have you seen that clip from PMQs doing the rounds? If anything is going to kill your meme off it's the new PM spluttering about signing a trade deal to export more stilton to South Korea.'

'Nope.' Caius flopped onto a chair. 'I'm done with politics. I'm going to live in a cave so I never have to engage with it again.'

'Fair enough,' Matt said, pouring the hot water into their mugs. 'I've put in a warrant request for the details of the PO Box owner to the Post Office. We won't hear back from them until Monday now.'

'Good.' Caius stared out of the window. 'I've let the Foreign Office know that we need to speak to Digby's mother.'

'You all right?' Matt recognised the distant look in Caius's eye.

'Yeah.' Caius didn't want to talk about it.

'Doing anything tonight?'

'One of Callie's friends is having a thing at their new house.'

'Oh cool.'

'You?'

'Pub with Yumi and her friends. Then I'm off tomorrow and will not leave my flat.'

Caius looked out at the street below and saw a bright red post box. 'A PO Box.'

'It's an affair.'

'Who has an affair conducted by letters these days? If you wanted to cheat, download an app, hang out in bars looking available or even go on one of those specialist websites. It's such a roundabout way of doing things.'

'Maybe they didn't feel safe giving away their address.'

'That's an idea.' Caius thought it over.

'They're not cheap though. PO Boxes are £40 a month.' Matt put Caius's tea down in front of him. 'What are you thinking?'

'A scam, maybe? Someone targeting old people. They're the ones who are more likely to advertise for a relationship in that way. They could be writing to multiple people. They lure them out on a date while an accomplice does their place over.'

'But Digby wasn't burgled.'

'Well, no, because he ate an accidentally poisoned salad. The date panics, flees and calls off the burglary. They'd know we'd be looking for them and they don't want us to see a pattern if they've done it before.'

'Isolde is a fake name, if ever I heard one.'

'It's either fake or they're super posh. It's from an opera by Wagner.' Caius wasn't going to admit that this fact had been new to him five minutes ago. 'It's based on an old story. I bet it's fake though. They've handpicked it based on their "culture vulture" mark. It says, "I come from a petit bourgeois family."'

Caius's phone rang. It was Amy. He put her on speakerphone while he and Matt caught her up.

'Me and Simm. You know Anthony Simm. Tiny Simm in uniform. The really lanky guy. Anyway, me and Simm have crossed off the downstairs rooms and half of the upstairs. The taxidermy stuff took up a lot of space so it didn't take as long as I first feared.'

'Great, you and Tiny Simm finish that off tomorrow.'

'Will do. Mrs Bourne the neighbour who I spoke to didn't see or hear anything, by the way. She said she bulk buys melatonin whenever she's in the US and takes one every night to knock her out. Were the door-to-doors any use?' Amy asked.

'No one on the square saw anything,' Matt said, checking over his emails on his phone. 'Half of the flats are empty. Investment properties. But one of the houses at the very end has a doorbell camera. It doesn't show the Institute, it's blocked by the trees, but you do get a portion of the pavement a bit further along.'

'Woo, that's my Sunday sorted,' Caius said.

'I've updated my playlists,' Matt said.

6

Richmond

Callie was tense. Her shoulders were braced, waiting for something terrible to happen.

'You all right?' Caius asked.

'Yeah, I've just not been to Richmond since Harriet's engagement party.' Callie looked out of the bus's window as they meandered slowly through Richmond towards Petersham and Dotty and Georgie's new place. 'The engagement lasted all of five weeks so I shouldn't be too bothered.'

Caius squeezed her hand.

On Callie's lap was a gift bag. Dotty was having a non-baby shower-cum-housewarming. She said the concept was too horribly American but she wouldn't be sad if you bought a little something for the little one.

'Are they doing a gender reveal?' Caius asked. He couldn't imagine Dotty popping a confetti-filled balloon.

'I don't think so.' Callie grimaced at the idea. 'I am bloody starving and yet also a little nauseous. I mustn't have eaten enough today.'

'What did you buy for the baby?' Caius asked.

Callie opened the bag and showed him. 'Teeny little socks from The White Company. It won't matter whether the baby has boy feet or girl feet if they're white.'

'They're so small.' Caius held the socks in the air.

'And a little cardigan thing with teddy bear ears on the hood.' Callie held it up for him and then neatly folded it and put it back into the gift bag. 'This is our stop.'

Caius rang the bell. They stepped off the bus and turned down the road. They were skirting around the bottom of Richmond Park.

'How much was the house?' Caius asked. Every one they'd walked past had been at least a few million so far.

'I haven't asked, obviously,' Callie said quietly, biting her lip. 'I'll look it up on Rightmove when we get home. I'll have to put the browser on incognito mode. It feels dirty looking up your friend's property.'

'Dirtier than porn?' Caius was sure that was what normal people used incognito mode for.

'Being caught watching a gang bang would be funny, being caught googling your friend's assets would be social suicide.'

'Social suicide? Hmm.'

'Oh yes,' Callie said, nodding gravely.

'It's a little Surrey around here for Dotty, surely?' Caius wasn't sure if he was actually the one being sniffy about the banker belt. What had he become. 'I mean, Georgie's low-key one of the East London mandem.'

'Shh,' Callie said, smirking. She stopped in front of a pair of shut gates. 'I think it's this one.'

Caius rang the buzzer.

A crackle came over the speaker. 'Callie, Caius! Come in,' said Georgie, his voice wobbled. He'd been on the sess all afternoon. 'Come round the back.'

The gate swung open and they walked down the driveway and along a path that followed the side of the house – a large red-brick family home with ivy growing over the front. It looked like a vicarage. For a moment there Callie had worried it was going to be mock Tudor. They turned the corner and stepped into the garden.

'Callie, dear heart,' Dotty said, kissing her on the cheek one after the other. 'Welcome to the new house. It's pleasant enough, for now.'

'Such a lovely area. Richmond Park is so gorgeous,' Callie said, although she did prefer being near to Hampstead Heath. She had yet to swim in the bathing ponds, despite her best intentions. The weather was perfect at the moment. Perhaps she'd go in the week.

'Isn't it. That's what sold the house to me in the end. But I have the worst pelvic girdle pain. I've barely been out and explored. Caius, darling, you looked divine on the old goggle box.'

'Hello, Dotty.' He kissed her on the cheek.

'Sodding Max. I can't stand the bastard. You were being so charming as well. Even Mummy messaged me to say how delightful you were and she hates fucking everyone and everything. I've got to say that you both handled it so well. And good old Monty.'

'Sodding Max,' Callie said, handing the bag to Dotty. Her Instagram account was going crazy. *Tatler* had shared the clip. She'd been followed by nearly five hundred new people already. A lot of the men sliding into her DMs were calling her things like 'Milady' and 'Fair maiden'. One even asked what a maid with such a fine pallor was doing with one of *them*. Instant block.

'This is for the baby.'

'Thanks, Cal. So kind of you. Come this way, everyone's down the bottom of the garden.' Dotty had started to waddle. The music grew louder as they approached a patio nestled between some overgrown conifers. 'It came with a bloody pizza oven and Georgie spent an insane amount of time proofing and then hand-stretching dough this morning. They've been drinking since lunchtime and predictably everyone is plastered. Except for me, of course.' She patted her growing bump.

'Bruv,' Georgie yelled at Caius from his preferred spot between the pizza oven and the barbecue. A gaggle of tipsy bemulletted men in tight short shorts and square-fronted baseball caps milled around the grilling meat, watching as Georgie turned rosemary-marinated pork chops over. Bubblegum electro-pop was blasting out of a speaker system that Georgie had set up.

'Your boyfriend's calling,' Callie said to Caius before turning to wave at a girl she knew from art school.

Dotty went and sat down at a table away from the smoke. She beckoned at Callie to join her. 'Darling, help yourself to drinks. We don't stand on ceremony.'

Callie got herself a glass of mineral water from the bar set up on the side of the patio. 'Can I get you anything?'

'No, thank you.'

Callie joined her at the table.

Dottie leaned in and asked quietly, 'Did you shag Casper?'

'No. Absolutely not.'

'Oh good. Couldn't remember. He's here.'

'And Nell?'

'His fiancée? Yeah, she's around.'

'Not a fan?'

'Oh Nell's nice enough. She can be very charming if she's in the mood but she's just so serious. Books, books, books. Far too intellectual for stupid old me.' Dotty watched the party unfold in front of her before whispering to Callie, 'You know, I had thought that parties sober would be no fun, but the things people tell you when they're blotto. I think I've even uncovered an affair.'

'You should be a detective. I'm sure Caius could get you on a fast track scheme or something.' Callie laughed. From what she gathered, most of Caius's work life was actually spent filling in paperwork. Dotty could never.

'Oh no, no, thank you.' Georgie waved at Dotty and she waved back. 'Georgie's convinced that he went on a reconnaissance mission with Caius the other month.'

'Ha, really?' Callie looked around the party, trying to ascertain the clandestine lovers. She turned to Dotty. 'Who's having the affair?'

'I'll tell you later.' Dotty raised an eyebrow. They were evidently nearby.

Caius looked over at Callie and smiled at her, before turning back to Georgie.

'Any good murders?' Georgie asked.

'Any good pictures?' Caius retaliated.

'Bruv . . .' Georgie handed Caius a craft beer.

Caius shook his head. 'I can't talk to you about my work. You know that.'

'If you need to go to another pub "for work", I can come. Also bars, restaurants serving any cuisine, anywhere that has booze and snacks, really.'

'That was just a pint and a hog roast. Are you reading too much into one friendly drink?' Caius laughed as Georgie handed him a hot dog bun from a bag next to the barbecue.

'Just say the word, mate. Let's have a code word. "Jolly Yeoman". Wink. Wink.'

'Are you guys still coming up to my parents' gaffe next week?' Caius asked, changing the topic.

'Absolutely,' Georgie said, holding a sausage up with a pair of tongs. 'Banger from the Ginger Pig.'

'Yes, please.' Caius held the bun open while Georgie dropped the sausage in.

'Onions caramelised with balsamic vinegar.'

'God, yes.'

Georgie plopped some onions on top of the hot dog. 'What are you reading at the moment? I'm bored of my studio and need a different sort of imaginative distraction.'

'Oh, um. Honestly, I'm in a bit of a slump. Work's been quite stressful so I haven't really got free headspace at the moment.'

'Oh dear.' Georgie was secretly thrilled by this apparent proximity to death.

'I should read some non-fiction perhaps. History or something.' Caius spotted Nell, who'd been watching him, gave her a weak smile and pointedly returned to listening to Georgie talk about a stream of consciousness novel he's been dipping in and out of while eating his hot dog.

Callie, who had watched the whole vignette unfold, stared at Caius. The creeping feeling that Caius's career was one day soon going to seriously impact their social life fell over her. Callie's phone went off. It was a private number. She sent it to voicemail. They called again. She let it ring out. They called a third time. 'Christ, what does anyone want me for on a Saturday evening.'

'I'll answer. What's the name of your fake assistant again?' Dotty took Callie's phone from her.

'Amelia.'

'Calliope Foster Millinery, Amelia speaking. How may I help?' Dotty took on a high-pitched, slow and bored voice.

'Eulalia?' Dotty made a series of protracted 'uh huhs' then pulled a face, opening her mouth wide in glee before returning to the bored tone. 'One moment.' She put the call on hold. 'Oh, my giddy aunt,' Dotty said.

'Eulalia as in the singer?' Callie asked, shocked.

'Yes! Got your number from someone at *Vogue*. She loves you, apparently. Adores you. Wants you.'

'Who loves, adores and wants you more than I do?' Caius asked as he sat down next to Callie with the remainder of his hot dog.

'Eulalia!' Dotty repeated.

'Shit, pass me the phone,' Callie said, receiving it from Dotty, taking the call off hold. 'Calliope Foster speaking. Ahum, yah, yah. Monday? Bear with me one moment.' Callie put the phone down.

'Amelia, yes I know you were supposed to leave two hours ago. I'm so sorry, darling, but we're just that busy. I'll make it up to you. Monday. How is it looking. Ah. Well move her, darling.'

She picked up the phone again. 'Monday at 10 a.m. is no problem. Yes absolutely, send over the details.' She gave them her email address. 'Delightful. Have a lovely weekend.' She hung up.

'Dinner and a show,' Georgie said as he joined them at the table with a pizza fresh from the oven. As well as stretching out the dough, he'd made the sauce from scratch and used *fior di latte*. 'I told you, darling, you should have gone on the stage.'

'I'd get so nervous,' Dotty said, taking a slice. 'Come on, spill, Cal.'

'Eulalia performs in those big bobbleheads, right?' Callie began.

'Sorry, who's Eulalia?' Caius interrupted. He didn't want to miss an important detail.

'What do you mean? Who's Eulalia? Do you live under a rock?' Dotty asked.

'She's a musician,' Georgie said, taking a seat and pulling a rather serious, considered face. 'Electro-pop, quite a heavy 1980s feel to the baseline but lyrically she's more akin to an evil version of Kate Bush. There's a dark whimsicalness, a morbidity to her lyrics, that offers a delightful contrast to the upbeat tempo of her oeuvre. Nominated for the Mercury Prize last year. Didn't win. She was robbed.'

'I take it you're a fan,' Caius said to Georgie, before turning back to Callie. 'And what does Eulalia want from you?'

'Her whole thing so far has been performing with these huge crazy heads. She has a different one for every venue. No one knows what she actually looks like. The girlies have been going mental trying to figure it out online. It's a mystery, until now. She's switching up the aesthetic for her next album and she has asked yours truly to help develop the whole concept.'

'That's amazing!' Caius said, thrilled for her.

'Oh God, too much excitement. I need to pee again.' Dotty got up slowly from the table and Georgie followed devotedly, leaving Caius and Callie alone.

'Let me get up Eulalia. I need to visualise this,' Caius said, opening up YouTube on his phone. 'This is cool.'

'Not your thing?' Callie asked, watching Caius's slightly bewildered expression.

'No, but this could be absolutely brilliant for you. You've been wanting to stop making hats and now you've got this opportunity to do something beyond the restraints of the Ascot dress code.'

'Yeah. It could really stretch me creatively. This brief is like building a little world, you know. A whole visual language.'

'The whole concept, right?'

'Yeah.' Callie looked a little spaced out.

'Are you OK?'

'No. I feel a bit off.'

'Eat some pizza,' Caius said, gesturing at the plate Georgie had brought over. 'Or how about my hot dog. I've only had a bite or five. You said you were hungry.'

'At least you didn't say it was my hormones.'

'Is it though? Your body runs like clockwork and there's a full moon tonight.'

'Get fucked.'

'Eat the pizza, you crazy, arty, genius, sexy, moody woman.'

'I'd like that to be the epitaph on my headstone.'

Caius finished off the beer he was holding. 'One more and then I'll stop. I've got a really boring day at work tomorrow and a hangover would make it a trillion times worse. Want one?'

'No, I'm good.' Callie picked up her glass of water. 'I'll stick to l'eau.'

SUNDAY

7

The Police Station

Caius poured himself a cup of green tea from the pot on his desk. He kept it in his locker for his own personal usage in desperate situations. He'd just heard from the Foreign Office that the consul couldn't get hold of Fenella Combe-Watson – she'd gone off on a spiritual retreat for a few days and hadn't left any details with her hotel's staff. Caius didn't want her to find out what happened from someone's third cousin's Facebook post while she was abroad. He started playing Matt's most exulted jungle playlist and pressed play on the doorbell cam footage from across the square. The quality wasn't bad, it was just from so far away. He'd zoomed in and could at least see the general outline of who was passing along that side of the square. Their height, build, anything particular they might have been wearing or carrying would all be ascertainable. Barry had said that the death occurred somewhere between 7 p.m. and 9 p.m., so he began watching from 2 p.m. on double speed, screenshotting anyone walking towards the Horatio Combe Institute. He'd seen Willow come and go as she described. She left with a book in her arms. So far no one had aroused any suspicion.

★　★　★

The pot of tea had been finished, and Caius had moved on to the flapjacks with dried strawberries and chia seeds that Callie had baked earlier in the week. He had watched up to 6.30 p.m. and Matt's playlist had looped around to 'Incredible' by M-Beat and

General Levy for a third time, when he saw something, namely a woman wearing an oversized cardigan and a pair of dark, baggy jeans. Her dark hair was cropped into a bob. She looked remarkably like Willow Bell, the intern.

★　★　★

Caius sat down in front of Willow. He put a large folder on the table. It thudded ominously. There wasn't anything in the folder, but he wanted Willow to think there was. He went through all the formalities again, thanking her for coming back to the station at such short notice, and started the interview.

'Willow, where were you Friday evening at around 6.30 p.m.?' Caius asked.

'At home.'

'At your student digs?'

'No, at my parents' house in Harpenden.'

'Can anyone confirm that?'

'My entire extended family and about thirty of my parents' closest friends. My dad retired on Friday. We had a big party at the cricket club to celebrate that evening. I caught the train from St Pancras mid-afternoon after I'd picked up my book for my essay. My mum dropped me off at the station before eight o'clock on Saturday morning.'

Caius looked at her. 'Willow, do you always dress like this?'

'What do you mean?' She pulled a face.

'Do you always wear dark jeans and an oversized cardigan. You had a red one yesterday, but this one is orange. It's the same one though, isn't it?'

'Yes. I have a signature look – oversized shirt, giant cardigan, tons of brooches. I have six of this specific cardigan, in different colours, and twenty-two others. Practically one for each day of the month. I have three pairs of the same shoes in different leathers. The only make-up I wear is red lipstick and brown mascara. I'm trying to do that whole Anna Wintour uniform thing. It's so chic. I actually find it really freeing, although I'm thinking of adding a miniskirt into the mix. I've been struggling in these jeans in the heat.'

He took out the screenshot he'd made of the recording and then he looked at her. She was diminutive. 'Willow, how tall are you?'

'Five foot two.'

Caius paused the interview and left the room.

'Amy,' he said, calling her from the corridor. 'Are you with Tiny Simm?'

'Yep,' she said, sighing. She'd realised that the Institute no longer smelled musty to her – she'd been there that long. 'We're getting there. We've only got the library left to do now. Why?'

'How tall are you?' Caius asked.

'Five foot five.'

He explained the photograph he wanted Tiny Simm to take of her and then waited five minutes for them to send it over.

'Willow,' he said re-entering the room. 'I know you said it was a uniform, but do you really wear this variation all the time?'

'Yeah. I document it. I've got a ton of fans. I have an Insta and I'm growing my TikTok following. I'm really popular in Taiwan. I'm the rainbow cardigan girl.'

'Do you talk about your life online?'

'Yes, but not really. I'm super wary of people forming para-social relationships so I don't let on where I live or study, you know. I pick and choose the information I give out about myself.

I'll take pictures all around the city, but I try not to take too many close to where I live in case someone works out that I'm nearby. I've never shown my boyfriend, or even mentioned him. Nothing about uni either.'

'And the Institute?'

'No, God no. Like I said, it was only the first rung on the ladder for me. I want to work at one of the big museums when I graduate. I'd love to end up at the V&A.' She swooned into her plastic chair. 'Could you imagine being there every day? Bliss, utter bliss.'

'Do you have any followers who are a bit too keen? Sending you too many DMs? Being a bit too into you?'

'Yeah but like I said, I'm popular in Asia. They don't live here.'

'Have any of your followers ever shown up in person?'

'No. Although I had noticed this girl I vaguely know has started buying cardigans like mine.' Willow laughed but then she leaned in across the table as the implication of what Caius was saying hit her. She got more wound up with each passing moment. 'Oh my God. Do you think I've got a crazy fan? Do you think they killed Digby? That's so scary.'

'There's no evidence to suggest so, but if you notice anyone behaving oddly or messaging you unsettling things then do call.'

★　★　★

At Caius's behest Amy had quickly returned to the police station. He'd shown her the screenshot from the doorbell camera and was now comparing the picture to the one that Tiny Simm had taken of Amy from the same place. Willow was still waiting for the interview to conclude.

'You're a couple of inches taller than Willow and this person is a couple of inches taller than you,' Caius said, comparing both figures to the iron railings.

'So what? They've dressed up as her?'

'Looks like it.' Caius picked up the image of Willow's doppelgänger. 'Is it a prank?'

'Maybe.'

'It's a lot of effort for a prank. Setting up a PO Box and corresponding with Digby by letter for weeks.' Caius had given the letters from Isolde that he'd found yesterday to forensics to fingerprint and to test the envelopes for saliva.

'Who would pull a prank like that?'

'Willow's boyfriend? Weirdly jealous that this older guy had tried to seduce his girlfriend down the pub? It doesn't stack, does it?'

'No.'

★ ★ ★

Willow was bored. She swung her legs in her chair.

'Sorry for the delay, Willow,' Caius said, sitting back down before introducing Amy. 'Is there anyone you can think of who might play a prank on Digby?'

'A prank?'

'Yeah, would they dress up as you to mess with him? Set up a fake date? Something like that. You said that he'd asked you out for a drink down the pub before.' Willow looked back at him blankly. 'You wrote to the Institute asking for work experience. Digby refused to use modern tech. Did he think you were a kindred spirit?'

'What?' Willow looked confused.

49

'Did Digby ever try anything more than going to the pub after a shift?'

'No, absolutely not. Nothing of the sort you're implying happened. We went for one drink. Mr Combe-Watson was friendly but nothing more. No hands. He was disappointed afterwards perhaps, but still cordial. It was just clear that he didn't see me as an option which I think he perhaps had done before.'

'Is it possible your boyfriend got the wrong idea, got one of his mates to dress up as you and fake going on a date with Digby?'

'Ex. I have dumped him since.' Willow chewed her nails. 'No. Definitely not. When I mentioned it to Tom at the time he was a bit put out but nothing more than that.' Willow looked amused at the idea of Tom being remotely bothered that some other man had hit on her. 'Tom's a marine biologist.'

'Where was Tom on Friday?' Caius wasn't sure what marine biology had to do with anything.

'Penzance probably. He's been in Cornwall for the last eight months with his tutor tracking basking sharks. Nowhere near London.'

'So you don't talk any more?' Amy asked

'No.' She rolled her eyes. 'He doesn't have it in him even if he still cared about me. Tom couldn't organise his sodding DnD group. He wouldn't be able to pull off a stunt with someone creating a fake date with a guy who doesn't even have a phone. Plus, it's mean-spirited. I can't stand him any more but I will say that Tom's goal in life is to literally save the whales.' Willow looked up at Caius, her eyes big. 'He was always more interested in aquatic megafauna than me.'

'Megafauna,' Caius said, wondering why a pretty girl like Willow had bothered with someone more interested in humpback whales than in humping her. 'Was there anyone who came into the Institute recently who put you on edge? Did they seem too interested? In the Institute? You? Digby? Or like they were scoping the place out?'

'No, not that I can remember. Like I said, I've been hiding away doing all sorts of random admin.'

'So you haven't seen anyone hanging around outside? Acting off?'

'I haven't seen anyone that weird. There's this girl who lives across the way who talks to me about romance stories in the square at lunch, but she seems mostly normal. I've been trapped in that attic. Mr Combe-Watson did all the tours. He liked showing off.'

'Apart from the Māori protestors,' Amy said.

'Apart from them. Fair play.' Willow sat back in her chair and fiddled with her brooch – a silver fleur-de-lis. 'You know, I don't think Digby did enjoy the tours. I know I said that he did before now, but thinking about it, I don't think he relished doing them any more. He'd started to look more and more fed up every Saturday. The change was incremental, so I guess I didn't notice it but looking back to when I started last year he'd changed. He'd begun moaning about the place. Jokingly at first, wondering how much the building was worth. But that all stopped the other week and he was suddenly all loosey-goosey. He was whistling when I saw him last. I only remembered because he didn't whistle normally and for a moment, I thought it was, you know, a presence.' She touched her necklace, a different tarot card than last time. 'But no, it was just Mr Combe-Watson being cheery. He must have been in love or something.'

'Did he talk about his personal life to you much?'

'No, as I said, not his thing. I think that would've killed him.' Willow realised her turn of phrase was not the most caring. 'Bugger. Sorry. You know what I mean.'

'I do,' Caius said. He took out the screenshot of the woman dressed like her. 'Do you know who this woman is?'

Willow paused, taking in the details. She almost laughed. Caius attributed this to the shock. 'She looks just like me.'

'Yeah.' Caius nodded. 'Do you know her?'

'I don't think so. It's a grainy picture. Maybe she's just one of the square's residents.' Willow looked up at Caius, but then switched her gaze to Amy. 'Or maybe I do have a weirdo fan after all?'

He ended the interview. Willow then gave her fingerprints so they could be eliminated from the crime scene. He suggested to Willow that she go and stay with her parents in Harpenden for a while and to call if anyone put her ill at ease.

* * *

Amy tacked the blurry screenshot onto the incident board and wrote 'Isolde?' above it in marker.

'Is it murder?' Caius asked, turning around to face Amy. 'No one else walked towards the Institute at the appointed time for the date.'

'Do you think someone tried to frame Willow?' Amy wondered. Willow had access to the building, but she couldn't fathom what sort of motive she could possibly have, let alone one that was worth trying to frame her for.

'Maybe? If they wanted to get into the house incognito then why mimic Digby's intern? They've just drawn our attention to themselves. I've got screenshots of ten other people who walked past in the two hours before Digby's death that aren't a priority any more.'

'It could be a coincidence? It's not an unpopular style of dressing. I know she said she makes content about her clothing but she's hardly unique.' Amy pulled up Willow's Instagram. She started scrolling down, looking for any recent pictures on her grid that suggested a connection between her and the Institute but didn't find anything.

'Isolde dressed up as the person who they likely knew would find the body.'

'Is it personal then? Are they taunting Willow?'

'I'm not sure.' Caius didn't think that Willow was the sort of person to inspire a vendetta, just the odd eyeroll. 'Maybe they thought they were in disguise and hadn't thought that far ahead. If someone was watching the house, say a neighbour or one of the protestors outside, they would probably just see a dark bob and giant cardigan. There's the height difference, but if you glanced across from the square you might reasonably dismiss them as Willow putting in a late shift. Isolde must have been watching the Institute for a while.'

'They'd need to know that Willow does her uniform thing.'

'She does have public social media.'

'Willow said that she's careful not to share too much about her personal life.' Amy opened up her page again. 'I'm just scrolling now. She's not an oversharer. There are no photos outside the Institute. There's one in the square garden but the caption doesn't give away that she's in the vicinity often.'

'She did know about "parasocial relationships".'

'You are such a sucker for people with big words. It might have just been one slip-up on a story six weeks ago.'

'True,' Caius said, staring at the figure who they had to assume was Isolde for now. 'I'm going to see if I can pinpoint Isolde's exit too. You all right to go back to the Institute and finish up?'

'I'd rather not but then I'm paid to so . . .' Amy saluted him and left the incident room.

8

Caius and Callie's Flat, Tufnell Park

Callie picked up a small cardboard box from the floor in the hallway. It had been shoved up against the wall behind the front door. The neon-pink box was from an online female hygiene subscription service that she'd signed up for and meant to cancel but kept forgetting. For a small fee they sent her a package in the post every month of organic cotton tampons and they donated twice as many to school girls in India. The tampons stopped them from dropping out of education. Callie had read all about it or something equally as noble when she'd signed up. It was the least she could do. Peter, her biological father, had made his fortune exploiting female garment workers in developing countries and all she was doing was sending them twenty tampons a month. Callie had at least convinced him to set up a charity. He hadn't taken much convincing. She suspected that that was because it could be societally advantageous for the old git now that he'd lost his footing after stepping down from Parliament and his acrimonious divorce. Despite her supposed place on the advisory board, she was rather fuzzy on the details. She took the packet of tampons to the loo and dumped them in the storage unit next to the bath. She hated to admit it but Caius had been right, she was bloody due. Any day now. Actually, probably yesterday. She'd been so tense over her television appearance that she'd probably skipped it. She looked at the calendar on her phone. She was late by a week. It must have been the stress of Chelsea.

Callie walked back into the living space and sat down at her laptop. She'd been reading past interviews Eulalia had given.

Most of them were ridiculous. Eulalia would answer straight-forward questions with pseudo-intellectual gobbledegook. Callie laughed as she read her most recent interview in the *Observer*.

Eulalia – the Mercury-nominated songstress whose catchy party songs are deceptively morose, her lyrics point to a deep loneliness as she questions complex philosophical positions while also being absolute bangers – won't give me a straight answer. When I asked how her burgeoning stardom felt she waxed lyrical for five minutes about everything but what I'd asked.

'Fame? What is fame? Am I famous? Am I a star? I don't have my own gravitational pull. I am not a source of heat or light. My body is made from stardust but then so is everything. No one is special if we're all made from the same inane building blocks that flew to Earth on a wayward asteroid. Did the asteroid mean to bring life or destroy it? Those poor dinosaurs. Fame? You asked what? There is no anagram of it, fame cannot be turned into another word. Metamorphised into another concept. Afem? Meaf? Feam? Fema? Emaf? Mafe? Letters mean nothing. I digress. No, fame is fame is fame. I'm talking of letters when you talk of renown. Of regard. Of people giving a fuck about a song that wails about the futility of it all. You can dance to it at least. Burn bright, bitch.'

I have no idea what any of that meant but Eulalia is the most disturbingly beautiful woman I have ever seen. You're going to go feral when you finally get to see her too.

Callie reread the email from Eulalia's people. It was pretty sparce in details – just giving her a where and when. All they asked her to bring was her sketch pad and an open mind. She'd also found a blog where a superfan had detailed all of the heads that Eulalia had worn on her last tour. There were a lot of wild animals, robots and even an anthropomorphised rocket but then towards the end of last year she started getting a bit mythical. The unicorn head with a twenty-centimetre horn was impressive but Callie's favourite had been Medusa, complete with a bloody neck and animatronic moving snakes. Eulalia had worn it at the Mercury awards last year.

Callie got up from the table. It was time to leave. She grabbed her trench coat, she'd embroidered the back so she wasn't entirely basic, and her trusty Mulberry bag. Taking out a soft matte lipstick in a warm rosy shade, she applied it in the mirror in the hallway. She was off to brunch with her old neighbour Innogen. Innogen's mother had been an actress and had insisted on giving her the correct form of the name and not the printer's mistake in the *First Folio*. Callie opened her front door but then realised she'd left her headphones, turned around and grabbed them. She was going to listen to Eulalia's debut album *Burn Bright* again and again on the tube. Callie wasn't going to be caught out.

9

The Police Station

Caius had watched to 3 a.m. and no Willow-lookalike had walked past a second time. He'd switched to Matt's house playlist. Jungle wasn't doing it for him any more. He got up from his desk and went to the break room. He did squats as he waited for the kettle to boil. Amy appeared.

'We've finished cross-referencing the catalogue with the exhibits in the Institute,' Amy said, sniffing her shirt. She could smell the damn place on her. 'Not a single thing is missing.'

'Good job,' Caius said, pouring water into the cup. He turned to look at Amy. 'There are three options here, aren't there? Firstly, Digby accidentally ate the salad with poisoned leaves in, he dies, Isolde panics and flees.'

'Secondly, Digby is murdered.'

'Specifically, because of something he's done or will do. Something personal. And thirdly, he was killed for access to the Institute.'

'I think three has been ruled out. What would they want access to? The boss-eyed kangaroo?'

'The basement level?'

'I don't know.'

'That's been sealed off for years.' Caius poured in the oat milk. It was his carton and his alone. He wrote his name on the side. 'So either it was an accident and Isolde fled, or Digby was murdered, possibly by Isolde but perhaps not. Who knows who could've had access to that food beforehand. Maybe the greengrocer in Dollis Hill hated him.'

'But the Willow costume?'

'Exactly. That's where I keep getting stuck.'

'I've had all of Digby's paperwork from his office brought here. Everything is being fingerprinted.'

'Great idea, Amy. Willow said that she did a lot of admin tasks for Digby so I would expect her prints to come up a lot,' Caius said, putting his precious dairy alternative away.

Amy poured herself a glass of water and the pair returned to the incident room. Caius put his tea on his desk and then, picking up a marker pen, wrote two words on a whiteboard. 'Money or sex,' he said.

'Which one?'

'Money.' He drew arrows coming off the word and started writing keywords as they spoke. 'We need to look into Digby's personal finances, but I doubt he had a couple of million in the bank. He was living in a studio in Dollis Hill. He wasn't loaded. A scam to lure him out so he could be burgled isn't impossible. Just no evidence to support it. It's a lot of effort for a seemingly small bounty.'

'The Institute then,' Amy said.

'The contents or the building?' Caius wrote both down. 'I think the building is worth far more than its contents. There used to be a lot of squats around that bit of Camden in the eighties and nineties, then it was Kate Mossified with Cool Britannia, and now it's been dullified by international finance bros in navy gilets.'

'It's worth a bomb.' Amy stared at the whiteboard. 'I wonder who inherits the Institute with Digby gone?'

'That's a good question,' Caius said, writing it down. 'Sex as a motive.'

'Isolde?'

'Yes. Solitary Digby, who refuses to deal with any technology developed in the last fifty years, puts a lonely-hearts ad in a magazine. Meets a woman who appears to be tailor-made called Isolde.'

'Bogus name,' Amy said.

'Bogus name,' Caius said, adding it to the board. 'The PO Box.'

'The Willow disguise.'

Caius sat down at his desk. 'Isolde didn't walk back the way she came. I think if she panicked there's a better chance that she'd return that way. It's familiar. Plus, most people are right-handed and turn instinctively in that direction. I don't know. I'm grasping now.'

'Is Willow in on it?'

'My gut says no. She's a bouncy twenty-year-old. What does she care. You?'

'I don't see it. She clearly sees her time at the Institute as only a stepping stone. Anyone else have doorbell cameras?'

'The neighbouring houses don't, and no one else has a view either looking down that end or with enough clarity that anything can be made out. Those magnolia trees block a lot of the square off and there's a huge skip.'

'When will you hear from Barry?'

Caius looked at his watch. The afternoon was slipping away. 'Not until tomorrow now.'

Amy's desk phone rang. 'Hello . . . Yes . . . Great . . . I'll come get them.' She hung up. 'Forensics are done with the letters from Isolde. No fingerprints. The envelopes weren't licked. No trace of the person who sent them.'

'Isolde is looking more and more like a killer.'

★ ★ ★

59

Caius had watched the camera footage to 10.30 a.m. on Saturday. The police cars had strewn past and blocked the pavement. The only thing of note it caught was the poor blonde girl Caius had nearly taken out after he failed to get into the basement. 'Urgh, I'm so embarrassing.'

'Huh?' Amy said, appearing at his elbow suddenly.

'Nothing,' Caius said wearily.

'I've gone through all the letters and I've made a key of their dates and contents. I'll send you a link,' Amy said, before handing Caius a plastic bag with the first letter in. 'Looking at the dates on the letters – which they both always wrote at the top because, old-school – Isolde would respond to him the following day. She was enthusiastic.'

'What about the contents?' Caius asked, reading over the letter.

'Isolde takes a huge amount of interest in his day-to-day life. She's asking him questions about the Institute, the book he's writing, his friends, what he's reading. Giving that ego a good, firm rubbing.'

'A book?'

'Yeah, she asks him what it's about.'

'Anything else jump out? Is there anything she keeps going back to?' Caius asked.

'Nothing in particular.'

'Is she grooming him?'

'Love bombing?'

'Yeah, I'm wondering.' Caius put the letter down. 'Is there any suggestion that they've exchanged photos? Old-fashioned I know but this is what we're dealing with.'

'No. Although she's very keen to meet face to face.'

'At the Institute?'

'It's funny.' Amy picked up a letter to show Caius one specific passage. 'She doesn't ask specifically to meet him there but she bookends the proposed date with a comment about the Institute and how interesting he is for running it.'

'She's suggesting it but letting him think it was his idea.'

'Yeah. Why there and not a restaurant?'

'A public place is safer, but that's a female way of necessary, precautionary thinking.'

'Exactly. I wouldn't arrange a date with a guy – at all but, you know, hypothetically – in a secluded place.'

'Matt thought she might be a goth.'

'Or a proper history nerd. Likes the idea of being allowed in out-of-hours, maybe?'

'Has she given away any facts about herself?'

Amy handed Caius her notebook. 'I've written a list. I'll type it up in a minute.'

'Let's see.' Caius began reading it out loud. 'Five seven; brown hair; a primary school teacher (English lead); wants to move to a small village for the peace and quiet; grew up in Dorset; Dad is big Wagner aficionado; used to do ballet until she fractured three metatarsals; has a brother called Richard; took up watercolours last year; allergic to strawberries but adores raspberries; big fan of Dickens novels; went to Exeter university.' Caius paused. 'Well, her height and hair colour match up with the footage at least.'

'I wonder how much of that is true.'

'Indeed.' Caius gave Amy back her notebook. 'She's perfect for Digby. Too perfect perhaps.'

10

Caius and Callie's Flat

Callie came home to the most delicious smell. She walked into the kitchen area to find Caius frying Korean veggie pancakes. He'd seen a video of someone doing it the other day and wanted to try it.

'Just using up the veg in the fridge before it goes soft.'

'Yum,' Callie said, taking an orange from the fruit bowl and beginning to peel it. She popped a segment in her mouth as she watched him cooking. 'Cast off tomorrow? Are you excited.'

'Yeah.' He didn't sound it.

'You have that look.'

'Which look?'

'I don't know how to describe it.' Callie ate another segment. 'Like you're lost in the back of your head. You're not quite here, whereas last month when you helped out on that gang stabbing you were sort of chill.'

'Chill?'

'Not chill, that's not the right word, but it was just your job. It's grim but you got on with it because you're a professional.'

'In some ways gang stuff is easier to deal with, there's a brutal logic to them, but murder is murder and it's always grim.'

'I hung out with Innogen my old neighbour today, and her husband is a whizzbang surgeon down at St Barts. She was saying he has this very zen vibe to his work considering he's literally dealing with life and death and that's you too most of the time.'

'Not this time?'

'No.'

Caius flipped a pancake over. He should've waited to make this tomorrow when his cast would be off and he wouldn't have to hold the pan with one hand. 'It's an odd one. I've had a bad run of funny cases. It's usually drugs and gang-related like you said, or domestic violence which is a special sort of awful but this one . . .'

'How weird?'

'It looks like a man was murdered by his date.' Caius was reluctant to go beyond that.

'We've all been there.' Callie sat on a kitchen unit as Caius went back to making dinner. 'I was worried it was going to be a kid.'

'No. Not this time.' He looked up at her and then quickly down to the pan in front of him. 'Thank God. I'm mean, well, you know. Varying degrees.'

'Maybe . . .' Callie shrugged. She let the words in her mouth fall to the floor unspoken. That was a decision for him to make. 'What am I doing with my life?'

'You're a milliner who's moving on to exciting creative consulting opportunities.'

'That makes me sound like a LinkedIn wannabe CEO.'

'Let me go again,' Caius said, feeling like he was being expected to perform but what, he wasn't quite sure. 'Artist, slow-fashion advocate, creative thinker. Warmer?'

'Maybe.'

'Is this regular existential dread or something more?'

'I don't know. I just feel off.'

'OK, let's play a game,' Caius said, plating the first pancake. 'You start moving around the kitchen and I will say hot or cold.'

'Are you treating me like a six-year-old?'

'Six-year-olds do not get PMT,' Caius said, watching her move towards the sink. 'Cold.' Callie turned around and walked in the opposite direction. 'Warm.'

'You patronising git.' She turned and walked towards the sofa.

'Warmer,' Caius said. Callie went towards his backpack. 'Boiling.'

Callie took out three full bars of Lindt milk chocolate. 'Did you buy this in anticipation of the arrival of my period.'

'Yes.' Caius poured a little soy sauce, rice vinegar and sesame oil into a small bowl.

'I don't know whether to be offended or grateful.'

'If you're offended you can give it back and I'll eat it.'

'Nope,' Callie said, opening one of the packets, breaking two squares off and putting the first in her mouth.

'Well then.' He added two cloves of crushed garlic, sesame seeds, chopped spring onions and gochugaru that he'd picked up from a Korean supermarket on Tottenham Court Road last week to the bowl.

'Are you happy?'

'Yeah.' He narrowed his eyes at her.

'But are you?' Callie couldn't help herself after all.

'My dad put you up to this?' Caius peered at her before flipping the pancake.

'No, you just begin to look a little hollowed-out after a few shifts in a row.'

Caius slid the pancake onto a plate. He began slicing it into pieces. 'All set for your meeting with Eulalia tomorrow?'

'Yeah, I think so.' Callie accepted the change of topic. 'Maybe? They didn't really give me much to plan for. I think I've read or listened to every interview she's ever given by now. I'm going to take my portfolio – I worked on a couple of editorial shoots back in the day – and just wing the rest. I have better ideas when I'm under pressure.'

'You are going to be brilliant.' He placed the pancake and the dipping sauce in front of Callie and then turned back to the stove.

MONDAY

11

The Police Station

Amy and Matt were busy arranging all the papers from Digby's office out in the incident room. They were organising them into personal or institutional. Caius appeared without his cast.

'Are we free?' Matt asked.

'We are free,' Caius said, showing off his arm. It was warm out so he'd rolled up his shirtsleeves.

'It's May,' Matt said, gesturing at Caius's forearms. 'Of course.'

'Huh?' Amy asked, looking up from the papers.

'I switch ethnicities right about now,' Caius said, holding up both forearms so Amy could the see the difference. 'I'll have one Jamaican arm and one Irish one for a month. It'll have evened out come the end of June into indeterminate Mediterranean.'

Caius's phone rang. He took the call. The jest fell from his face. 'Digby's mother Fenella is downstairs. Appears the Foreign Office failed to get hold of her in Goa.'

'Oh dear,' Matt said, sucking in his breath.

'Turned up at the Institute and got informed by uniform out front what happened,' Caius said.

'We don't have tea strong enough for that,' Amy said.

★　★　★

Fenella Combe-Watson appeared much younger than Caius had expected. She was a former nineties raver type turned sleek Pilates teacher. After seeing how Digby lived, he'd expected her to be an ancient old lady in a twinset, a matching pleated skirt with a humped back, but no: Fenella was a sixty-something in Sweaty Betty leggings and a pair of Hokas.

'Ms Combe-Watson, I would like to sincerely apologise for the manner in which you found out about your son's death. We asked the Foreign Office to get in touch with you while you were abroad.'

Fenella did not speak. She couldn't. She had barely registered what Caius had said. She was clearly in shock and Caius wasn't going to get anything out of her yet. Caius left the room, signalling for the family liaison officer to take over. Telling them to call him when she was able to talk.

★　★　★

Matt, who had taken charge of the institutional pile of paperwork, was reading through a glossy booklet when Caius came back into the incident room. He passed it over to Caius. 'Digby had the property valued last week.'

'Two million pounds. Imagine what it'll be worth once they put electricity in,' Caius said.

'It's got all the original features and then some,' Amy said, grimacing. She'd bathed in menthol Epsom salts after washing her hair twice last night, to shake the decrepit smell that her girlfriend Fi said she'd brought back with her to their flat. The cats had been delightedly sniffing her all over. She must have smelled like mouse wee.

'That's a pretty good motive if Digby isn't the only person who has a share of the property,' Matt said.

'His mum wrote to him saying they'd talk about the future of the Institute when she got back,' Caius said, remembering the postcard sent from Goa on the fridge.

'What would they do with the collection if they did sell the house?' Matt asked.

Amy held up a letter and began reading it aloud.

Dear Sirs,

I am writing to you with regard to the repatriation of human remains within the Horatio Combe Institute.

As you may be aware the Institute is in possession of seven toi moko or mokomokai from New Zealand. It is the wish of the trustees that they be returned to their ancestral land. If someone from the department would be good enough to advise us on the proper channels et cetera, et cetera.

Yours faithfully,

Digby Combe-Watson
Curator and Executive Chair
The Horatio Combe Institute

'When was that dated?' Caius asked.

'It hasn't been dated, or signed yet,' Amy said, looking the letter over.

'He was waiting to speak to his mum,' Caius said.

'There was another letter kept in the same folder, offering the rest of the collection to the Royal Geographical Society,' Amy said, scanning the other letter. 'Also unsigned and undated.'

'He was serious if he was offloading the collection.'

'Oh and there was a letter from some academic asking to set up a meeting. That was from two weeks ago.'

Caius's desk phone rang. 'Fenella Combe-Watson feels up to talking.'

★ ★ ★

'Again, I'm so sorry for your loss, Ms Combe-Watson,' Caius said.

She gently folded, unfolded and then refolded the tissue in her hand like it was an act of prayer for the weeping, finally placing the reliquary tissue into her lap.

'We're just trying to ascertain why anyone would want to harm Digby.'

'Harm?' she whispered. She tried to hold her pain back, but somehow found herself shouting at Caius. 'They killed him. That is far beyond harming someone. They didn't pinch him on the arm. They murdered him!'

Caius nodded. 'I understand.'

'Do you?' She didn't believe him. She knew that terrible things happened to people all the time, but this time it had happened to her and it was a singular hell.

'Yes, I do.' Caius gave her the look that only the violently bereaved understand.

She calmed herself, taking in multiple rounds of deep breaths for counts of five. 'You wanted to ask me some questions, I believe.'

'Yes, madam,' Caius said, taking out the postcard and reading aloud what she had written. 'Could you explain the context around your message, please?'

'Digby had written to say that he had a plan for the Institute. I think he wanted to wind it down.' Fenella shook her head, thinly veiling disgust. 'Finally.'

'You disliked the place?'

'It gave me the creeps.' Fenella turned in on herself for a moment. There was no family left besides her any more. 'It's a mausoleum. My father was curator before Digby took over. I spent far too much time there as a child. Hated it. Utterly hated it. I wanted to dispose of it when Daddy died but Digby had graduated the summer before and was at a loss because of the recession so he took it on. He adored my father. I think he felt a duty towards him to carry it on.' She picked up a tissue from the box on the table. 'They adored each other. Digby was working on a book about the Institute.'

'Had you seen a draft at all?' Caius remembered that Digby had been talking to Isolde about a book. It would explain why Willow got bumped up to research assistant from intern. Although he was certain that was not an official title.

'No, he mentioned his idea for the book but I don't know whether he had started it yet.' A little light found its way back into her eyes. 'It would've been such an interesting work. Quite brave, I suppose. Noble.'

'And what was his idea?'

'He called it "Our Apologia". He had begun to feel uncomfortable with the collection. We both did. What was in it and how it had been obtained. Rather unsavoury at times but we both agreed that it was healthier to talk about it rather than sweep it under one of the Institute's motheaten rugs. The book was going to be him meditating on what it feels like to directly inherit a colonial horror. He kept mentioning some man called Edward Said as a point of reference.'

'Right.' Caius understood. 'Is there a trustee board? Anything like that?'

'It's just the two of us now. My aunt had been on the board

until she died three years ago. I told Digby we should let it go
then too, no shame in the world moving on, but he was still at
a loss, you see. He was a child out of time. He wanted simplicity
so he clung to the past instead of moving forward.' She sighed.
'God knows we could've done with the money. I kept telling
Digby that he could use his part to go and have adventures of
his own.'

'If you don't mind me asking, were you aware whether or not
Digby had made a will?'

'Not that I know of. He was young.' Her neat hands unfolded
the tissue for a final time and swept up the tear that fled down
her cheek. 'Young men always think they'll live forever.'

Caius nodded. 'Did Digby ever tell you much about his social
life?'

'His university friends all live in the North still. They were
close.' Fenella scrunched up the tissue in her hand, the whites of
her knuckles showing. 'He went to visit a couple of times a year.'

'Do you know how we can contact them?'

'No. Nathan's a nice boy. Yes, Nathan was his best friend.'

'Nathan. Nathan what?'

'I might have a number somewhere. Maybe. I'm sorry, I can
check. I'm sure Digby will have an address book.' She looked
down at her hands. They looked older to her all of a sudden.
'Nathan came to stay with us in Dollis Hill after graduation.'

'Was that your house originally?'

'Yes, I broke it up into studios when I moved with my partner
to Oxfordshire six years ago. Digby lives in one rent free and I
let the others out.'

'I see.' It was the same arrangement he had with his parents.
Caius made a note to look for the address book. 'Did Digby tell
you about his love life?'

'Not really. And what mother wants to know the details.'

'He hadn't told you he'd met anyone recently?'

'No. Had he?' She leaned forward with a bittersweet eager-ness to know that her son had lived more than she had believed. That there might be someone who would miss him almost as much as she did.

'We think so.'

'Oh.' She sank back into her chair, her vertebrae-stacked-on-vertebrae Pilates posture failing her. 'We were going to meet up this week once we were back. If he had met someone and it was serious he probably would've told me about it then. Would have . . .'

12

Tate Britain

Callie had initially been given an address in Primrose Hill for the meeting but Eulalia had decided that she wanted to meet 'somewhere awe-inspiring', and had changed the venue at the last minute. Callie walked past the shrapnel-damaged walls between the gallery and Chelsea College of Arts and went into the building. She walked up the swirling staircase, popped into the gift shop to buy a postcard for reference later on and then found the painting she'd been told to meet Eulalia in front of. She held the postcard up in front of the real thing, her eyes flitting between them as if she was trying to 'spot the difference'. Callie was anxious. She checked her watch – she was five minutes early. She still had no idea what Eulalia bloody looked like.

Callie sat down on the bench opposite *Ellen Terry as Lady Macbeth*. Lady M's strong arms held her ill-gotten crown above her head. The cobalt flashes on the dress were made from thousands of jewel beetle wings. Callie wondered how they killed the poor things. Had they gassed them before they plucked them or had they torn their wings off when they were alive? There was a still and yet frenzied quality to the painting. On the cusp of madness. Only her tremendous, pooling eyes rippled with the terror, the gravity of the crime she'd committed. Lady M, driven by her ambitions to murder her king, upsetting the natural order of the world. Beyond subversive. If Eulalia wanted mad, Callie wondered, then why Lady M and not Ophelia. Her own work aligned more with Millais who was in an adjoining room. She liked Rossetti's work too, but she thought he was a wanker. Callie checked her phone. She had heard nothing from Eulalia's people since the venue change. She put it on loud and back in her bag, taking out her lipstick – a sheer russet she'd bought from Liberty's when she'd been in a rough patch with Max two years ago – and a vintage 1950s compact mirror. Callie couldn't abide it when people used their phones to apply make-up. She touched up her lipstick and checked her reflection. She jumped when she saw a young woman staring at her intently from behind.

'Jesus Christ on a bicycle,' Callie said, closing the compact and standing up. 'I take it you're . . .'

'Yes, that's me,' came a small sotto voce.

'Calliope, delighted to meet you at last.' She held her hand out. Callie smiled at the barefaced young woman in front of her. She was perfect. Quite odd, but utterly perfect. Her eyes were perhaps a little too large; her nose a little too snubbed; her mouth a little too wide and plump. Her teeth, which looked like her own, were too white, a little too symmetrical. She had a little too much of everything. She was trying to hide it too – dressed-down and mutely, swathed in excess fabric, hiding beneath a baseball cap. She was unearthly – a goddess, hiding – Venus beneath baggy tracksuit bottoms and a 2XL men's T-shirt.

'I'm so excited to meet you,' Eulalia said, taking her hand. Eulalia's handshake was limp. She didn't care for such formalities. She dropped it and flopped onto the bench. Eulalia ignored Callie; gazed up in silence at the painting. 'She's so fucking angry. I love it.'

'Is it her air of unpredictability that you like?' Callie placed herself down next to Eulalia. She kept her posture erect while Eulalia slouched as if the public gallery were her private residence.

'Women should be unpredictable. We already are. We have hormones that move us. We can grow life. Men are constants; they're boring. Stagnant. Insipid pools of still water. They're entirely bacteria at this point. Cholera in trousers.'

'In my experience that depends on the man.' Callie took out her notebook, a little leather-bound Smythson that she'd bought a bunch of disgustingly cheap from a sample sale a few years ago. She only used them for client consultations. She felt like they lent her authority. She wrote down 'unpredictable', 'female anger' and 'wild-eyed'.

'I'm so happy you agreed to this. I've been feeling really lost.' Eulalia in a total change of pace grabbed Callie's hand as Callie gazed back, unsure about what to do about this overfamiliarity. 'My sister Mel is amazing; she organises everything for me. My deals with my label, all the business stuff.'

'Cool.'

Eulalia leaned in and said even quieter, 'But she doesn't have that creative mindset. She's phenomenal at planning the practical stuff, you know, the shit that has to happen to get things moving, but she can't freewheel ideas. She doesn't get aesthetics, you know. She doesn't understand the pursuit of beauty.'

'We all have our strengths,' Callie said diplomatically. She looked up to see a woman staring at them from next to the painting. She gave Callie a wry smile and rolled her eyes. Callie wasn't sure where she'd appeared from. She wondered if Mel had been summoned by her sister's criticisms. It was quite likely she had been there the whole time but Callie had been so engrossed in Eulalia that she hadn't noticed.

'Mel, this is Cal; Cal, this is Mel.'

'Hey,' Mel said. It was clear to Callie that Mel had been studying her. She was wearing a plain white shirt tucked into a pair of tailored black trousers, and a pair of black heels that Callie thought were last season's Louboutin's, but she couldn't see the sole from where she was without making it obvious. Low-effort chic. It was hard to be poorly dressed when dressed like that. Although Callie wondered why she was barefaced but then that was a choice. It was all very predictable for a manager. All very safe. Expensive. There was money here, but Mel knew she wasn't the star of the show and she wasn't going to even try and make too much of herself. She wasn't a good-looking woman, especially so when in the vicinity of her sister. Their family resemblance was clear but they shared no regular features.

'Hello, Mel, lovely to meet you,' Callie said, standing up. She didn't think Mel liked her very much. Callie held her hand out anyway. In contrast to her sister, Mel grasped her hand firmly.

Mel looked at her watch. 'I'm going to go meet the people at PCQV. I'll see you at home later. You need to be back by 3 p.m. at the latest. Have you got your Oyster? Your phone in case I need to reach you.'

'Yep.' Eulalia patted the pocket of her tracksuit.

'OK then.' Mel nodded at Callie who smiled back. Mel was checking that the name of the giant French luxury conglomerate had landed with suitable weight.

'Bye, Mel,' Eulalia called after her. She turned to Callie conspiratorially. 'Don't mind her. She's really stressed with all the deadlines looming.'

Mel turned back around and handed Eulalia a bottle of water from her bag. 'Don't get dehydrated. It's far too hot out there.'

Eulalia winked at her sister, making a clicking sound as she pretended to shoot her. Mel sighed but then fired an imaginary shot back.

'Where in the North are you from?'

'How could you tell?' Eulalia had been trying her hardest to sound posh-like. Mel had advised her to so she'd be taken more seriously. She'd gone as far as to get elocution lessons for the pair but Eulalia knew she couldn't keep it up as well as Mel could.

'The humour in your work feels northern. I expected you to be from Yorkshire.'

'God's own country.' Eulalia rolled her eyes.

'See, only people from Yorkshire say that.'

'All right, you've got me. I'm a Yorkshire lass born and bred.'

'My mum's family are from out that way.' Callie closed her notebook. 'Is it just the feeling in the painting or do you like the aesthetic too?'

'Both. I love the look. The whole vibe.'

'Do you like Millais?'

'No. I don't care for him.'

They walked through to the adjoining room and stopped in front of Millais's *Ophelia* – mouth agape, drowning slowly.

'Too inactive?' Callie asked.

'Yeah. She's pitiful. Ophelia has things done to her and doesn't do a thing for herself. She's beautiful, I grant you, but she's fucking weak. I hate that she goes mad and that makes her fuck-able. You know?'

'Viragos not damsels.'

'Yes, exactly. I don't like guys at the moment. I'm all about the divine feminine.'

'How about Joan of Arc?'

'Love her. What a queen. I like the meek but not the weak. I'm a fan of Julian of Norwich. I adore those crazy women. Anchoresses and the like. Batshit-crazy nuns. That whole thing. Straight-up schizophrenia channelled into religious revelational energy. I sympathise with them. God's a woman. God's a mother.

Love it. I love love love it. That's why I bought my house.' Eulalia stepped away from Ophelia. She was disgusted by her pathetic death. 'Let's go for a walk while I explain the business and what I need from you.'

They walked out of the gallery and down the main steps to Millbank, meandering slowly towards Westminster.

'Have you ever been to Westminster Abbey?'

'No,' Callie said. It was one of those touristy things to do that she'd never got round to, despite having lived in London for well over a decade. She'd probably enjoy it – she'd ask Caius to take her. She was still at that point where she felt that making little demands every now and then put her in good stead. 'I've never been to the Tower of London either.'

'Really?' Eulalia shook her head. 'I swear you can feel Anne Boleyn's spirit there.'

'Poor thing.'

'Poor thing indeed.' They sat down on a bench overlooking the Buxton Memorial in all its neo-gothic, proto-woke glory. Eulalia took out her phone and began reading from it. 'What I want from you is the thought behind a cohesive aesthetic that includes both my creative work and my brands moving forward.' She looked up. 'I hate it but I'm a brand. We estimate that I have five years to make all the money I can before I can go make the weird art albums that I'm desperate to create and not starve. I'm going to get fabulously rich and then I'll make my legacy works.'

'What exactly do you mean by creative work?' Callie took out her Smythson notebook again and started taking notes. The action hid a growing sense of inadequacy.

'Visually. Don't worry about the music, I can handle that, obvy.' Eulalia looked at her phone again and the message Mel had sent outlining all of this for her. 'I mean my costumes; my album covers and associated artwork. Oh and don't forget the merchandise. Merch, merch, merch. That's where the money is. Even social media posts, I guess. By brand I mean packaging, logos, all that boring capitalist shit that makes the world go round and people buy stuff they don't need but desperately want.'

'Is your label not doing all that for you?'

'They tried. There was a lot of neon latex and glitter. It felt very inauthentic. Mel and I agreed that it was chopped. They've given me two weeks to come up with a better alternative.'

'I see,' Callie said, nodding. 'And PCQV, where do they fit in?'

'That's all Mel. She had the great idea that we should line up a series of commercial deals and pitch the aesthetic to them first so that then the label will be forced to go along with what I want and not fluorescent-pink pineapple bras. Nothing wrong with inflatable tits, it's just not me. At the moment we're looking to launch a make-up line. Same old, same old. Lip oils. Cream blushes blah blah. It'll be sold in high-end department stores and in Sephora. Mel is in the early stages of those negotiations. We need to pitch the brand feel to them next week. All of their mock-ups of products are super clean-looking with soft and gentle pinks whereas I'm a violent-colour-riot sort of girl. Bright reds. Oranges. Anything flammable, you know. They went futuristic, clean and sleek, where I want it to be unrealistically anachronistic. Theatrical almost.'

'Performance art meets Renaissance fayre?'

'Exactly. I knew you'd get it. As soon as I saw that video of you in that garden with that awful man trying to steal your moment, I thought, that girl is like me, with your little hat and flower language. You're an ancient soul trapped in the body of a hot thirty-year-old. I knew you'd understand.'

Callie wasn't sure whether to laugh or cry. 'That was quite a day.'

'The guy in the cast, that was your boyfriend, right? What is he? He looked so embarrassed, but he really wanted to rescue you. It was sweet.'

'It's his job. He's a professional dragonslayer.'

'He rescues a lot of damsels?'

'Oh yeah, me included.' Callie remembered the look that Nell gave him on Saturday evening. 'He's a police officer.'

'A hero then.'

'Don't ever tell him that. His little head will explode.'

'Did I read something about his family?'

'Yeah, probably,' Callie said. She wasn't keen to talk about the Beauchamps but it didn't look like she'd get away with brushing Eulalia off. Eulalia was peering at her with a childlike expectation. 'His dad is a baronet. He's a Sir. It's a title passed down the male line. Caius's grandfather inherited it last year after the previous titleholder's parentage came to light. It was a whole thing.'

'So one day you might be a lady?'

'Maybe.'

'Maybe Lady. I like the assonance.' Eulalia took out her phone and quickly wrote the phrase down. 'How did you meet?'

'We sat next to each other at the theatre one evening.' Callie chose to give her the short version.

'That's so sweet.' Eulalia scrunched her face and her shoulders up. She thought it was adorable. 'So, Westminster Abbey? It's just there.'

'Fancy it?'

'Yasssss.'

They got up from the bench and marched over to the abbey, joining a chaotic queue that made them both anxious. They were at the front after twenty minutes. Eulalia had got to the lady at the ticket booth first and ordered two tickets with additional hefty guidebooks. She then turned and looked at Callie expectantly. Callie paid the £70 with a smile on her face.

'Thank you so much. Invoice Mel for the tickets.' Eulalia scrunched her nose up again. Callie realised that she did it when she wanted to affect cuteness. 'I don't have any money on me. Only my Oyster card.'

'Don't you just tap in and out with your phone?' Callie asked. She was confused why Eulalia didn't have anything on her.

'No. I, well, I don't have contactless.' Eulalia turned away quickly and picked up a set of headphones and a guide. 'Retro. So Y2K.'

Callie collected a pair of headphones for herself too and followed Eulalia into the body of the abbey.

Callie followed Eulalia around the abbey. They got stuck behind a group of schoolboys who weren't suitably reverential, considering their location, towards the pair. The giggling gaggle of teenage boys received a sombre history lesson at the Tomb of the Unknown Soldier, which Eulalia and Callie decidedly took as their moment to leave them behind. They paused in front of Sir Isaac Newton. A group of tourists were taking pictures of Newton's monument, loudly proclaiming their love of *The Da Vinci Code*. Eulalia pushed on, determined to find where the old queens of England rested. She stopped in front of Catherine of Valois.

'Samuel Pepys was a creepy little fucker,' Eulalia said.

'What?' Callie asked, perplexed. She'd been admiring the Italian woman in front's bag.

'Catherine of Valois's tomb fell into disrepair and the bastard peered in and kissed her on the lips. The poor queen had been dead for hundreds of years. He thought it was funny. He put it in his sodding little diary.'

'That is so gross.'

Eulalia marched on, and then stood reverentially at the feet of Elizabeth I. 'Such a baddie.'

'It's so funny that the government tried to introduce ruffs as our national dress.'

'I like them.'

'Do you?'

'They take up space.'

'True.'

'I want to take up space.'

'As you should,' Callie said, nodding along. They whipped round the Lady Chapel and into Poets' Corner.

'Do you have a favourite?' Callie asked, peering at the names of poets on the floor.

'The Brontës. I'm from Yorkshire. It would be treason to say anything else.'

They meandered slowly towards the exit, via the gift shop, and left the abbey. Callie turned to look at the gothic grand dame once more, silently taking in the twentieth-century martyrs above the door.

'That was so fucking cool.'

'It was,' Callie said, trying not to frown. She wasn't a prude, she swore like a sailor at the best of times, but something about Eulalia's flippant tone rankled her while she stared up at Martin Luther King. Eulalia linked her arm through hers and practically marched Callie back towards Westminster station. They stopped at the lights in front of Parliament while Big Ben chimed the hour.

'How do you want to proceed?' Callie asked, trying to

steer the conversation back to the professional and away from either the personal or the profane.

'Mel said she'd email you a list of all the creative assets we need to pitch to the label. She said mock-ups are too much but definitely visual reference points. Something about mood boards, influences – something to give to their product design team. Let's meet again this week before the presentation. We've got a short turnaround on this.' Eulalia hugged Callie. Callie hugged her back but was keen to release her. 'This was a great meeting, Cal. We're going to work so well together.'

'Yes, absolutely,' Callie said, released from the hug. She watched Eulalia scamper away towards the Embankment.

As Callie entered Westminster tube she wondered, not whether she had bitten off more than she could chew but whether it was going to choke her to death. Eulalia was sweet, she supposed. A lot of creative people were intense, with slightly loose personal boundaries and undiagnosed ADHD. Callie didn't think she'd be too difficult to work for as long as she kept her distance slightly. She wasn't going to get sucked into thinking she was a friend. Could she pull this off? It was such a short turnaround. The project was pretty ill-defined. Callie wasn't feeling at her absolute best. Then she shook her head. Callie wouldn't tolerate such nonsense from a friend, so she shouldn't tolerate it from herself.

<h1 style="text-align:center">13</h1>

The Police Station

'What have you got today then?' Matt asked, peering into Caius's stainless-steel lunch box with suspicion.

'A sandwich,' Caius said, brushing off Matt's sceptical tone.

'Is it a super-duper sandwich that will give you telepathy or something?'

'No. It's a regular chicken salad.'

'Is the salad sprouted.'

'Nope, just lettuce and cucumber. It's not even organic. Just grabbed it from the little Sainsbury's.'

'And the chicken?'

'Leftovers from the other day.'

Matt narrowed his eyes. He'd bet with Amy that it was going to be weird today. If he was correct, he scored a point but if he was wrong then Caius gained it. At the end of the month whoever had the lowest number of points bought lunch. Matt and Amy switched out every other month with the other adjudicating. The rules were straightforward by British standards and so far, no one had endeavoured to cheat.

'OK fine, Callie baked the rolls using live Greek yoghurt. It was a recipe she saw online from a gastroenterologist-cum-chef. But it was just from M&S. In fact, it was their basic range. We're trying to improve our gut health.'

'How many types of seeds are sprinkled on top?'

'Only seven.'

'Not eight?'

'I'm slipping.'

'You know, if I squint that looks like normal food.'

'It is. It's flour, yoghurt, a pinch of salt and seven different types of seeds. It's normal food.'

'Normal food, eh?' Amy asked, walking in with her leftover pasta salad.

Caius gestured to his stainless-steel lunch box, inviting her to investigate its contents.

'It looks normal enough,' Amy said, peering at it. 'I'm giving today's point to Caius.'

'What?' Matt said, putting his head in his hands. 'Seven types of seeds, Amy.'

'I feel like I could buy that as a packet mix in a big Tesco. My ruling stands. Caius 11, Matt 7.'

'Bugger it,' Matt said, shaking his head.

'Sorry, Matt, I'm going to call it. You've lost this month's "how weird is Caius's lunch" contest and will have to buy us all bánh mì on Friday.'

'It's a god-tier sandwich,' Caius said.

'Are you not worried your lettuce might have hemlock?' Matt asked, pointedly glaring at the offending chicken salad roll.

'Nope,' Caius said, picking up his sandwich. 'Just had an email from the Food Standards Agency. They've investigated the farm where Digby's bagged salad originated and there was no trace of hemlock in their polytunnels whatsoever. It was murder.'

★ ★ ★

Matt had gone back to Digby's flat to locate his address book so they could get in contact with his friend Nathan while Caius and Amy filtered through the papers from the Institute.

'Barry's report has come in,' Caius said, opening the document.

'And was it hemlock?' Amy asked. She came to his desk and began reading over his shoulder.

'As expected.' Caius scrolled through the document. 'This is interesting. They eliminated Willow's and Digby's fingerprints from the ones they've found and there were two partial prints that match each other. One on the library door and one on the door to the basement that has been painted over.'

'Have the partials flagged anyone with a prior?'

'No.'

'Isolde?'

'Possibly. Although Willow and the Māori protestors have all said that there weren't many visitors, it could have been someone just having a look round.'

'There's a big red rope across the final set of stairs with a sign saying "Private" on it. I don't think even the most brazen of tourists would step over that.'

'I doubt Digby dusted that place. Lord knows how long those prints might have been there.' Caius remembered how immaculate his own home had been though. 'He was neglecting it. He'd had enough. Those two partial fingerprints could've stuck around for quite a while.' Caius looked up at Amy, who was still hovering at his elbow. 'Nothing was missing from the library, was it?'

'Not according to the catalogue. We accounted for everything. Most of the books were the reports of other "gentlemen explorers" and their escapades. There was a whole section on Captain Cook, but I can't imagine they were valuable. Just musty.'

'Was there anything by Horatio Combe himself?'

'There was a set of his handwritten journals. I looked in one of them but it was barely legible.'

'Those are what Willow was typing up. Digby was using them as research for his book.' Caius called Matt, placing him on speakerphone. 'Hombre, are you still at Digby's flat?'

'Sí.'

'Can you find a draft of the book Digby was writing?' They could hear Matt shuffling around. 'His mother wasn't certain that he'd actually started writing it up.'

'I've not found anything that looks like a manuscript. I would've thought that he wrote while at work. It's not as if he had much else to do there.'

'What about Willow's research notes?' Caius asked.

'Haven't found them yet. Most of the paperwork in his office was financial,' Amy said.

'Do you think someone nicked it?' Matt asked. The others heard a cupboard door open and close.

'Isolde honey-trapped Digby to steal the research and a dodgy first draft?' Amy asked.

'Not much of a motive,' Caius said.

The call ended and Matt set off for the station with Digby's address book.

★ ★ ★

'Hi, is that Nathan?' Matt asked. He'd returned to the station and called Digby's best friend from university. He had him on speakerphone.

'Yes. Fenella told me what happened. I can't believe it. Poor Digby.'

'Fenella told you?' Caius asked, slightly suspicious of the fact that she had previously said that she wasn't sure how to contact him.

'Yes, she told me to call you. That you would want to speak to me.' Nathan paused. 'I can't believe it, I really can't.'

'I'm so sorry for your loss,' Caius said, his suspicions abating a little. 'Is it OK if I ask you a few questions? It would really help us get to the bottom of what happened to Digby.'

'Of course. I just . . . I mean . . . How does this even happen?'

'That's exactly what we're trying to ascertain, Nathan.' Caius stopped for a moment to let Nathan gather his thoughts. 'When was the last time you saw Digby?'

'He came to visit us two weekends ago. There was a real ale festival on in our town. We had a good time; terrible hangovers though.' Nathan sighed.

'Did Digby talk about his love life? Anyone he said he was dating?' Matt asked.

'He said he was talking to a girl called Isolde and that they were hopefully going to meet up soon.' Nathan paused. They heard him sigh again. 'Poor Digby hadn't had much luck with women. He always seemed to pine after the ones with boyfriends or the ones who generally had no interest in him, while ignoring the girls who actually liked him. My girlfriend kept introducing him to her friends but it never went anywhere.'

'Did he tell you much about Isolde?' Caius asked.

'Digby said that on paper she was perfect for him. Cultured. That was a big thing for him. He wanted someone who'd traipse around ruins with him and go to plays.'

'Did he share what she looked like?' Matt asked.

'No, I don't think he knew. They hadn't met yet. Digby was culturally atavistic, I suppose. They were writing to each other. She'd described herself as dark-haired, something like that. You know, a nondescript description.'

'Did Digby tell you about his plans for the Institute?' Caius asked.

'Yeah, he was going to fold it. He had to get his mother's approval but he thought she'd agree. Then he was going to sell the building and move back up here to Yorkshire. I never left after uni. I liked it too much.'

'What was he going to do in Yorkshire?' Caius asked.

'He was going to write some sort of memoir about his family and having to deal with the legacy of his ancestor. He was telling me about this one journal where Horatio had gone proper off the deep end and got into seances. Lots of creepy occult stuff. He said he thought he was sniffing powdered Egyptian mummy and all sorts. He said his granddad dismissed it as old Horatio having a bad case of malaria the year before he died but Digby thought it was sinister.' Nathan thought of the diplomatic way to explain it. 'He'd had a change of heart about the place in the last year. He said he had these protestors outside and it had made him think. He became horrified by the place. He felt quite guilty. The book was him trying to do something about it.'

Caius understood, he was in a similar situation himself, but the fact that Digby would've had a handsome payout for ridding himself of the guilt rankled him. Would Digby have ever felt comfortable in a delightful cottage in Knaresborough bought with the proceeds of the sale? Would writing a book about it and then retiring to the shires have absolved him? Caius knew that Britain was fine with it. This windswept little rock clinging to the edge of Europe has the sixth largest economy. Could such legacies even be given away? 'So Digby was moving back to York then?'

'Yeah, York's cheaper than London and it's infinitely more pleasant. He was going to buy a nice house and live off the interest from his chunk of the sale while he wrote.'

They thanked Nathan and ended the call.

'Where does that leave us?' Matt asked.

'Willow's notes and the draft of his "Apologia" are missing. Is that why he was killed?' Amy asked. She'd heard of stupider reasons.

'If he even wrote a word,' Caius said. From what Nathan had said it sounded like Digby had yet to put finger to typewriter. He didn't think Willow's missing notes added up to make much of a motive for murder. 'What would Digby, or even his weirdo ancestor, know that was worth murdering him for?'

'Any legendary treasures the British Museum didn't get their hands on?' Matt asked.

'The Horatio Combe Institute wouldn't be that shabby if that were true and Digby wouldn't have been living essentially in one room in Dollis Hill,' Caius said, remembering the peeling paint on the window frames at the Institute. 'Horatio didn't "find" an Indian diamond like my charming nabob ancestor.' He'd been swatting up on the old paternal line. Between the horrors of enclosing the commons and a failed plantation in Antigua, one of his illustrious ancestors whose older brother died suddenly had had rather too much fun in India before claiming the title.

'What are you going to do about that?' Matt asked.

'I really don't know. We gave a Turner painting to the nation, but knowing my dad that was just a tax thing. Write an Apologia? You can't inherit blame, but you do inherit responsibility.' Caius looked at the whiteboard. He didn't feel like pulling apart this now. What would he do at 3 a.m. otherwise. 'Isolde isn't real. She responded to an ad. Maybe a scammer. "Fake Isolde" wore a "Willow costume" because she'd been watching the place and calculated that she wouldn't look suspicious entering the building dressed as the intern.'

'What next?' Matt asked.

'It's a long shot if it'll throw up anything useful, but we really do need to check that every woman called Isolde within a hundred miles of London isn't murdering their dates. One for us tomorrow, Matt, while Amy is off.'

'I bet there's no more than fifteen Isoldes in the country,' Matt said.

Caius looked at the time on his watch. 'Pub?'

'Yeah, go on,' Amy said.

'Monday Funday,' said Matt.

14

The Red Lion Public House

'What are you having, Amy?' Caius asked.

'A dandelion and burdock, please.'

'Matt? Craft beer with the best pun for a name?'

'Yes, sir.'

Caius walked over to the bar, leaving Matt and Amy alone in the conservatory.

'Caius mention anything more about that stupid special unit?' Amy asked Matt.

'Nope.' They'd been summoned to the Chief Superintendent's office a little over three weeks ago and had been informed of its closure. Little fuss had been made. They'd all seen it coming since Arthur Hampton, its originator, had gracefully bowed out of the Cabinet and caused a leadership contest.

'I'm so glad it's been closed down.' Amy was relieved to no longer have the possibility of being compromised hanging over her. Although to her mind the threat of being dragged into a truly heinous conspiracy would never quite go away now.

'I wonder what will replace it?' Matt said off-handedly.

'What do you mean?'

'Something will. Hampton's down but he's not out.'

Amy nodded. She watched Caius at the bar. He hadn't mentioned the unit closing beyond uttering 'Well, that's that' in the lift afterwards. 'I feel like I know everything about Caius, and yet I somehow also feel like I know nothing about him either.'

'He's taken the end of the special unit harder than I thought he would. I think he saw it as his chance to work out what happened to his sister. The whole tit-for-tat off-the-books thing meant he could've actually had a go but he never really got a chance.'

'Do you still think he's going to quit?'

'Yeah.' Matt watched Caius from across the pub. 'His family will make him or maybe even Callie.'

Caius arrived at the table holding three glasses in the classic triangle formation and two packets of crisps wedged between his chin and neck. 'Matt, I went with a pint of "And Ale Tell You One Thing". It's a guest IPA.'

'I'll try anything once,' Matt said, gladly taking the pint.

'And a dandelion and burdock for Miss 1932, here.'

'I like it, it tastes like medicine. Like an old-fashioned health tonic. It's probably good for me.'

Caius sat down at the table. 'What were you talking about?'

'Hampton,' Amy said, before Matt could change the subject. 'Heard from him?'

'I have. I left him on read.'

'That's probably for the best,' Matt said. He didn't think it was possible for Hampton to not be mad with Caius, even subconsciously. 'How's Callie?'

'On edge. She's had this special commission come in on the weekend that she's excited for but it's stressing her out.'

'I bet she's still upset over her dickhead ex.'

'Oh yeah, but Callie's got a more general air of minor violence about her than usual. Hormones. Has to be.' Caius turned to Amy. They didn't really have boundaries any more. 'Do you get really bad PMT?'

'Well, I'm a reformed Regina George type so I just let every-thing out when I play netball.'

'Callie's not really one for contact sports. She's a floaty yoga and a stroll around Hampstead Heath sort of woman.'

'How's the house and all that?' Matt asked, waving his hands to demonstrate the enormity of Caius's new-found ancestral pile. 'Your dad still trying to get you to work for him?'

'Yeah, but he'd drive me insane,' Caius said, before taking a sip of his pint. 'I'm getting used to it all. I think I'm going to get too used to it. I'd invite you guys up, but I appreciate that you might not fancy it.'

'One weekend perhaps,' Matt said, being diplomatic.

'Yeah,' Amy said, sipping on her dandelion and burdock.

15

Caius and Callie's Flat

'I can't be arsed with cooking tonight,' Caius yelled as he walked through the hallway into the living space. 'Let's celebrate me being castless. Want to go to that gastropub you like on Fortress Road that does those arancini?' He fancied one of their aubergine and San Marzano tomato ones.

Caius found Callie crying on the sofa.

'Hey,' she said, sitting up straight. 'How was your day?'

'What's wrong? Is it Max?' Caius asked, sitting down beside her and putting his arm around her shoulders. 'Did he turn up here?'

'No, not Max.'

'What then, sweetheart?'

'Work . . .'

'But your text said the meeting with Eulalia went well.'

'I thought it went well at the time, but I think I'm actually just really good at talking.'

'No, you're not. I mean, yes you are disgustingly charming. What I meant was that it went well because you're brilliant.'

'I don't know that I am. I'm just a fraud who knows a few people and sounds right.' Callie showed Caius a piece of paper she'd printed out. 'It's the list of all the things Eulalia . . . Eulalia, her real name can't be Eulalia. It's every asset she needs to have a coherent visual concept for in less than a week. She's basically using me to go over her record label's head. It could go spectacularly wrong.'

'Or it could go spectacularly right. Who cares if she's getting

98

you to tread on a few precious toes? It's her career and it could be the making of yours. Besides, she's paying you well, right?'

'We didn't get round to fees, actually.' Callie was kicking herself. That's rule number one for freelancers. 'I forgot.'

'Whatever you want to charge her add a zero, and get "Amelia" to send it.' Caius kissed her on the forehead.

'I need to get a contract over to her ASAP.'

'Get dressed, and I'll buy you all the arancini a girl could possibly want. If you like you could use me to soundboard some of your ideas about . . .' He picked up the printout. 'Fonts, LP album sleeves or whatever while we're at the pub. A change of scene helps me think.'

She perked up. 'I'm into the idea of that old medieval font; you know the one. They use it in Hollywood movies to denote the Middle Ages.' Callie got off the sofa and picked up her laptop. 'But I'm worried it's clichéd, so I've spent the last couple of hours looking through digitised editions of illuminated manuscripts on the British Library's online archive for inspiration. I've got a few images that I can show her that I think she will go mental for.' She spun her laptop around to show him. 'Here's a picture of a nun picking penises from a tree. I think Eulalia would get a kick out of it. It's weird and amusing in the original context but it would be so provocative to reproduce that image now. It's cheeky.'

'I don't remember being taught about these trees in GCSE biology,' Caius said, staring at the picture. 'What was Eulalia like?'

'She was cool. I guess. What you would expect from someone who writes lyrics like that.' Callie wasn't going to describe her. She wasn't going to say that she looked like a baby angel. Caius didn't need to know that. 'Her sister deals with all the business stuff and I guess she just floats around being tickled by the muses.' Callie took her pyjama top off. 'So the same dynamic as us really.'

'New bra?' he asked appreciatively.

'Nope.'

'Let's just order in.' He went to unhook the clasp.

Callie batted him away. 'I want arancini now you've said it.' Callie leaned over and kissed him in lieu. 'You've already been to the pub.'

'Team bonding. Only had a swift one, then I rushed home back to my darling girl,' Caius said, pulling her back onto the sofa and kissing her neck. 'I'll buy you all the arancini in Sicily tomorrow, how about that?'

'But crispy Italian rice balls . . .'

'Is it because you're on?'

'No, I'm late, actually?'

'What?' Caius sat up.

'I'm late. I think I was so stressed worrying about the TV thing going wrong and then it did so my body just went "Haha, no, not this month."'

'You're not . . . ?'

'Pregnant? No, I can't be. I'm baby-proofed.'

'You've still got that thing in your arm?'

'Yeah, Nexplanon.' Callie took her handbag from the table and fished out her purse, finding the card with details of her contraceptive implant. 'Shit.'

'What?'

'It ran out three months ago.'

'You can have all the arancini you want.' Caius stood up. 'And we'll just stop by the Sainsbury's Local on the way. I bet they sell tests. They must do.'

'Are you OK?'

'No. Are you OK?'

'No.'

'Look, it'll be fine.'

'Yeah.' Callie paused. 'Will it?'

'We're not seventeen-year-olds. No one is going to yell at us for being irresponsible.'

'Your mum is still going to kill you though.'

'Oh God yeah. Get dressed. Sainsbury's, pub, all the arancini in the world, pee on a stick. We've got this. Absolutely. We have got this.'

★   ★   ★

'I can't see the tests,' Callie said, staring at the 'lady problems' shelf in Sainsbury's. Tampons, and pads, even a moon cup but no pregnancy tests.

'They're probably behind the till. They get nicked a lot.'

'Schoolgirls?'

'Maybe. I don't know, but the baby formula, steaks and cheese have security tags in here so . . .' Caius glanced over to the adjacent vitamin aisle and spotted a box with a toothy blonde smiling while holding her bump. 'Do you want a pack of those?'

'Pregnancy vitamins?'

'Do you want them?'

'Um.' Callie froze. She looked up at Caius.

'If it is positive, do you want the vitamins?'

'Do you want me to get the vitamins?' Callie asked, aware that the vitamins were tangential to the real question.

'It's your choice.'

'Whether I buy the vitamins?' She just needed to hear him say it.

'All of it. It's all your choice.'

Callie silently picked a packet off the shelves and they walked to the checkout. They got to the front of the queue. Callie placed the vitamins down and the sales assistant scanned the packet. 'Please may I have a pregnancy test?'

'Sure.' The sales assistant took one down from the shelf, scanned it and placed it on the counter. Callie slipped both items into her bag. 'Anything else?'

'A packet of condoms,' Caius said.

'Stable door,' Callie said.

'Never mind,' Caius said to the bewildered sales assistant. 'The horse has bolted.'

'Oh, and twenty Marlboro Lights and a bottle of your strongest whisky as well, please,' Callie said. The sales assistant tried to not be judgy but froze at the combination.

'What?' Caius asked, turning to look at her.

'I'm only joking,' Callie said as the sales assistant began turning around to get them. She took out her Nectar card hurriedly. 'Sorry, I thought I was being funny.'

The sales assistant gave a polite laugh.

'You're going to kill me,' Caius said, tapping his card on the reader.

'I do hope so,' Callie said as he slipped his arm around her shoulder.

'Arancini? Arancini. You can have all the arancini as long as they take Amex.'

TUESDAY

16

The Police Station

'Maidin mhaith,' Caius said to Matt as he walked in.

'Ni hao.' Matt sat down at his desk. 'What language is that?'

'Irish.'

'Do you speak much?'

'Not really. A few phrases here and there. I should learn.' Caius swung around on his desk chair. 'In good news, there are only ten Isoldes in the entire UK. One is in a nursing home in Surrey. Seven are in primary school within either Chelsea, Fulham, Putney or Chiswick. Names have geo-social currency, I guess.' He paused for a moment as he considered baby names before getting back on track. 'That leaves one each for me and you.' Caius handed Matt a printout.

'Isolde Wallis, resident of Marlow,' Matt said, getting his phone out and searching for the postcode. 'You all right?'

'Yeah.'

'You just seem a bit . . .'

'A bit?'

'Cheerful. We're running out of leads and you look less bothered than you normal would do.'

'I got a good night's sleep.'

★　★　★

Caius knocked on Isolde Burrell's front door. She lived in a terrace in Walthamstow Village off Orford Road. There was a for sale sign outside. The house had been renovated recently and the windows replaced with dark grey frames. He never quite got why people did that. It was like they were asking to be broken into. Nothing said I'm here to raise the property prices and be burgled quite like grey window frames.

'One second,' came a voice from inside.

Caius waited patiently for a good minute before ringing the bell again.

'Hang on.' The door slowly opened. 'Do you need me to sign?'

'Madam, I'm not here to deliver anything.' Caius introduced himself and showed her his warrant card. She took down his number and closed the door to ring the station to check he was who he said he was.

'Sorry about that,' Isolde Burrell said, opening the front door and allowing Caius in. 'You can't be too careful.'

'There are an awful lot of scams around,' Caius said, looking down at Isolde's leg which was encased in an orthopaedic walking boot. He followed her into the house, noting the crutches in the hallway as he went. She had long blonde hair. Not a short bob like in the footage.

Isolde limped over to the sideboard and turned off the music that was playing. Caius observed that she hadn't been streaming a Spotify playlist but was instead using a record player. That was a choice he thought Digby would have appreciated.

'Is that Eulalia?' Caius asked. Callie had been playing her album this morning before he left for work.

'Yeah, I can't get enough,' Isolde said, gently lowering herself onto the sofa, gesturing for Caius to sit down on the opposite one. 'She really speaks to me at the stage of my life I'm in now.'

'When did you break your leg?' he asked, glancing down at the moon boot.

'Foot. I've got a stress fracture on my second metatarsal. I've got a weakness there from my ballet days. I am training for the Bristol half marathon. I was out running when I did it.'

'Sorry, that must be quite frustrating.' Caius had been considering signing up for a half marathon but he was concerned that his knees were beginning to creak. He should start lifting more weights and drop his mileage to avoid surgery in his sixties. 'When was that?'

'Friday evening after work. I spent hours waiting in A&E. We got back at 5 a.m. I thought it was just a pulled muscle or something, but I was convinced to get it checked out and here I am.'

'Wow,' Caius said, making a note of her fledgling alibi. 'We?'

'Me and my ex-boyfriend, Andy. We're still good friends. If you don't mind me asking, detective, why do you care?'

'Have you ever met this man?' Caius showed her a picture of Digby.

'No, why?' Isolde shrugged off his question.

Caius thought she was telling the truth. 'You haven't responded to any recent lonely-hearts ads, have you?'

'Certainly not.' Isolde laughed. 'Maybe in a year. Give me time. I'm still in the post-break-up "finding myself" phase. I'm thinking of travelling around Italy. Less wanky than *Eat Pray Love* though. I'm going to tour all the old churches, drink good coffee and paint some landscapes for a month.'

Caius noticed a pile of children's books on the coffee table.

'I'm a school teacher,' Isolde offered up.

'Where do you teach?' Caius ticked her profession off in his head.

'I'm doing substitute work at the moment. I'm moving out of London soon and I'd had enough at my old school. The staff room politics made it quite unpleasant in the end and I didn't want to start at a new school to only leave six months later. I've had a bit of a shake-up this year.' She shook her shoulders as if freeing herself again from the shackles of a whole generation of children raised by Cocomelon on their iPads and her codependent and yet evasive ex. 'It's feeling good.'

'What's your brother called?' He didn't feel the need to ask whether she had brother at all.

'Richard.'

'Does your dad love Wagner?'

'Yes, not in a weird way. His music. Not his politics. What's going on?' Her disbelief that the police had arrived at her door at all had until then stopped her from really considering why he was asking all these peculiar questions. 'What has that got to do with that man in the picture?'

'Are you sure you've never met this man before?' Caius held up Digby's picture again. 'Take your time.'

'I really don't think I have.' She peered at the picture. 'I'd remember a moustache like that. He's very characterful.'

'How tall are you exactly?' Caius thought she was about the same height as Amy.

'Five foot four. I'm sorry, but what has that got to do with anything? Why are you here?'

'Digby, the man in the picture, was catfished.'

'Catfished? Like when people fake an identity online? Are you saying they used my pictures?' Isolde Burrell asked aghast. She was appalled that a stranger had stolen her image for some nefarious purpose, but then again she was also mildly flattered. She hadn't thought she was hot enough to be the victim of something like that, but she had been exercising a lot more recently. Isolde was then in turn duly appalled at her own vanity.

'Not that we're aware, but I do think they've used your life.'

'Oh my God.' Her pictures were one thing but the facts of her existence were something else. 'My life?'

'Yes, is there anyone you know fairly well that might potentially dislike you enough to use details of your life? Or the other way? They like you a little too much perhaps?'

'What on earth are you talking about?'

★　★　★

Caius formally took a statement from Isolde Burrell at the station after he had explained enough of what had happened to Digby. As it turned out her brother Richard was a solicitor, and another solicitor from his firm had accompanied her. Her friend Keisha, from her running club, had also arrived to formally alibi her. Keisha stated that she was out running with Isolde who had landed funny on a dodgy paving stone and went over. Keisha had helped her get home sometime around 6.30 p.m. – she couldn't be more precise than that – and had sat her down on her sofa with a bag of frozen peas. It was now the turn of Isolde's ex-boyfriend Andy who had so gallantly taken her to A&E later that evening when it became apparent that Captain Birdseye hadn't helped the situation. Caius saw Andy react slightly at his name. It appeared even the intelligentsia were up to date on their memes.

'What time did you pick Isolde up from her flat?' Caius asked Isolde's knight in shining armour.

'I walked to Issy's about 9 p.m., I guess. I was marking essays that evening – first years who can only just string a sentence together. I'd turned my phone off. I end up playing some stupid game or reading the bloody news otherwise. It's all so shocking, isn't it? One thing after another. Russia invading Ukraine. What next?' Andy, who was an innocuously dashing academic at King's with floppy hair and a habit of talking with his hands, had rushed over to the station and alibied Isolde as soon as he was called upon. His warm brown eyes appeared bemused by the situation. 'This is all so very bizarre. A catfish?'

'And what happened when you got to Isolde's house?'

'Issy thought it was merely a sprain. Her foot had really swollen up so I talked her into getting an X-ray at least. She's the sort to pretend there's nothing wrong when there blatantly is.' Andy shook his head and widened his eyes. Caius wondered if this was the cause of their relationship's demise. 'I booked an Uber and had it drop us off at Whipps Cross. We were there for bloody hours. I should've brought the rest of my marking. Mind you, there were both piss and crackheads everywhere. It's hard to focus when someone's on a comedown and is claiming to be able to see Jesus. Although strangely relevant to the essays I was marking.'

'If you don't mind me asking a personal question, isn't Isolde your ex? Not your current partner? Why were you the one to take her to A&E?'

'Correct. We were together for thirteen years. We first met in Freshers. It's hard to go from that to nothing and we're actually still really good friends. She comes and feeds my cat when I go away for conferences. I have her spare keys, she has mine. We outgrew each other in many senses, but we'll always be connected.'

'Right.' That went over Caius's head. He could understand staying friends, or rather being friendly, with an ex if you had a child together, or being cordial if you bumped into them out and about, but other than that, nope. No, thank you. He was making a note about their relationship when he suddenly looked up. For a moment he thought Andy was furious with him. That fell away rapidly when Andy gave him a civil smile before glancing at his watch. Caius assumed he just had better places to be than in this windowless room being questioned on his very grown-up, amicable split.

Caius ended the tape and Andy forwarded him the Uber receipt he had for the Uber journeys to and from Isolde's place, and he went ahead and requested the CCTV footage from the A&E waiting area to be on the safe side. Caius was always curious about academics, erroneously feeling in awe of them, and had made small talk with Andy when escorting him out of the station. He asked him about his area of expertise. Andy, perhaps being modest, said that he was a mere early modernist, but he'd just had a broad history of Britain published. A work of popular history to help him gain wider public appeal and possibly a TV show on BBC Four. Caius ordered a copy online afterwards.

Matt was waiting for him in the incident room. 'My Isolde was a mum of three under three who laughed in my face when I asked if she had been sending love letters to Digby Combe-Watson. She was at a family wedding all weekend. Her mum was there trying to wrangle a toddler onto a potty and alibied her there and then. Yours?'

'I found her, but it's not our Isolde. She's a different Isolde.'

'What do you mean?'

'She's called Isolde, brother's Richard, dad likes Wagner, primary school teacher, is moving to the country, grew up in Dorchester, wanted to be a ballerina growing up, went to Exeter uni, paints watercolours and is allergic to bloody strawberries.'

'Those are the facts that Amy listed out from Isolde's letters.'

'Exactly, but it couldn't have been her. Isolde has a broken foot, and a watertight alibi from the friend she was with when she did it. Then she was in A&E until the early hours with her ex-boyfriend. He has the Uber receipts to prove it and I have no doubt that there will have been CCTV on her the entire time.'

'So someone used her life as the backstory for this "fake Isolde".'

'That's what it looks like to me. It's similar to how they dressed up as Willow.'

'Do they know each other?'

'I showed Willow's Instagram to Isolde and she didn't recognise her. She gave me her account name. She's a teacher so her name online is Issy Lara not Isolde Burrell. Lara being her middle name. She chucked a couple of numbers on the end too for good measure. It's locked down. She said because she's a teacher she knows everyone who follows her personally and she doesn't think she knows anyone who'd be capable of catfishing Digby let alone murdering him.'

'What's the commonality between Isolde and Willow?'

'Both female, under thirty-five and living in London. That's it.' Caius stared at the whiteboard. 'The killer, "fake Isolde", planned this out. She's chucked two red herrings at us to slow us down.'

'Stealing Willow's look makes sense, but how did she pick Isolde to imitate? She must know her.'

'I don't know.' Caius played with one of his Muji fine liners. 'Copying Willow is practical. It's a costume in case any of the neighbours see her. "Fake Isolde" could've easily found out about Willow through watching the Institute.'

'Or from her socials.'

'Maybe. Bugger . . .' Caius chewed on the pen. It leaked and he got ink on his lip and spat it out. He grabbed a tissue and dabbed his lip. 'What I don't understand is if they wanted access to the

Institute, why didn't they just break in after hours? Digby doesn't live there and she's already casing the place.'

'They must have wanted something from him,' Matt said.

'But what?' Caius checked his shirt for a stain. He was relieved to see it was clean. 'We've only got one lead left for discovering who "fake Isolde" is. Matt, chase the Post Office. We need to find out about that PO Box.'

17

The National Portrait Gallery

Callie had been sitting in front of a portrait of Elizabeth I for the last half an hour. She had her sketchbook out. She wasn't copying the image of the golden-age queen, she was just picking out the details that she liked. Earrings. A pattern on a sleeve. Jewels in her hair. The textures and the motifs. The opulence. All of them crafted to signal strength. The body of a weak and feeble woman, yada yada. What a piece of rhetoric. Feminine or rather feminised armour. There was perhaps something in that idea. Eulalia liked viragos, after all.

But Callie had had enough of drawing for now. She checked her phone and saw that Mel had replied to 'Amelia's' email stating that Callie was happy to take on the consultation work as long as the fee was commensurate with the short deadline and wide scope of the project. Mel had offered a handsome fee that Callie's impostor syndrome was too proud to reject. 'Amelia' emailed back confirming that the offer was acceptable. Mel had then sent over a contract and a lengthy NDA for Callie to sign. She'd skimmed through it then sent it over to her dad's solicitor to check. She may as well make use of them and Peter had said he had them on retainer for family usage. Callie was already picturing the sun lounger in Sicily that this commission would pay for and they could eat all the arancini they dared straight from the source. Or rather than a beach holiday she should use some of the money on a good pram. Something they could use for all their children. Although she thought that her father would make a show of buying the baby one from Rolls-Royce. Not that they made prams, but she thought there was a chance he would ask them to make an exception for him. She needed to work out how she'd tell her mother, but that was a problem for another day.

Callie packed up her sketchbook and drawing pencils and wandered around the gallery, stopping in front of any portrait that caught her eye. She hated being that person but she took pictures too. Without the flash – she wasn't a barbarian. A very serious-looking woman who didn't even work there, wearing an ill-fitting cardigan (in this weather), gave her a dirty look and was ready to pounce and tell her that the flash would damage the pigments in the paintings, but she was disappointed. Callie flicked her hair in her direction when she turned abruptly to find the loos. She'd suddenly started to feel a bit sick.

Callie stared at the white porcelain bowl for a moment, not sure if she was going to be sick or not. The wave of nausea seemed to abate and she stood up. Judging by the tutting, quite a queue was forming outside. She performatively flushed the empty toilet and went to wash her hands. Callie left the gallery and got the Northern line home. She bailed at Camden Town and caught a black cab the rest of the way. The nausea had returned and she didn't want to puke in one of those clear plastic bags attached to a hoop that passed for a bin. She'd rather have the taxi pull over and throw up on the side of the road. She made it home, although the cab driver couldn't help but comment on the shade of chartreuse she'd turned. He even helped her out after she had paid.

Callie was lying on the sofa listening to a Radio 4 broadcast on Eleanor of Aquitaine when her phone rang. It was Eulalia.

'Cal, hi it's Eulalia. Can you talk?'

'Absolutely.' Callie sat up, aware that she didn't want to sound ill on only her second day. 'Have you had some more thoughts after yesterday?'

'Yes,' Eulalia said. Callie thought she sounded a little unsure but then that chipper brightness reappeared. 'I saw something interesting.'

'Cool, what was it?' Callie waited for a response but didn't get one. 'Do you want to do this over Zoom or Teams instead? That way you can share your screen with me and we can talk about it.'

'I can email it to you.'

'Great,' Callie said, waiting for Eulalia to elaborate her new idea. Callie reached for the iPad and opened her emails. 'What was it you saw?'

'OK then.'

'Oh, sure.' Callie refreshed her email – still nothing. 'Are you going to send the thing over?'

'Yeah, yeah, yeah. You still good to meet on Friday morning to discuss initial concepts with the guys from PCQV?' Eulalia asked. It sounded clear to Callie that Eulalia didn't want to hang up. 'Plus Chic Que Vous . . . Zut alors.'

'Yeah, I'll bring mood boards with me as agreed,' Callie said, waiting several seconds for a response but not getting one. 'Are you all right?'

'Do you want to get dinner this evening? There's this new Korean place that's opened up nearby and I really want to try it.'

'I can't tonight,' Callie said. She didn't have anything on, she just felt rough. 'I have plans.'

'Tomorrow then? Let's do tomorrow evening. You should come see my place.'

'Brilliant, see you then.'

'OK. I'll send you the details.'

'Marvellous.' Callie hung up and lay back down.

Callie didn't expect the world's most mysterious pop girlie, who had gripped a certain section of the internet with a whole lot of unprocessed trauma and obsessive tendencies, to be lonely, let alone to see her as a source of comfort. Callie remembered reading on some blog somewhere that Eulalia had studied at the Royal College of Music. Surely, she had friends from her course who were still in London? But then again, London was such a transient city with a lot of international students. A lot of people from her own course had disappeared after graduation. She checked her email for the 'thing' that Eulalia had seen but nothing came through. Her phone pinged with the address of a restaurant that had a bit of a buzz to it. Then came a meme. And another. And another. Just shitposts about how awful men were. Callie sent a non-committal but polite reply with a couple of random emojis thrown in for good measure. Callie turned the show about Eleanor of Aquitaine back on as she started working through the contents of the mood boards in her head. Pausing the recording periodically, unsure as to whether she was going to have to run to the loo to puke or not.

18

Eulalia's House

Mel laid out a selection of goodies on the dining room table for Eulalia to choose from.

'PCQV have sent over samples for you to try,' Mel said, gesturing at the forty-odd products neatly arranged by type. There were death-scented perfumes, over-ripe peach-flavoured lip oils, highly pigmented cream blushes, powder highlighters that shone like the blood moon, lipsticks that made your pout juicy enough to bite, a tubing mascara in five wacky shades that promised to make your lashes look like spider legs and eyeshadow palettes whose colour story were inspired by the world's most deadly creatures.

'I hate the packaging.' Eulalia wrinkled her nose at how 'clean' it looked.

'That's just what the sample comes in from the factory.' Mel had to stop herself from rolling her eyes at her sister's predictability. She'd told her that before, that this was the whole point of hiring Callie, but Eulalia refused to ever see the big picture and preferred griping instead. 'It won't look like that in the end. They're really open to our input.'

'It's so refreshing to work with people who get it, who get what we're trying to achieve. Of course they'd get it, they're a French company. Duh.'

'I thought we should start with the perfumes first.' Mel gestured at the bottles lined up.

'I love perfume so much. Scent is the most provocative sensual input. It's so transcendental.' Eulalia picked up the first bottle and sprayed it. 'Love it. Smells like rotting plums.' She worked her way through the other two bottles in front of her, equally delighted with their sickly sweet, heady smell of decay. Eulalia swatched every lipstick shade down her arm like a plump, semi-matte ladder climbing up her flesh. Globs of lip oil ran down the back of her hand. She tried a sheer purple one on. It tasted like Palma Violets. Anyone she kissed while wearing it would succumb. Eulalia smeared every high-pigmented glitter eye-shadow from a palette inspired by poisonous jellyfish down her other forearm, followed by every cream blush that looked like bruising and every mercurial highlighter. She was utterly delighted by everything, but she was most of all delighted that she'd been understood by the mega luxury goods conglomerate. Mel made notes.

Eulalia flitted back upstairs to her room to shower off the gloopy excesses of hyper-profitable vanity and then to listen to music in her bedroom. She was searching for inspiration for the lyrics of a new song her sister had already bashed out a melody for. Eulalia blasted Fleetwood Mac as Mel was left downstairs to manage everything else.

'Hey, Venetia, it's Mel.' She disliked speaking to Venetia. She found it hard to maintain her new accent around someone who spoke in such a heightened way. 'From Eulalia's team. She was thrilled with everything you sent over. Loved it all. I'll email over the final choices, but yeah she picked everything I said, sorry, I mean everything I thought she would. Yes . . . let's final-ise the meeting. You know Calliope Foster? Yeah, yeah, so lovely. Milliner, but did a lot of fashion editorial a decade ago. Oh you know her personally. You're old friends. Small world. She's working with Eulalia on concepts. They've really gelled.' Mel smiled as she spoke; it hid her true feelings. She wasn't comfortable with an outsider being so close to the process, so close to their mutually held deceit. 'Eulalia has made it quite clear to me that her visual concept for the album and the associated lines need to be at least partially taken on board when considering the cosmetic line. I know, I know. That's why she chose to work with you and not one of your competitors. She knows that you value true artistic vision. Between you and me, we all just need to listen to the presentation and nod along, telling Eulalia she's a genius. I think realistically what you'll end up incorporating is a font or a colourway, you know. Artists huh. Great chat.' Mel ended the call and smiled to herself. She was pulling it off.

19

The Police Station

'I've got the information from the Post Office,' Matt said, opening the email. 'The PO Box is located in Barnet and was paid for by a Mrs Beverley Parkin, her address is in Harrogate. They only bought it for three months.'

'Oh that's a lovely part of the world. Very fancy.' It was just the sort of place to go for a weekend away. A baby moon, maybe? Caius checked his watch. It was coming up to the end of their shift.

'Do you think it was some sort of identity theft?'

'Possibly? Although Digby was going to move to York, wasn't he? Maybe there's a connection there?'

'I'd say with a name like Bev though there's at least one generation difference between her and Digby, and probably a social class or two.'

'Call back his friend Nathan and see if he's ever heard Digby mention a Beverley or anyone else called Parkin.'

Matt put Nathan on speakerphone. 'Hi, Nathan, I have a few more questions for you.'

'Sure,' said Nathan.

'Did Digby ever mention anyone called Beverley to you?'

'Beverley? No. A bit too school dinner lady for Diggers. He was my mate, and you know I loved him like a brother, but we all called him Posh Digby at uni. Not that you needed to use the word posh. Digby isn't a name you'd find on a council estate. He was culturally posh, you know what I mean, even if he wasn't loaded. Liked opera and that, although he wasn't averse to the odd bit of low culture either.'

'Right,' Matt said, making a note that he liked opera. 'Any connection between Digby and Harrogate?'

'We went there together once.'

'You went with Digby?'

'Yeah, we went for the day. Had tea at Bettys. It's a lovely place.'

'Did anything eventful happen?'

'Not really. Well apart from going to the Wetherspoon's.'

'What happened?'

'We got very drunk. It's the nicest 'Spoons you've ever been in. It's inside the old baths.'

'Right.'

'It was a Saturday evening and we were a little worse for wear. There was this girl there with her troll of a sister. It started out as normal flirting. I've got a girlfriend so I was a hands-off and extremely respectful wingman. I was chatting away to the ugly sister, all very nice. I can talk to women like they're people too.'

'OK,' Matt said, shooting Caius a look.

'You know, it was funny because they were very clearly sisters but the younger one was the most beautiful girl I'd ever seen. Looking at her made me uncomfortable. Digby was enamoured the moment he saw her. He was telling her all about his life, trying to impress her with saying that he was a curator in a museum down in London and all that. The ugly sister wasn't impressed and kept trying to get her little sis to leave but she wouldn't go. It was as if Digby was the only man who'd ever seen her and she'd gone wild for the attention.'

'Sure.'

'I'm a good wingman so I kept buying jugs of cheeky woo woos for the table while the ugly sister told me about her music or something. We were all plastered by the end and Digby declared his undying love for her, said he'd rescue her from her sister, the dragon. The beauty got pulled away into the night by her sister who'd got pissed off and was never seen again. We were so twatted we nearly missed the last train back to York. It was a fun day. I'm going to miss him so much. He'd bring that girl up every now and then.'

'When was this?'

'Three years ago.'

'Thanks, Nathan.'

'Was that helpful?' Nathan sounded hopeful.

'Sure.' Matt hung up. 'That was painful.'

'I'll get hold of Barnet Post Office and get the CCTV for the days that the letters were posted,' Caius said, shaking his head.

Tiny Simm came into the incident room.

Caius smiled at him. 'Amy said you did a great job checking the collection.'

'Thanks, sir.' Tiny Simm moved on the spot. He felt like he was sticking his head above the parapet. Caius had a reputation for being a bit of a bastard when he wanted to be around the station, but he liked the guy. 'I thought you might want to know that a break-in was reported on Priory Square this morning.'

'A break-in? What number?'

'Seven.'

'Anything taken?'

'No, the guy who reported it was apparently half-cut. I just thought you might maybe think it was related. It's rare for two things to happen in one small square like that so close together.'

'You're not wrong.' Caius gave his best winning smile, while Simm gave him an awkward thumbs up. 'Thanks, mate.'

Simm left the room buoyed.

Caius turned to face Matt. 'Do you fancy a trip up to Harrogate?'

'Are you taking me on a little mini break?'

'Solo travel, mi amigo.'

'Fine, I'll go home and grab my toothbrush.'

'And clean pants.'

'Do you think? I was just going to wear the ones I've been wearing all year. Bonne nuit.'

'Arrivederci.'

20

Caius and Callie's Flat

'Can I have an omelette for dinner, please?' Callie asked. She'd given up on the sofa and had retreated to bed.

'Anything for you.' Caius had got in under the covers with her after he'd come home. 'When can we tell people?'

'The old adage is that you wait for the twelve-week scan because most miscarriages happen earlier than that.'

'I see.'

'I feel horrendous. I'm no longer in denial so the nausea has really kicked in.'

'My darling.' Caius stroked her hair. 'Did you call the doctor's?'

'Yeah, I've got an appointment with the community midwife on Thursday.'

'Want me to come?'

'Oh no, it's OK. I think they just do a blood test and weigh you or something.'

'What do you want in your omelette? Ham, mushrooms, onion, cheese?'

'Everything, please. Is there any more unicorn in the fridge? A bit of that grated on top would do me wonders.'

'I'm sure we've got a whole multipack of mythical animal meat in the freezer from Costco that I can add.' Caius sat up from the bed. Callie's sketchbook had slid onto the floor. He picked it up. 'What have you been drawing?'

'Bits and pieces from portraits,' Callie said, sitting up. 'I think that a sort of Renaissance-era portrait of Eulalia could be really interesting.'

'You should speak to Georgie.'

'Yes, I thought the same, but I doubt there's time for a full-blown portrait. I love the idea of sketches. Not Vitruvian man exactly, but something along those lines.'

Caius stared at the sketchbook. 'You are so talented. Why are you even with me?'

'Because of your massive . . . house.'

'Ha ha.' Caius got off the bed. 'I've been thinking about names.'

'What have you come up with?'

'Mostly it's a list of names to avoid. People I hated at school, people I've arrested, Chelsea players, you know. The worst people in the world.'

'No exes.'

'Yeah. Definitely not baby Max. I quite like the name Charles. It's solid. You can shorten it to Charlie. No nonsense.'

'Dated one. He was a nonsense person.' Callie shook her head. That had been a terrible three weeks in 2011. 'I'll start a list. Just pray that it's a girl because I've been on a lot of second dates with utter bellends.'

'Am I on that list?'

'Yeah, but you're a bellend that I can tolerate in small doses.'

Caius kissed her on the forehead. 'One unicorn omelette coming up.'

Callie decided that she'd had enough of staring at the cornicing on the ceiling and made her way to the living space to stare at the cornicing there. She sat down on the sofa. A large bunch of white roses had appeared on the coffee table.

'Are these for me?'

'No,' Caius said, slicing the vegetables.

Callie reached out for a petal, rubbing it between her fingers. 'They're beautiful.'

'Well, I did accidentally knock you up so it was the very least I could do.' He put the knife down and came over.

'Flowers are a good start.' She shot him a look to let him know that this was only the beginning.

He wound his arms around her waist. 'What do you think they'll look like?'

'Like a cross between me and you.'

'They could be ginger. I don't know what recessive genes I've got lurking in my nuclei.'

'Why did you say ginger like it was the same as having six fingers? Red-headed babies are adorable.' Her phone buzzed.

Tabs

18.13

Hey Callie, it's Tabitha! Saw that video from Chelsea. That dress was stunning on you. Where's it from? I'm doing more stylist work atm and am always on the lookout for new designers. Honestly though, that video was so funny. Was it a set-up? If so you were very convincing. If not your ex illustrated your point very well. Fancy a coffee this week? Would be great to catch up X

'Tabs wants to go for coffee.' Callie reread the message twice. She didn't know what to do. She didn't want to be rude, Tabs was a nice girl, but she also didn't think it was wise to get sucked into that circle. 'I'm not sure.'

'Go, if you want to,' Caius said as he cracked an egg into a bowl. 'You like her, right?'

'Yeah, she's nice. Plus she works in fashion so she may be useful at some point. Mercenary, I know.'

'There you go,' Caius said, whisking the eggs together and adding them to the pan. It might not be the worst thing if Callie heard the odd account of Arthur Hampton's goings-on. 'Meet up with her.'

WEDNESDAY

21

The Police Station

Caius was at his desk reading over a report on an attempted burglary that had been made by a certain Benedict Carr-Ridge who lived at 7 Priory Square. His name was familiar but Caius wasn't sure why. It became apparent quite early on in the report that Benedict wasn't a reliable witness. The officer who had interviewed him wasn't even convinced the incident had happened. The empty bottles littered about the place hadn't helped his credibility.

'Morning, morning,' Amy said as she entered the incident room. 'Did I beat Matt in?'

'He's been sent to Harrogate.'

'That's better than being sent to Coventry. Why Harrogate?'

'The PO Box was paid for by a woman called Beverley Parkin who lives there. We think it was some sort of fraud,' Caius said, rapping his fingers on the desk. 'The Post Office in Barnet where the PO Box is located has security footage but only covering the days that the last three letters were likely sent or received.'

'Are you telling me that I have to watch three days' worth of footage of people returning online orders?'

'Well, I found out this morning that the Met is trialling a computer program that can track faces across multiple pieces of footage. I've requested that we are put on that trial. I've forwarded you the details. If you could sort that out when they get here.'

'That sounds terrifying but I really, really hate watching CCTV so I'm going to let that particular little piece of apocalyptic programming off.'

'I'm going to go check out a burglary on Priory Square. Tiny Simm flagged it.'

'Anything stolen?'

'Apparently not.' Caius grabbed his suit jacket off the back of his chair. It was too humid to wear it but he would once he got to Priory Square. It made him feel like an adult. 'It could be a coincidence but we are running out of leads fast with this one.'

22

Harrogate

Matt knocked on the door of a 1930s semi-detached in a pleasant cul-de-sac. It had rained overnight. The air was muggy. A middle-aged woman opened the door.

'Hello, are you Mrs Beverley Parkin?'

'Who's asking?' She inched back behind the door.

'DS Matthew Cheung, from the Metropolitan Police,' he said, holding his warrant card up for her to see. 'May I come in for a moment? We think you may have been a victim of fraud.'

'Nigel.' The woman demurely called once for her husband to no response and then again with operatic gusto. 'Nigeeelllll.'

A bald man appeared behind his wife at the door. He was flustered, his cheeks red; he had a trowel in one hand and a pair of gardening shears in the other.

'What is it, Beverley?' He stopped and looked at Matt in his shirt and tie. 'Jehovah's Witnesses? Or is it double glazing? No thank you, not today. I told you, Bev, just shut the door.'

'No, Nigel, he's police.'

'DS Matthew Cheung, from the Met.' He showed him his warrant card. 'We think your wife may have been the victim of fraud.'

'You best come in then.' Nigel moved aside to allow Matt into the house.

Beverley walked into a neat living room and gestured at Matt to sit down on the leather sofa opposite, while she and Nigel sat together on the other, larger one.

'You said something about fraud?' Beverley asked.

'Yes, perhaps.' Matt looked about the room. It was a normal house. A cheap chandelier hung from the ceiling. 'Did you rent a PO Box in London recently?'

'A PO Box?' Beverley asked, picking at a bobble on her cardigan. 'Like where you send competition entries to?'

'They're frequently used for that sort of thing,' Matt said.

'Why would Beverley need a PO Box?' Nigel asked. He didn't like the implication that Beverley was up to something untoward.

'I don't know. Did you purchase one, Beverley?'

'No, definitely not,' Beverley said, mystified.

'Especially not one in London. Why on earth would she want to go there?' Nigel puffed.

'I've not been to London since the Royal Wedding. Oh she did look lovely. I was stood right in front of Westminster Abbey. Me and my cousin camped out the night before. What a fairytale.'

'Kate Middleton?'

'Oh no, Lady Di,' Beverley said, gesturing to a commemorative plate in a cabinet. 'Taken too young.'

'Have you been phished recently?'

'I beg your pardon, young man,' Nigel said. He took 'phished' to be some modern innuendo.

'It's a type of internet scam. Often the criminal will pretend to need your help, usually by imitating a friend or relative in trouble. They try and get you to click on a link and give them your bank details.'

'Oh no. I've got an account but I only really use it to get my bills and emails about the Next sale,' Beverley said. She turned to look at Nigel and furrowed her brow. 'Hang on, Nigel. I think I dropped a card in M&S Food the other month. I had to get a new card, but perhaps I wasn't quick enough. It was such a hassle. It can't have been an expensive charge or I would've

noticed and challenged it with the bank. I hadn't noticed anything, actually.'

'Do you not have two-step verification?'

'What's that?'

'When the bank texts you if you're making an online
purchase.'

'I do have that I think. Maybe. Oh, I'm not sure.'

'Bev, did you leave a little piece of paper with the PIN number
on it with the card?'

'I might have done, Nigel.'

'You've got to be more careful.'

'Right,' Matt said. He took another look around the room.
There was a graduation photo of a young woman on the
mantlepiece. There was nothing remarkable about it other than
the girl's spectacular plainness that she had tried to hide under
a chunky fringe and a layer of caked-on make-up that didn't
match the colour of her neck. Beverley looked like she would've
been pretty when she was younger. Her daughter must have
taken after her doughy father. 'Well, I recommend speaking to
your bank as soon as possible, they have a lot of advice on
avoiding scams, and if you notice any other odd charges to
your account then please notify them and then call me.' Matt
handed Beverley his card and left for the four-hour drive back
to London.

Beverley closed the door. She turned to her husband who was
perched on the stairs.

'A PO Box? What does Jenny want with a PO Box? She said
she just wanted to buy a cardigan. And why are the police
interested?'

'A cardigan? Why can't she buy her own cardigan?'

Beverley shrugged. 'She said she didn't have any cash.'

'I thought they had plenty of money.' Nigel stood up and took his phone out of his pocket. 'Can't buy a cardigan? I thought the whole idea of Jenny moving to London too was that she'd get a bit of independence while her sister kept an eye on her. Made sure she was OK.'

'I know.' Beverley nodded. She thought it was for the best too for Jenny to be a bit more independent and away from them. It also meant that if Jenny had another turn with her nerves the neighbours didn't have to see or hear of it like last time. Besides, they had better doctors down there.

'She's supposed to be paying her to be her assistant now that things are taking off for her. I'm going to call and find out what this is really about. They've not been back to visit in ages either and there's no way I'm going all the way to bloody London.'

'Hang on, Nigel.' Beverley took the phone from her husband and placed her other hand gently on his chest. She spoke in the soothing manner that had calmed most of his bluster over the last thirty years. 'It's no big deal.'

'Of course it is, Bev, they don't send policemen up from London for one little dodgy payment like that.'

'I'll call later, love.' Beverley looked at the time on her watch. 'They'll be busy and I don't want to upset anyone.' She really didn't want to upset the little bit of 'housekeeping' she was sent on the sly every month without her tight husband's knowledge, which had paid for her new highlights and a pair of new leather boots and all the other little treats that her husband had been convinced had come from the back of the wardrobe.

23

Eulalia's House

Eulalia was sitting on the floor of her bedroom, her MacBook nestled between her crossed legs. She replayed the footage again.

Monty Don:

My understanding is that to the Victorians flowers had specific meanings.

[Callie, wearing a boater, holds her
grandmother's ancient copy of Kate Greenaway's
Language of Flowers aloft.]

Callie:

Exactly so. The Victorians were a privately romantic if not publicly restrained people. Floriography was a way to discreetly communicate your feelings. It imaginatively harks back to the age of chivalry. A lady might choose to signal to her lover that she wants to see him again by wearing a Michaelmas daisy which means 'farewell'.

[Monty Don spots Max jumping over the rope
around the show garden. Max then creeps up
into shot and gets on bended knee. Max wobbles;
he is drunk. Monty is calm.]

Max:

Calliope Foster, will you marry me?

> [Callie spins around, her face turning from
> surprised elation to horror.]

Callie:

No, definitely not. I don't ever want to see you again. This is a Michaelmas daisy. Do you understand me? [She starts laughing, turns to Monty, rolls her eyes and tries to regain her composure by continuing her trail of thought. She takes her hat off.] In this arrangement I've also included a musk rose which—

Max:

The new man!

> [Max wobbles as he raises his fists as he marches
> across the shot to Caius. A production assistant chases
> after him. The cameraman has given up on floriography
> and has chosen drama.]

Caius:

[Speaking quietly and trying to back off from the shot.] Let's get you a glass of water, mate.

Max:

I'd punch you but you've got a cast on your arm.

Caius:

If anything that makes it a fair fight.

[Max swings at Caius who easily dodges it and in turn
catches him, restraining him one-handed. Caius, realising
how this looks, glances pleadingly at Monty Don to end it all.
Monty Don turns to camera.]

Monty Don:

Chivalry isn't dead.

Callie:

You know, right now I rather wish it was.

Monty Don:

Do you? But what about your work?

Callie:

My work? My work is about aesthetics, it's not a code of
conduct . . . I'm aware that it may seem a little fanciful, but it's
about the idea of a pure love rather than the reality of it, isn't it?
It's the romance not the consummation, it's the yearning for an
impossible love, for a truly perfect feeling. For the sublime. It's the
difference between art and things. All I'm trying to create is poetic
poignancy. That wasn't chivalry, it was just my stupid ex who
appears to have spent the day drinking on his corporate credit
card.

Monty Don:

Men, eh?

Callie:

Tell me about it, Monty.

Monty Don:

You should get a dog.

Callie:

Better conversations.

Monty Don:

They're loyal.

Callie:

Unwavering loyalty was a key characteristic of chivalry.

Monty Don:

Perhaps women should replace men with Golden Retrievers?

Callie:

They would shed less.

Monty Don:

They're more likely to chew your slippers.

Callie:

I don't know, Monty. It's rough out there.

'Are you playing that again?' Mel asked from the doorway.

'What?' Eulalia asked, turning round to look at her sister. 'Seriously? What? I think it's funny.'

Mel rolled her eyes.

'I like her vibe.' Eulalia jumped up in defence of Callie's honour.

'I know you do, that's why we've got her on board. She sent over the signed contract and the NDA, by the way, so you can continue to play with her without her leaking your bra size to the *Mail.*'

'Good.' Eulalia looked up at her sister and started pacing. 'I just feel like she gets it. Cal understands me. She understands what I'm trying to do.'

'Are you OK? You seem a bit manic.'

'Yeah, I'm good, just excited to start on this next phase.'

Mel nodded, although she wasn't convinced. 'You've got to stop having little crushes on these girls who aren't interested in you. It's sad,' Mel said with a sigh. 'Is it even love? I don't think you're capable of love per se. I think you just get obsessed or even jealous of them.'

'Shut up, Mel. I'm going out,' Eulalia said suddenly, putting her laptop down, grabbing a slim volume from beside her bed and dashing out of her room, past Mel who stood patiently at the top of the stairs. 'I'm not gay.'

'No one would care if you were.' Mel slowly descended the stairs, yelling after her flouncing sister. 'To be fair, a nascent proclivity for bisexuality would make you a much more interesting person. Might be worth pretending you are in the next round of interviews anyway. We can get you a PR girlfriend for a few weeks.' Mel waited for the front door to shut before descending all the way down to the basement, where her final meeting of the day was waiting for her. When the house had been purchased, extensive work had been rapidly done underneath the property with a gym and a soundproofed recording studio having been dug in.

'Her ladyship gone out?' asked DJ Sonikk, the former boarder turned DJ turned producer who was working on Eulalia's soon-to-be-released sophomore album.

'Yep.' Mel looked at the time on her phone. 'She'll go mooch around one of the wanky shops on the high street so we've got at least an hour and a half of peace. I wound her up a bit and she left with a volume of poetry, so maybe two if we're lucky.'

'OK.' DJ Sonikk pursed his lips tight.

'What?' Mel asked, glaring at her producer. 'We've been through this. The label said you're totally fine with the arrangement. You're being paid enough. She's the face, I'm everything else. The division works well. No one would buy anything with me on the cover.'

'I don't really have a problem with the deceit,' Sonikk said, staring at Mel. He took her in. It was such a shame she didn't look like her sister. 'Eulalia' had this otherworldly beauty, partially due to the fact that she wasn't always in this world. When the label had first approached him about working on Eulalia's second album he'd been excited – but then he'd signed the NDA. The situation was then explained to him in full and his enthusiasm plummeted. He understood why 3lectr0, who had produced Eulalia's stellar first album, hadn't returned. He knew before he took the job that the situation was a bit off, he'd been euphemistically warned as much by 3lectr0 himself, but he hadn't been expecting this. He'd thought 'Eulalia' was going to be bratty or a cokehead, not a sweet girl who possibly had a personality disorder and her hyper-gifted, sow-faced big sis. 'Is your sister all right? She seems pretty OK but then she'll just say something weird. When I got here she was telling me all about this artist she's got on board. She believed 100 per cent that she was in charge of the look, everything. Then she was rapidly talking weird shit about nuns being burnt alive.'

'She is in charge of the look. To an extent. She's got some input. She can't be expected to prance around miming without feeling like someone listened to her at some point. We don't want her getting fed up and exposing us all.'

'Who even is this Calliope Foster?' He wondered if he'd met her at a party or whether that was a Penelope Carter and he was getting confused.

'She's a jolly nice sort of gal. One of yours, I suspect,' Mel said, affecting Callie's heightened accent. 'To be fair to Calliope, she is legit. Went to art school. Spent time at the big magazines early on in her career before settling into being one of society's premier milliners. I don't doubt she's got the chops, especially when it comes to costumes. The label vetted her and see no harm in it. If working with darling Calliope for a week and getting her silly little notions heard – which might not even be that dreadful, she does care about how things look – gives "Eulalia" a feeling of control then it's worth it. The label and PCQV are both aware and they're fine with it. They're willing to implement a few of them, if possible. "Eulalia" doesn't know that though. Don't tell her that they've already agreed. It needs to feel like a victory.'

'But she seems, for want of a better word, a bit delicate.'

'She's not delicate. She's more robust than most people you'd meet out on the street.' Mel was making sure she took her medication, after all. Perhaps it was time for a review with her psychiatrist just to be sure the dosage was right though.

'I'm not saying she's stupid.' He wanted to say that she was impressionable, even vulnerable. She seemed so isolated when he saw her. She acted like he was her new best friend when they'd barely spoken.

'Oh no, she's intelligent in a raw animal sort of way. She's constantly writing and reading these silly little stories on her laptop. Half of what she says is word salad.' Mel paused. She was aware that she was coming off as mean. That she looked jealous of her stunning little sis. 'It's useful for interviews.'

Sonikk took a deep breath. 'I just think it'll be easier to have a conversation now where she's put more in the loop with what the label think, rather than in five years' time while she's having a breakdown at the loos of the Grammys and sobbing all over Taylor Swift's shoes while Adele tries to comfort her.'

'Fuck the label. They're just the bank. We do write the lyrics together. We genuinely co-write them. She comes out with a couple of key phrases or an image that I build around and make coherent. I'm the musician. I'm the one who understands the cadence. I just focus the chatter on what she's contributed and her ego fills in the rest. She's Ringo and I'm George and Paul and John,' Mel said, playing with the cord on her headphones, affecting a pathetic tone to her voice that Sonikk wasn't buying. 'Unfortunately, God gave my sister the face and the body and me the talent and tenacity. My sister's face could launch a thousand ships; mine could maybe inspire one very mediocre man to drive a Peugeot down two junctions of the M42. I'm a realist and so is she. Together we make one phenomenal popstar.'

'As long as she can hold it together.'

'She will. I will always make sure of that. No harm will ever come to her. I love my sister.' Mel turned and smiled. 'Now let's go from the top.'

Sonikk went to play the backing track but stopped. 'What do your parents think of all of this?'

'They don't care as long as they get cash in their bank account every month. Now are you finished?' Mel, who had had quite enough of this, gave Sonikk a small nod. 'May I remind you that you're being paid bloody good money to play along, and that you also signed an ironclad NDA. If you violate it I will sue you to Hell and back.'

Sonikk played the track and Mel began to sing. She may not have had a face that could launch a thousand ships but she had a voice that could lead each and every one of them to wreckage.

'Fuck me, this is good. We're all going to be so rich,' Sonikk said, listening back to Mel nailing the vocals in one perfectly haunting take.

★ ★ ★

Mel walked up the stairs and knocked on her sister's door. She'd heard the front door slam ten minutes ago. Barely waiting for a response, Mel opened the door. Her sister was watching the footage of Callie again.

'Perhaps having Calliope work for you was a bad idea? Should I speak to the label?'

'No.'

'Then maybe you should stop obsessing about her. Treat her like a normal person and then she might actually want to be your friend.'

'I'm not obsessed. I just think she's terribly romantic. Her boyfriend will be a knight one day. An actual knight. His family have a big house in the country.'

'Not this Downton Abbey nonsense again.'

'I've been reading about him. It was in all the papers last year. Remember? His grandfather inherited this house and stuff because someone else was illegitimate. They had no idea it was going to happen. It's like a fairytale. In fact it is. His family are descended from a branch of the Plantagenets and therefore from Melusine. You know, she's a fairy. I think she's half snake or something . . .'

'Who's Melusine? This is what I mean by obsessed. Don't say this stuff to her. She'll think you're weird.'

'I'm not obsessed, see.' Eulalia closed the tab. 'I'm going to read instead.'

'I brought you some lunch – quinoa with black beans and roasted squash and grilled chicken breast.'

'Chicken again. Really. I never want to see another grilled chicken fillet again. Can't I have lasagne? Or cottage pie? A cheeseburger? What about a roast? Let's have a roast on Sunday! We could go home? I've not seen Mum or Dad in ages.'

'The label want you in your best shape ever for the tour so they've had this amazing chef prepare all your food. It's all organic, high protein. It's nutritionally balanced to perfection. You're going to look amazing. You're going to have to do a lot of performances. You're going to need to be fit.'

'I know.' Eulalia took the plate of food. 'Are they going to send me a new choreographer?'

'Soon. They're looking out for a good one. They're in talks with Beyoncé's choreographer's assistant. Only the best for you. The last guy tried to sell your pictures to the press. They've upped their vetting process.'

'That's so sad. I really liked him. I thought he could help me.'

'Help you with what?' Mel's weight shifted.

Eulalia paused. 'My flexibility. I'm so much stiffer these days than I used to be.'

'That'll come back with training. How about yoga? What if I get us a yoga teacher who'll come here to the house. I can do it with you. It'd be fun.'

'That would be fun. So much fun. Could Callie come too?'

'Let's just have quality us time.' Mel looked at her sister picking over her lunch, reading some brain rot story on her laptop.

'Callie's coming over for dinner, by the way. Thought we could brainstorm or whatever.'

'Here?' Mel wasn't keen on having her in the house. She didn't want her poking around or trying to get her sister into the recording studio downstairs for a cheeky preview.

'I thought we could go out?'

'Sure.'

'Can I have some money then?'

'I'll leave some cash on the hall table.'

'Amazing.' Eulalia didn't look up from the computer.

24

Priory Square

For the third time Caius rang the doorbell of Benedict Carr-Ridge's town house. He tried to peer into the windows but they hadn't been cleaned in years and the railings shaped like spears stopped him from leaning further round. He rang for a fourth time.

'What the fuck do you want?'

'Benedict Carr-Ridge. *The Pursuit of Hostility*.' It had finally come to him.

He slammed the door shut.

Caius rang the doorbell again.

'Did my editor send you?' He looked through the letterbox at Caius with his smudged, horn-rimmed glasses. Yes, the bastard looked literary enough. 'It's been thirty years; they should've just sunk the cost of the advance by now.'

'DI Caius Beauchamp. I'm here about the break-in.'

'Oh, a DI.' He swung the door open to reveal himself standing with his arms aloft beckoning him in. 'I am important. Oh and a detective who reads quality literature. Well, I never. I suppose you may enter.'

Caius followed him down the hallway. Stacks of books clung to the wall. One wobbled as Benedict walked past and a pile of twelve hardbacks fell in front of Caius.

'Just step over them,' Benedict said, turning into a room filled with even more books. He flopped onto a chaise longue. 'So, you've read my novel?'

'I have.' Caius hadn't but he nodded enthusiastically all the same. He had a paperback copy he'd bought for £1 from an

Oxfam bookshop a couple of years ago lying around the flat somewhere, but he'd never got round to actually reading it.

'What did you think?'

'Well . . .' Caius, still nodding although now he was doing it in a more thoughtful manner, grasped for any vague snippet he knew about Benedict and the book. He knew there was something controversial. 'It was . . .' he fumbled. Instead of saying anything, he sat down in a battered armchair, took a deep breath and looked pensive.

'Yes. It often has that effect on first-class minds.'

'Fuck Martin Amis!' The literary spat that ended Benedict's career came back to him.

'Attaboy. Whisky?' He stood up and wandered over to a shelf in the alcove that had become a makeshift bar.

'On duty, I'm afraid.' He raised a hand to stop Benedict from pouring one anyway.

'Such a shame. I rarely meet another kindred spirit. Granted, I don't go out much.' Benedict rooted around for a bottle of whisky and poured himself a healthy glass. 'Fuck Martin Amis indeed!'

'I've actually come to ask you about the break-in you had recently.'

'I'm not going to lie, I'd had a few. No more than my usual few, mind you. My normal few. I fell asleep in my chair. The very one you're sat in now. I woke with a start and there peering out at me was a face in the dark, white like death herself. I couldn't tell you what they looked like. I gave a start, as well as one might, but they fled. I fell asleep again thinking that unusually the gin hadn't agreed with me.'

'Are you sure you saw someone?'

'Well here's the thing. I woke up in the morning and my back door was wide open. I forget to lock the damn thing all the time but I wouldn't leave it like that. Not conclusive, I know, but it was flapping about and so was the door to my basement. I never go down there. It depresses me too much.'

'What's down there?'

'It used to be the pantry and the kitchen when the house had servants, but now it really is just a makeshift library.'

'May I?' Caius asked, standing up.

'Of course you may.' Benedict stood and ambled over to the staircase. He turned the light on and started down the stairs. He was still holding his drink. 'It's quite a large space as you can imagine, but as a noted man of letters one cannot have too many books and the buggers need to go somewhere. I've read them all down here, but I can't quite seem to let them go. I always said that I'd read one more book and then I'd get editing. But then there's always something else to read. Other people keep writing bloody books. Some of them are even passable.'

Caius stared around the space. That much paper was highly flammable. 'You think the wannabe burglar came down here?'

'Yes, like I said, the basement door was open. I haven't been down here in a while.'

'What's that?' Caius asked, looking at a mark on the wall revealed by a layer of paint peeling away. It looked to him like a pentagram. Maybe Matt was right and the goths of Camden were really involved in whatever was going on in Priory Square.

'Oh that, ha. This square has a history, you know.'

'It's London, show me a road that doesn't.'

'Touché.' Benedict smiled. He'd never warmed up to a flatfoot before. 'Priory Square is so named because it is built on the site of, well, a priory. Lots of nuns nunning about until Henry VIII declared himself head of the church. The land was then parcelled off to a loyal courtier. His descendants still own my fucking leasehold.'

'Like Covent Garden.'

'Far more exciting than that. No one was ever burnt alive in the middle of Covent Garden for being a witch, were they? Go and have a look at the monstrous statue in the middle of the square. A horde of unwashed, hairy feminists erected it in the 1970s in homage to the madwoman they executed.'

'Madwoman?'

'Oh some nun who had visions. Poor thing was probably a schizophrenic. Most onsets of psychosis in adults are accompanied with religious mania. I read a novel about it once. It was a dirge. Of course it won the fucking Booker.'

'What has that got to do with the pentagram on the wall?'

'Well, I was told by the old lady I bought the house off in 1973 that her mother had told her that the lady who lived here before their family did, had performed seances down here. The Victorians were mad for all that spiritualist nonsense. I've thought about turning that into a novel too, but alas I've never got round to it.'

'I'd read that.' Caius had had enough of the smell of old books. He would've thought that was impossible before, but the lack of air in the basement was getting to him. He climbed up to the top of the stairs. 'You're not missing anything, are you?'

'No, not that I've noticed.' Benedict turned around, taking in the space before shrugging at Caius.

'A manuscript perhaps?' Caius remembered that they hadn't yet come across Digby's fabled 'Apologia', if indeed it existed.

'Only thirty years' worth of manuscripts. Only a career. They didn't steal that from me. Martin fucking Amis did.' He gestured towards the door. 'Thank you for taking me seriously.'

'Lock your doors properly,' Caius said, handing him his card. 'Call 999 if you have another uninvited guest and call me if you remember anything else. I'll send someone round to take fingerprints from the back door and the door to your basement, and then we'll take your own so we can compare them.'

Benedict read over the card, turning it in his hand.

Caius started down the steps to the road, turning when he reached the bottom. 'Oh, and I meant it. Fuck Martin Amis. One article in the LRB shouldn't ruin a man's career. Send your editor all those manuscripts in the drawer. One of them will be publishable at least.'

'I've got one about lepers, actually. That should get me onto the longlist of something. Everyone loves a good leper story,' Benedict said, waving off Caius. 'I could add in a pair of impoverished Indian sisters.'

Instead of getting straight back in his car, Caius walked into the garden in the middle of the square. He sat down on a bench in front of the memorial that Benedict had mentioned. The sculptor had decided against a figurative statue, instead creating an amorphous globule. He read the plaque attached to the base of the sculpture.

In memoriam
For Alice and all the other women
philosophers that we lost to the flames

A bunch of chequered fritillaria had been left at the base. He only knew they were fritillaria because Callie had pointed them out at some point during a Sunday morning stroll around Regent's Park.

25

The Police Station

'Over the three days of footage that has been searched through, a handful of people appeared multiple times,' said the specialist running the program that matched faces. 'The program has isolated their images along with their time stamps.'

'Cool,' Caius said, watching the demonstration.

'Two women both came in on two of the three days and one man came in on all three.'

'The women both have multiple packages as they're entering the Post Office,' Amy said, peering at the image. 'They're probably eBay sellers or something.'

'But the man only has a letter,' Caius said.

'The next step for the program will be to run the footage against our databases,' the technician said, clicking a button on a side panel. 'We're ironing out a few bugs still, but once it's completed it will pull up matches from driving licences and passports of individuals whose facial features are a close match and flag if there are any alerts.'

Caius nodded as the technician clicked a couple more buttons. He wondered if the technology was equally as good at identifying some people as others. 'What a game changer.'

'I'll need you to fill in a feedback questionnaire based on your experience.'

He nodded. He'd pass that on to Amy to complete later. Questionnaires weren't his thing – he always answered them sarcastically even when he sincerely tried. Caius thanked the technician and they left the incident room, taking their laptop with them.

'Anything we can tell about the guy from the picture?' Caius asked, looking at the stills he'd already been emailed.

'His tote bag.' Amy leaned forward as she inspected the image. 'It's really familiar. The handles are a different colour from the rest of the bag.'

'I can't see all of the name printed on it.' Caius checked a different day's footage, pausing it. 'Something "ery".'

'The Purple Toad Bakery. I knew I recognised it. Everyone in Primrose Hill was shuffling their baguettes around in them. I went there the other day for lunch when I was going through the Institute's catalogue. It's on the high street. It makes Gail's look like Greggs.'

'So he's local.'

'More than that,' Amy said, pointing at a small, blurry image on the breast of his T-shirt. She went over to her computer and opened up the website for the bakery. She found a picture of all the staff outside the bakery cradling a variety of different-shaped loaves. One of the unpixellated faces looked familiar. 'All of the staff wear these T-shirts.'

'Baguette, Amy?'

'You know I love bread.'

★　★　★

The Purple Toad Bakery was chaotic. Steam was coming off the solitary barista as she frothed milk for flat white after flat white, while another woman was frantically taking orders for pastries. The last Gruyère and walnut cheese straw was sold and a groan went up from the fifteen-strong queue at the till. There was not a seat to be had at any of the tables. There were prams blocking the fire exits as newborns snuggled into their mothers sipping decaf cappuccinos. He peered at tiny fingers waving upwards at a black and white toy dangling from the hood of their pram. He wondered why it was black and white. He'd need to do research on baby toys later.

'Sorry, folks. We're short-staffed today,' said the woman behind the till that Caius took to be the manager. 'Another tray of cheese straws came out the oven fifteen minutes ago. They're just cooling down.'

'It was calmer when I came in before,' Amy said, joining the back of the queue.

Caius, who was looming by the side, caught the eye of the manager and showed her his warrant card over the heads of the hangry, self-absorbed horde. He nodded, indicating that she should clear the queue before they chatted. The new tray of cheese straws was brought out and promptly disappeared; spinach and feta rolls, crustless butternut squash quiches, almond cronuts and rose petal-dusted brownies were all carefully placed in paper bags, and the queue ebbed to a more manageable level. The manager left her colleague to it as she took Caius out the back through the kitchen and into the office.

She introduced herself as Jodie, the co-owner of the bakery.

'Do you know this man?' Caius asked, showing Jodie a still from the Post Office footage.

'It's Scott. Isn't it?' She peered at the grainy CCTV image. 'Yeah, that's him.'

'Scott what?'

'Scott Brown. Something happened, didn't it?'

'Hmm,' Caius said.

'I knew it when Scott didn't come to work yesterday and again today. I hoped he was sick maybe and forgot to call.'

'Would that be uncharacteristic of Scott?'

'Yeah, very. He's never been late before. He's very conscientious. Is he in trouble?'

'Do you have his address on record?'

'Yeah,' Jodie said, opening her laptop and retrieving the details. She wrote them down and handed them to Caius.

'If Scott gets in touch, call me,' Caius said, giving her his card.

He found Amy waiting near the entrance. Amy handed him the mozzarella and mortadella ciabatta with a pistachio pesto that she'd grabbed for him. They walked back towards Priory Square where they had parked and sat in the square overlooking the globular feminist sculpture.

'That took us all of five minutes to walk from the bakery to here,' Amy said.

'There's a fair chance that Digby and Scott may have known each other. If Digby's technological atavism extended to his diet then I bet he was a repeat customer.'

'The bread rolls he bought for his date,' Amy said, remembering the poppy seeds swirled on the top of Digby's untouched roll. She looked down at her honey-roasted goat's cheese, sun-dried tomato, spinach and tapenade baguette uncertainly. 'I think they were selling them there just now.'

★　★　★

Caius banged on the door of Scott's flat for a third time. It was ex-council in Enfield. He turned to look at Amy. 'I have that feeling.'

'Me too.'

He banged the door for a fourth time. Still nothing.

★　★　★

Caius waited to the side as the front door to Scott's flat was broken down. They smelled him before they saw him. Barry went in first followed by forensics.

'Did he catfish Digby?' Caius asked as they waited outside the flat, giving Barry space to make his initial assessment. 'Met him at the bakery, got obsessed, created "fake Isolde" based on real Isolde and then killed him?'

'How does Scott know the real Isolde in order to steal her identity?' Amy asked.

'That's a good question. That's the problem for me in all of this. Why did the killer steal all the details of Isolde's life down to taking up watercolours and how do they even know that? The killer could've just made a dream woman up. It's not as if Digby wouldn't have fallen for a comparable facsimile. Cultured, middle class and pretty, right.'

'Your type.'

'I guess that's my type but with the added ability to really yell at me if I'm being a git. I need a little safety valve.'

'Regulate your own emotions and behaviour, bitch.'

'Amy,' Caius said, looking at her. 'Are you hungry?'

'Starving, but the point still stands.' She hadn't eaten much of her baguette. She'd kept thinking about poisonings, and wondered if the spinach in hers was what she thought it was.

Barry appeared. 'Afternoon, afternoon.'

'What have we got, Barry?' Caius asked.

'Stabbed in the gut. I'd say they nicked his liver. Not a nice way to go. He would've gone into shock quite quickly though,' Barry said, looking down at the body in front of him. 'One stab wound. The killer thought they'd done enough.'

'Professional kill?'

'Oh no, I should say not,' Barry said, standing back as the

body bag was being zipped up. 'They were lucky. A professional would've gone straight for an artery like the carotid. No one would survive that.'

'Is it sexist of me to say that this doesn't feel like a feminine crime and yet the poisoned salad does?' Caius asked.

'I love salad. It makes me happy,' Amy said. She mimicked a stock photo of a woman eating a bowl of lettuce. 'I think I could stab a man to death.'

'Yes, but you're not the average broad.' Caius and Amy stepped around the scene in the narrow hallway.

'Neither is "fake Isolde".'

'Amy, just check that Scott's laptop and phone et cetera have been taken into evidence. We need to review them ASAP.'

'No problem.' Amy began searching the room.

Caius looked around the room. There were a couple of generic prints on the wall. Although there were a lot more empty nails where picture frames had been removed. On the mantlepiece was an empty photo frame. It was in pride of place and yet showed nothing off. A bottle of open but untouched Chablis was sat on the side table that Scott's ex apparently thought was too ugly to take. Two glasses were sat next to it and an optimistic condom.

'He's just gone through a break-up,' Caius said to Amy as she re-entered the room. 'His ex moved out and took half the furniture with them. There's no dining room table but the marks where one had rested on the carpet are there. I'm worried, Amy. They either killed Digby for some yet unknown, awful but logical reason and then killed Scott because he knows too much about them from delivering the letters to the PO Box or . . .'

'Or you think they've got a taste for killing blokes on dates?'

'What do Digby and Scott have in common? They were both lonely men. Digby had a sexual interest in "fake Isolde", poor Scott with his hopeful condom looks like he might've too.'

'So she seduces lonely men and then kills them?'

'Yeah.'

'And she has a hunting ground around Priory Square.'

Caius stared down at the indent the old dining room table had made in the carpet. 'Is she spiralling?'

'She sounds cool. I'd like to be her friend,' Amy said.

26

The Police Station

'These are fat rascals,' Matt said, opening the box of scones he'd quickly purchased on his way out of Harrogate.

'They're so cute,' Amy said, picking one up and taking a bite out of its big, fat head.

'How was Harrogate?' Caius asked. He placed a cup of tea in front of Matt and Amy each before sitting down at the break room table with his own.

'Delightful. Might take Yumi for a break in the summer. The climate was different, cooler, and yet I definitely saw a lot more men in shorts than down here.'

'I love Yorkshire. I went to uni up there.' Caius took one of his fat rascal's eyes and popped it in his mouth. 'The tea's shit though.'

'That's tantamount to treason against God's own country,' Matt said.

'They'll never know I said it. Neither of you southern Jessies would dare rat me out,' Caius said.

★　★　★

Matt looked up at the new whiteboard that had appeared for Scott Brown's murder. 'So she's what, some sort of black widow?'

'I can see the *Daily Mail* headlines now,' Caius said.

'And all the girly edgelords on Tumblr will lose it,' Amy said, wondering how long before someone would be selling merch on Etsy. 'At least no one will be sharing memes with your face on, mate.'

160

'Is that still going on?'

'No, you were a flash in the pan.'

'Thank God.'

'Do you think they're a spree killer?' Matt asked.

'No,' Caius said, although he hesitated. 'Digby's murder was thoroughly planned with a very personal, if not opaque motive. Scott was killed because, well because anyone with half a brain would realise that we would find the footage of Scott at the Post Office. Once we'd found him, Scott could easily identify them.'

'Why did he help? Do you think he knew he was an accomplice?' Amy asked.

'I doubt it,' Matt said, staring at the board. 'It was transactional. He was taking the letters to get in her good books.'

'Also known as her knickers.' Caius's desk phone rang. 'All right. Thank you.' He put the receiver down. 'Uniform have collected his new starter forms from the bakery. We've got contact details for his mum that he gave to them. I'll deal with that. Matt, get the staff from The Purple Toad in. Scott might have talked about his date. Amy, please chase up where his electronics have got to. It's going to be a long night.'

27

St John's Wood

Callie was walking along the top of Regent's Park when Caius rang.

'I'm going to be back late,' Caius said over video. He was calling from the break room at work and had that look he had when he'd had to tell someone devastating news.

'That's OK. I'm out tonight having dinner with she-who-must-not-be-publicly-named,' Callie said, flicking her hair over her shoulder as she walked past the zoo. She could hear the monkeys howling. She turned the camera to face the enclosures. 'We should get membership to the zoo when the baby is a toddler. We could go every weekend.'

'That's a lovely idea. My mum has a picture of me in multi-coloured dungarees at the penguins,' Caius said, smiling. 'How are you feeling?'

'Well, after that initial "what the fuck" moment, I actually think we'll be pretty good parents.'

'Yeah. I mean, yeah.'

'Hmm.'

'It's terrifying.'

'You deal with hardened criminals all the time. How bad can a newborn be?'

'I don't know. I read online about this thing called colic.' Caius was ready to share a link but then thought better of it. 'Did you walk from ours?'

'I got the bus down to Camden and have walked the rest of it. I needed the air after closeting myself in the flat all day.'

'Don't push yourself too hard though. Get a taxi back.' Caius looked away from his phone and up at someone else in the room. 'How's the "project"?'

'I'm getting there with the mood boards. It's all very thirteenth century. Be warned, there's velvet all over the dining room table. It looks like a mess but it's organised to me. I read this article about this poet called Marie de France. She was this spectacular poetess, so forward-thinking in terms of gender politics. There's a theory she was an abbess. It was a whole vibe.' Callie had been thinking about nuns all day – the singular clarity of purpose they have. 'When I was thirteen I seriously considered becoming a nun. It only lasted a week, but God what a phase that was.'

Caius laughed. He could imagine Callie as a nun but it wasn't a pious thought. 'Got to go, babe. Have a lovely dinner. Don't wait up for me.'

'Love you, byeee.' Callie put her podcast back on as she turned north towards St John's Wood. She had slid down a medieval rabbit hole. It was about Julian of Norwich. Eulalia had mentioned her by name so she thought she should gain a basic grasp of her life, listening desperately to anything she could find on the era between frenzied mood board sessions – when the nausea allowed. Now that she'd met Eulalia she couldn't bear to listen to her music. It felt weird. Too personal. She sang about trying to kill herself metaphorically, physically and emotionally. That album was destructive. She must have broken and then remade herself to get there. Callie thought that would explain the sort of ethereal detachedness that Eulalia had when you spoke to her in person. She'd stared into the bleak abyss and come back 99 per cent a complete and yet fragmented person, and 1 per cent a soulless dream. The podcast came to an end as she arrived at her destination – a well-reviewed and yet overpriced Italian restaurant with chichi decor, low lighting and plump, padded booths that you could get lost in. Eulalia was already waiting for her outside. Callie wasn't expecting that. She'd expected to be kept waiting, to be told that she was the lowly freelancer whose time wasn't important. Callie wasn't one for such power play and it seemed Eulalia wasn't either. That was probably why her sister dealt with the business side.

'Hey, you,' Callie said, kissing Eulalia on the cheek.

'Cal. How are you? Do you fancy Italian? Or Korean barbecue, maybe? There's a sushi place across the road that might be better? What do you think? Are you a sushi person? You look like a sushi person but then you also look like a Botticelli painting. You're sort of pearly, aren't you? Did you pop out of a clam fully formed?'

'Here looks good.' Callie didn't think she was up to sushi, as much as she usually loved it. She could almost feel Caius being over-protective and telling her that in her state the lasagna was far safer than salmon and avocado maki. She wasn't sure that was true, but she did think there was a possibility that there was some sort of pistachio-based pudding on the menu at the Italian. She wasn't keen on dithering, and Eulalia was clearly in an odd, frenetic mood, so she firmly made the decision. Callie walked into the restaurant and up to the maître d'. 'Table for two, please.'

A waiter seated them to the side near the bar. It was pretty busy for a Wednesday.

'So many first dates.' Callie leaned in and whispered, 'My favourite game is to work out who's going to ghost who.' This was an old trick of hers. Drag the other person into a piece of speculative people watching and force a conspirative intimacy.

'That's a fun game,' Eulalia whispered into Callie's ear. She stayed a little too long in Callie's orbit and to her surprise, Callie blushed. She turned to look at their fellow diners. 'That couple in the window.'

'Blondie in the olive-green shift dress and the office drone in the Ralph Lauren polo?'

'Yeah. She's into him more than he is her. He's going to sleep with her tonight, promise to text her about drinks next week and then disappear into the ether.'

'Do you think?' Callie wasn't sure. He looked to be in his mid-thirties and she was younger. 'Five-year age gap. He's getting on. Aware that he needs to settle down. There are worse girls to marry than her. She looks after herself. She'd probably look after him. Well, as long as he keeps getting those lovely Christmas bonuses. They'd have pleasant-looking children.'

'What a horrible way to live.'

'If that's all they want . . .'

'I take it that isn't what it's like with your boyfriend? He is your boyfriend, you're not engaged, right?'

'I refer to him as my "paramour" and he refers to me as his "missus". It's an equal partnership.'

'I'd destroy a man like that.'

'Caius?' Callie didn't think Eulalia knew enough about him, could not have even possibly seen him for longer than the ten seconds he was on screen.

'No, Mr Polo. They're easy to break. All bravado but their insides are fragile. Like they're made of glass.'

'I don't doubt that you've broken a few hearts in your time.' Callie picked up the menu.

'A few skulls too.'

Callie laughed. A waiter appeared and asked for their order. Eulalia tried to order a carafe of wine but Callie said her dermatologist had told her to stop drinking for the sake of her complexion, so Eulalia had had to settle for a solo glass of Valpolicella while Callie daintily refrained and ordered a Limonata.

'How's recording going?' Callie asked. She had hoped to hear a little of the new album. She was worried that her work would jar with the finished sound.

'Phenomenal. I had a session with Sonikk yesterday. Do you know him?' Eulalia shifted about on her seat. She was trying to hide her discomfort. Callie assumed that Eulalia didn't like her new producer.

'Not personally.' Callie was vaguely aware of a dance track of his that had been played at every party that she'd attended last summer. She thought he might be the cousin of the girlfriend of someone she knew, but she wasn't sure.

'Well, you should. He's so much fun. I'll introduce you. There's bound to be a launch party for the album. You will of course be invited. Bring your "paramour" too. I'd love to meet him.'

'Would it be possible to hear the album? It might help me with my process.' Callie's process was usually procrastinating until the week before and then she'd chuck herself at it, but the turnaround on this project was so tight there'd not been a mental warm-up and she'd had to go straight to frenzied. Just listening to a couple of bars of a melody would be enough to assuage her fear that she was off course.

'I don't know.' Eulalia looked up at Callie innocently and pouted. 'I don't think Mel would like that.'

'That's OK.' Callie poured them each a glass of water from the tiny jug on the table. She whispered, 'I don't want to get you in trouble.'

'Mel is such a pain in the arse.'

'Looks to me like she's just protecting your interests.' There was something of the lost child about Eulalia, a certain blissful naivety, that made you think she was being taken advantage of continually. Besides, you did hear of these young starlets who were exploited by their friends and families, who were seen by them as not a beloved daughter or sister or childhood bestie but as a cash machine. 'You have to be careful. There will be people who want to get close to you because of how it'll benefit them, not because they like you. Awful, I know. A lot more people are out for what they can get than you'd think.'

'Do you like me?' Eulalia asked, with such earnestness that Callie was mildly shocked.

'Geewhizz, I think you're swell,' Callie said, faking an American accent. She changed the subject. She did not want to make friends, only to get paid. 'Are you excited to lose the headgear?'

'I really want them gone.' Eulalia let out a guttural 'eurgh'. 'I hate those stupid heads. They're smothering.'

'I thought that was the plan?' Callie was confused. Eulalia had said as much on their first meeting and Mel's very clear brief had left them out.

'Mel is now saying that the label's plan is for me to perform in them when live but when I'm doing photoshoots and inter-views it'll be my face.'

'Right,' Callie said. She hadn't been aware of that. She'd have to pull something out of nowhere ahead of the meeting on Friday morning. 'It wasn't included in the document that Mel sent over but I can think of something. My first instinct is doll heads. Rosebud lips and humungous eyes. Too clichéd, maybe? They could be pretty dark. Although if your team decide to go with what we've already discussed then it would be quite effective visually.'

'Oh my God, I love dolls. Cute little creepy ones. I knew you were the right person for me.'

Their food arrived. Callie had a plate of pappardelle with beef shin ragu and a side of garlic sautéed broccolini while Eulalia had a caprese salad. The waiter brought a basket of bread over but Eulalia waved him away.

'They've got you on no carbs?' Callie asked. She dreaded to think of the food and exercise regimes they had Eulalia on to keep her looking like she did.

'Mel says I can't eat bread. I've got to bring the receipt back with me.'

'Mel eats bread,' Callie said, frowning.

'Oh yeah, she loves it. She's a piglet. But then she'll say stuff like "Flour and water together make glue and what does bread do? Stick to your hips?" It's kind of sad.'

'I say eat the bread and get a boyfriend who likes a little jiggle.'

'But you're not fat, you're curvy and in all the right places. I could eat you up. You look like a Renaissance painting, you really do. I meant that when I said it before. It's no wonder you've got such an "eligible paramour".'

Callie balked at the word 'eligible'. 'You should read some Susie Orbach, it'll help you sleep at night.' Callie lifted her plate for Eulalia to pick some pasta off it. 'I won't tell if you don't.'

Eulalia took a forkful and shoved it in her mouth. 'Oh my God.' She had another forkful and then insisted that Callie try the burrata on her salad.

The waiter reappeared with two limoncellos. 'Courtesy of the gentleman over there,' he said, gesturing to a man sat eating at the bar.

Callie nodded; that was the polite thing to do, after all. They were nearly finished with dinner anyway and would be leaving soon. Eulalia instead put her arm around Callie's shoulder and kissed her on the cheek. Having marked her territory, she turned to look again at the man and flipped him the bird.

'Can we have the bill, please?' Eulalia asked the bewildered waiter, who was still standing at their table, releasing Callie as she did so.

The bill promptly came. The waiter sensed the tension between Callie, Eulalia and the man at the bar who thought he was being cute but now felt like shit. Eulalia took out £60 from her pocket, put it on the table and got up without waiting for her change. She walked out of the restaurant, leaving Callie sitting there bewildered.

Callie hadn't realised that Eulalia didn't have a bag with her. She'd never met a woman who just pulled cash out of her pocket for dinner before. But then she knew she was sheltered. Callie hurried to gather her things up, regrettably leaving her pasta unfinished, and followed Eulalia out. She shoved her quilted jacket on. The heat of the day had begun to wane. Eulalia was standing on the pavement, emptily staring at the traffic. For a moment as Callie walked towards the door, not stopping to thank the maître d' as she normally would, she was gripped by a vision of Eulalia stepping in front of an oncoming car.

'Hey,' Callie said, rushing over and gently taking her arm. 'Are you OK?'

'Yeah, I'm fine.' Eulalia wouldn't look at her.

'Are you sure?' Callie said, watching as Eulalia stared at the front of an oncoming double-decker. She didn't think Eulalia's behaviour was really about the limoncello or the pass the guy made, but more that his interruption represented all the ones that had come before it. It wasn't being hit on that specific time but all of them. 'You must get shit like that all the time.'

'Just trying to have dinner in peace.'

'It'll only get worse once the world sees you without those heads on.'

'I know, but I hate them so much. I told Mel that I wouldn't do it any more if I had to keep wearing them.'

'You must get so much attention all the time. Not all of it good.'

'Why?'

'Why? Because you're painfully beautiful. My eyes hurt looking at you.'

Eulalia laughed and touched Callie's cheek. 'Fat lot of good it's done me.'

'Men can be awful.' Callie turned her head and looked at the ground.

'Yours isn't.'

'No, but there have been a lot of frogs.'

'Before you found your literal knight in shining armour.' Eulalia turned to Callie and began talking quickly. 'Does his family live in a castle? Is there armour everywhere?'

'There's a bit of armour.' Callie didn't want to talk about that. If Eulalia was worried about fan attention then perhaps Caius should be too. It hadn't really occurred to her. There were always going to be snobs – England will be England – who'd try to cosy up to him because of his new-found status. Dotty had had a lot of that sort of thing at uni. She'd sniffed out Callie quite quickly as the only other former boarder in their tutor group and that had been that. There had been a girl who Dotty used as a byword now. If someone was being a bit too keen, too much of a brown-noser, she'd call them a 'Laura'.

'What's he like?'

'Umm.' Callie was getting a little annoyed now. Eulalia wasn't picking up on her unwillingness to talk about Caius. 'He's a sweetheart.'

'Sure, but what's he really like? He's a policeman, right?'

'Caius has a really strong sense of public duty,' Callie said, rather stiffly.

'He's a good one though, right? He's not one of those bastards you see on the news fitting people up for crimes they didn't commit.'

'Yes, he's one of the good ones. Caius's parents' backgrounds are Irish and Jamaican, he knows how they were treated which has made him hyper aware to injustice. There are a lot of men out there, especially rich white ones, who just coast on through without a fucking care in the world. They don't try. Caius tries and he fails, but he keeps on trying.'

'God loves a trier.'

'You bet He does.'

'I think God's a woman.'

'Do you?' Callie didn't know enough about it, quite frankly, to debate the statement. She changed the subject while looking out for a passing black cab. 'I was listening to a thing about Julian of Norwich today. You're making me vibe my way around medieval history.'

'Julian! I love Julian! Did you know that there was a mystic nun who was burnt at the stake not too far from here?'

'I didn't know that.'

'There's all this lore around her.'

Callie nodded; the nausea was returning. 'That's fascinating.'

'You look a little pale.'

'I've had such a lovely evening,' Callie said, finally spotting a black cab with its light on. She waved it down. 'Thank you so much for inviting me out.'

'Oh you're going?' Eulalia looked disappointed. 'I thought you might want to come back to mine and listen to records.'

'I can't, unfortunately. I've got a big day tomorrow ahead of Friday's meeting.'

'Sure. You'll have to invite me round to yours soon.'

'Absolutely.'

'And I'd love to see your boyfriend's house.'

'One day, perhaps.' Callie grinned that specific polite smile that was meant to gloss over the fact she was only saying maybe to save her feelings. She opened the door of the cab, and got into the back as she gave the driver her address. Eulalia waved at her from the pavement as she texted Caius from the back of the cab that Eulalia was kind of weird.

THURSDAY

28

The Police Station

Caius had his head on the desk when Matt walked in holding a half-eaten croissant.

'You all right?' Matt sat down and took a final bite, crumpling up the paper bag.

'Yeah. Same old same old.' Caius sat up straight and pulled an exaggerated smile that was more of a grimace.

'Don't even bother lying to me.'

'It's been a weird week.'

'The case?'

'Nah, ish, not really.' Caius sat up in his chair. 'I'm not supposed to say this, but—'

'Callie's pregnant, it's too early to say anything but you're chuffed and have chosen to tell me, Matt Cheung, beloved colleague, cherished friend. You're excited but also scared. Understandably. The responsibility is huge. But you're naive and you think that being a dad will be sunshine and lollipops. What's scaring you most is how you can reconcile doing this,' Matt gestured at the incident room, 'with the hope that new life represents, all the while resisting the forthcoming leviathan that is your family's estate.'

'Yeah that's it. Pretty much. How did you know?'

'You left your phone unlocked yesterday while you went to the loo. You'd been staring at a picture of a pregnancy test. Don't worry, I've not told anyone and I won't do. Obviously. I fully expect to be made godfather for my silence though.'

'Thanks.' Caius smiled at Matt. 'How are things with you?'

'I'm good. I bought some paint for my living room online last night. It's called sandblasted linen. It's barely any different to the colour in there at the moment but I need a project and I've already put up shelves in every conceivable place. Yumi may move in when her lease runs out at the end of the summer. I've downloaded *Letterboxd* because my attention span is fried. I suggest you add me and then we can discuss art house films.'

Caius smiled.

'Congratulations on the bambino, bambino,' Matt said, patting Caius on the shoulder.

'Why are we congratulating Caius?' Amy asked, coming into the room.

'New PB on my 5K,' Caius said, looking pleased with himself. He actually had done his fastest run ever that week.

'Good for you,' Amy said, sitting down at her desk. She slyly caught Matt's eye and wiggled her ring finger. Matt shook his head and mouthed 'not yet'.

★ ★ ★

'Again, I'm so sorry for your loss,' Caius said to Scott's mother Mandy. The shock hadn't worn off. She had a grey tinge to her face, apart from a redness swelling around her eyes and nose, the remains of weeping. 'I know we spoke yesterday briefly but I wanted to get you in formally.'

'Do you know who did it yet?' Mandy asked.

'We have an idea of the type of person they might be but we're working towards finding a definitive identification.'

'So, no then.'

Caius grimaced. 'Do you mind if I ask you some questions about your son?'

She nodded.

'Did he talk to you about his love life?'

'No, not at all. I'd find out about a girl eventually but only if they'd been together for six months and he thought it was worth introducing her.'

'Had Scott been seeing anyone recently?'

'I don't know.' She looked at Caius who clicked his pen and put it down with a finality. 'Is that all you've got? He was dating a bunny boiler?'

'For now. Unless there's anything else you think is important? A stalker, for example.'

'No nothing like that. Scott was a normal boy. He worked in a bakery, for God's sake.'

'Any previous relationships? Any girls he'd dated before who were a bit off?'

'His ex, Jessica, dumped him six months ago and is having a glorious time backpacking around Thailand according to her mother. I bumped into her in Tesco's last week.'

'Right.'

'I don't understand what you're trying to imply. I don't get it. From what you said last night he was murdered by some sort of scheming femme fatale. Why was she interested in him?'

'What do you mean?'

'I loved Scott. He was everything to me but he was a normal kid. He wasn't rich or famous. What could she have got out of him?'

Caius ended the interview. He was equally perplexed by this. It couldn't have just been that Scott was willing to go to the Post Office for her, could it? 'I will do my damned best to give you all the answers I can.'

Mandy didn't want to believe him, but he held her eye contact for a little too long and she felt like she had no choice but to cradle a little hope in her heart that he might have answers and maybe even justice.

★　★　★

Matt looked up at Angus, the burly Scottish baker in front of him. He looked like he belonged on the front of a porridge packet throwing a caber.

'So, Scott, eh?' Angus said, taking a deep breath and shaking his head knowingly.

It was unusual for the person opposite him to initiate conversation. Matt wondered whether Angus would be one of those self-stylised truth-tellers that yells at everyone or if he was just that blunt.

'I barely knew him.'

Matt found this hard to believe. 'But there are only four of you who work at the bakery?'

'Aye, I'm out back with the bread. I don't want to deal with people. My wife Jodie does that. She's great at it, whereas all I care about is yeast.'

'Right.' Matt wrote yeast in his notes to stop himself from visibly reacting. 'Did you not spend time together on breaks?'

'What break? I own the place.'

Matt nodded. Amy had told him how popular it was. 'Did he ever talk about his dating life with you in passing?'

'That was the only thing he ever did speak to me about. I used to try to stick to sports whenever we did cross paths, to be honest, because he was one of those "females don't want good guys" sorts.' Angus laughed at the absurdity. 'I mentioned to Jodie that he was like that, but she said he was good at making a flat white and kept to himself during shifts so she couldn't complain.'

'Any "female" in particular?' Matt asked. He'd made sure to roll his eyes at the word 'female' like Angus had.

'Aye, there was a girl in the last couple of weeks. He tried to tell me the details of how she was stringing him along but I put my headphones in before he could really start. I like listening to politics podcasts while I work. I don't know why, it makes me anxious. I get a better crumb when I'm anxious.'

'Did you catch a name?' Matt asked, poised to capture a new lead.

'No. I know nothing of the girl other than she was daft enough to be associating with him.'

'Have you ever met this man?' Matt showed him Digby's picture.

'He looks sort of familiar. Does he live nearby or something?'

★ ★ ★

'Scott rarely served customers,' Jodie said. She felt oddly numb. It was obviously awful but she didn't actually care that Scott was dead. She felt terrible about her apathy but she wasn't great at faking emotion. She decided to put her indifference down to the shock of it all. 'Only if we were short. Leigh takes the orders most of the time. I step in during the rushes. Scott did the coffee. He was a bit of a personality vacuum, if I'm being brutally honest, but my God could he get a decent head of froth on a cappuccino.'

'Did he chat much to you in your quieter times?' Caius asked.

'If it was quiet then I was out the back bulk ordering butter or doing the accounts.'

'Right. Did Scott have a girlfriend?'

'I don't know, to be honest. It didn't bother me but I don't think he liked me much on a personal level. He never engaged me in small talk. I was just his boss. I was a pay cheque, that's it.'

'Scott was a twat,' Leigh, the cashier at the bakery, said. She'd spent the whole bus ride over trying to think of a diplomatic way of saying that, but she'd accidentally talked herself full circle. 'Not to speak ill of the dead but he was awful.'

'What do you mean?' Amy asked.

'He used to write his number on takeaway cups. Even if they were eating in. He wouldn't give them a proper china cup like we're supposed to. Scott had a type too. It wasn't always the super gorgeous girls. You know where we are, there are fucking supermodels wandering around our neighbourhood. No, Scott had a type. He always did it to the girls who were pretty but off.'

'Off?'

'You know, those girls. There's something a little broken about them. They seem a bit sad or lonely. He liked pretty ones with low self-esteem. It was predatory.'

'Did you tell Jodie?' Amy didn't think that was behaviour many employers would tolerate, let alone a woman who owned a small business reliant on yummy mummies.

'I was going to. I threatened to twice, but he said he'd tell Jodie that I hand out the pastries that she thinks I've put in the bin to the local homeless community. Bags every day. Angus is cool with it, I think, he saw me doing it once and never said a word, but Jodie is super worried that the bakery's "polished" reputation would take a bashing, so we have to bin them. I can't afford to lose this side hustle. I'm a jobbing actor and Jodie is pretty chill with me dashing off to an audition last minute as she'd cover. It's really hard to find a job that allows that and pays over £12 an hour.'

'Do you remember any of the girls recently that Scott hit on?'

'No, he did the coffee and I did the tills and the bread. We'd both clear up the tables. I wouldn't always know he'd done it that day until I'd find a cup left behind by the drinker.'

'Any blondes?'

'It's NW1. You can't throw a three-day-old cronut without hitting one, natural or not.' Leigh shrugged. 'I'm sorry, I really don't know. I wish I could be more helpful. We didn't exactly "chat" about his fantasy woman, you know?'

29

Running Latte Coffee Shop, Dartmouth Hill

Callie quickly pulled the cotton wool that had been taped to the inside of her elbow off and put it in her bag. She felt weird about putting it in the café's bin. She'd had blood taken, been weighed and had her height measured by a community midwife. She had decided that she may as well make the most of the make-up on her face and the shining sun and work from their local independent coffee shop. They had opened their windows fully so she had sat at the front, soaking in the sun's rays and banishing any potential lingering vitamin D deficiency from the winter months.

Before she left the house to be prodded, Callie had spent an hour that morning cobbling together enough images of porcelain doll heads onto a page to freak even the most cynical person out. Then she'd spent another hour adding to the doodles she did last night when she'd got home after dinner with Eulalia – she called it doodling, but it was a drawing and she was selling herself short – of six different doll heads. Each of them was equally adorable and macabre – slashed throats, bleeding eyes, pointed little teeth. She had a set of watercolours at home that she hadn't used in years that she was going to crack out when she got back, to add a pinch of colour to their ghoulish faces. Callie was feeling quite proud of herself, although as she sat in the spartan whitewashed coffee shop sipping lemon and ginger tea, she realised that she actually was also starting to feel relieved. This project for Eulalia had come from nowhere, wreaked havoc for an intense week and then after tomorrow morning would be gone again. She was glad of its transience.

She'd encountered Eulalia through her music and had assumed that it was hyperbolic in nature, but there was something about last night. A desperation to have Callie like her, an outlandish performativeness that she felt Eulalia was trying hard to control, but that had burst out after the limoncello appeared that Callie was too old to deal with. In her early twenties she'd been a magnet for girls like that. She'd indulged them too. It felt lovely to have someone want you to like them. Callie was always the one who the poor thing had acted out their latest calamity to in the loos in a nightclub, but she was entering another phase in her life (one preoccupied with keeping a tiny human alive) and she didn't care for it any more. She also didn't care for celebrity. It was all an empty glimmer, a distraction from the more diffi-cult and real business of getting on with living.

Callie began packing up her bag. Two women sat down at the table beside hers. 'I know this sounds crazy but I think I'm missing some of my underwear?'

'Eaten by the tumble dryer or what?'

'Taken from my washing line.'

Callie turned to the woman. 'Sorry to interrupt, but I couldn't help but overhear. You should report that.'

'Do you think? I might have just misplaced it.'

'Maybe,' Callie said, feeling silly all of a sudden. 'Sorry again, enjoy your coffee.'

Callie left the coffee shop in embarrassment. She turned down her road composing herself. She'd started to see danger every-where since meeting Caius — not that she didn't see it everywhere anyway. You can't go through life as a woman and not be aware that a lot of men hate you for existing. She smiled sororally at the woman (Caius's parents' tenant) who lived on the floor above them as she walked in the opposite direction. She stopped Callie.

'Be careful,' the neighbour began.

'Oh?'

'There have been reports of a creepy guy at night round the neighbourhood.' She mouthed the word 'flasher'.

'Gross! Thanks for letting me know.' They parted ways and Callie returned to the flat, shutting the door firmly behind her and being sure to put the chain on. She went into the bedroom, got changed into the floaty white cotton night gown that she adored – it made her look like she was about to be bitten by a vampire – and retired to the sofa with the vapours. She texted Caius about what she'd just heard. The ginger tea hadn't fully suppressed the nausea – it was possibly just a placebo, an idea she refused to entertain lest her self-awareness make it fail – but if she was lying down then she could sort of work. She started tweaking the mood boards again. Moving images around ever so slightly until the slide was only a little imperfect. The doorbell rang. Callie reluctantly got up and answered it.

'Calliope Foster,' the delivery man asked.

'Yes,' Callie said, taking the bunch of flowers from him. He handed her a pen and she signed next to her name. 'Thanks.'

Callie took the flowers into the living room. They were a chaotic arrangement from a florist she recognised as being based near Sloane Square. Callie thought they were perhaps from her father. Caius had already sent her a bunch that week. She opened the card.

Dear Cal,
I had such a great time. E x

Callie took a picture of the card and the flowers and sent it to Caius.

Her message was left on one tick. Caius's frequent unavailability was usually something she just accepted but today it pissed her off. She put on another Radio 4 programme on Christine de Pizan and her *City of Ladies* and tried to forget about it.

30

The Police Station

'Nothing makes a girl feel special quite like the scattergun approach,' Amy said, reflecting on Scott's coffee cup trick. She'd sent uniform to the coffee shop and a poor forensics technician returned with thirteen bin bags full of rubbish. So far they'd counted sixteen attempts in the first bag alone. They were now poring over the crumpled napkins and soggy paper cups in the hopes of finding a full print that matched the partials left at the site of Digby's murder.

'Looks like it only worked once,' Caius said. He had Scott's phone in front of him. There were plenty of women's names saved in his contacts but none of the messages were recent and none of them had responded to his last communication – usually a request for nudes or for phone sex after very little initial chat. There were a few messages to friends, mostly about video games. Those were seemingly normal. 'Oh dear.'

'What?' Matt asked.

'He's an incel,' Caius said.

'Oh no, not another one,' Amy said, the fuckers just keep on popping up.

Caius had found a host of notifications in Scott's emails that a post of his on a notorious forum had lit up and was getting a lot of responses. 'He's one of the "good guys". Staceys. Chads. Mewing. Looksmaxxing. Oh boy.' Caius scrolled down through the chat to find the original post. 'He was doing an experiment.'

'The coffee cups?' Matt asked.

186

'Yep, he was giving out exactly thirty cups per shift and recording the responses.'

'Which were few and far between?' Amy said. She didn't need to see Scott's write-up of his 'experiment' to know the outcome.

'He's used PowerPoint to create graphs of his findings,' Caius said.

'Those poor women were just trying to have a moment's peace while they drink a coffee. They're not going to reject him, are they? That won't confirm his bias,' Matt said, peering over Caius's shoulder to read the odious replies.

'Everyone else in the forum is asking for an update, because he finally posted a success a few days ago.' Caius scrolled through the posts, summarising them to the team. 'Scott had "scouted an opportunity" a few weeks previously. He'd written his number on "the opportunity's" cup. "The opportunity" hadn't messaged him but she kept coming back to the coffee shop and flirting. She eventually got him to run errands for her. He called it an "act of service" to show that he was a "good guy". Scott was trying to prove how manipulative she was by asking him to jump through all of these "crazy hoops" before he could have sex with her. In the last update Scott said that he'd written his address and a time for her to come to his. He didn't think she was going to show but he was bored of the flirting. He thought she was going to reject him once he tried to actually initiate sex.'

'To be fair, you really would have to be something to go to a random guy's house like that.' Amy shuddered. 'It's the beginning of a horror movie.'

'By "something", do you mean a spree killer on the hunt for vulnerable men?' Matt asked. From where he was sitting it was predator versus predator.

'Amy, get forensics to prioritise the search for a cup with

Scott's address on,' Caius said, closing the lid on Scott's laptop. He'd seen enough for one sitting.

'I wonder how many hemlock poisonings there have been in the last decade,' Matt said, wondering whether, jokes aside, they really did have a black widow on their hands.

'Can't be many. I'm not sure how important that is. I imagine any hemlock deaths will be the odd forager who got confused,' Caius said. He thought the method of Scott's death reflected the urgency of the killer rather than any special preference. 'Digby's death had been planned out meticulously whereas Scott's was opportunistic. They killed him in the hallway. In and out. Have a look though, and for men murdered on a first date too. That's what Digby and Scott have in common.'

'I can't imagine there are many of those either. Although, considering all the ghosting that goes on you'd think there'd be corpses everywhere,' Amy said, juggling a set of imaginary balls.

'Put a quid in the tin,' Matt said, gesturing to the 'bad joke jar' on his desk. Caius had implemented it after one too many low-quality puns. They were going to spend it on a meal at Christmas.

'Seconded. A new round of "Is Caius's Lunch Wanky?" resumes on Monday too.' Caius's desk phone rang. He nodded along. 'Absolutely. Send the details over to my DS who will get in touch with the person who reported it. I'll be along in twenty minutes.' He put the phone down and looked at Matt. 'Saddle up. There's another one.'

'Another break-in on Priory Square?' Matt got up from his seat.

'And another body.'

31

Priory Square

'A safe and well check, huh,' Matt said, getting out of the car and looking up at the house. It was identical to all the others in the square and had the exact same layout. 'Who alerted us?'

'A fan, apparently.' Caius sat on the bonnet of the car reading the initial report that he'd received while he was driving over. He emailed it to Amy and asked her to get in touch with the fan. 'Jimmy Jones, forty-eight years old. You may well remember him from mid-two-thousands late-night panel shows.'

'The guy who asked some woman to flap her minge live on Radio 2.'

'The one and the same. I'll get up his Wikipedia.' Caius searched for 'Jimmy Jones'. 'Not just any woman, she was one of the Queen Mother's ladies-in-waiting. She was ninety-four at the time. Apparently, Jimmy is doing weird little livestreams for a handful of fans these days. Hasn't toured in four years.' He put his phone back in his pocket. 'He was in the middle of a live-stream when an intruder was spotted on camera. He gave chase and never returned.'

'And everyone watching thought what? That it was a bit?'

'Yeah, but one concerned fan called it in when they realised that he was still livestreaming at 8 a.m. this morning.'

They walked up the stone steps – Caius's third set that week on the square. He got to the top and looked out across at the other houses. The magnolia trees in the central garden blocked the view of the Institute but he could tell they were directly opposite. Both houses were in the middle of their row. He could, however, see Benedict Carr-Ridge's house in the middle of the western side of the square. Caius wondered whether he was actually writing about lepers like he said he would or was he just drinking more whisky. The feminist blob monument in the middle of the square gleamed through the shrubbery in the unrelenting sunshine. He stepped into the house and followed the sound of activity to the garden. 'All right, Barry,' he said.

'What is this case you're working on?' Barry asked, getting up from crouching over the latest body found in the square. A forensic technician was swabbing the corpse's T-shirt as another took pictures of the surrounding area.

'I don't know, mate.' Caius was beginning to wonder if he'd got it all wrong somewhere. 'But I wouldn't want to live on this square. I'd be worried I would be next.'

'This one looks like an accident. The poor guy simply hit his head on the iron railing after slipping on the crumbling stone steps.' Barry pointed to the middle step which had split in half and then to Jimmy's left trainer which was covered in dust the same colour. 'I'll obviously be a little more thorough than that in my report, but there's no evidence of foul play.'

'Use all the Latin you need, Barry,' Caius said, looking around the garden. It was paved over with a few empty plant pots, one of which was next to a garden chair and filled with cigarette butts. He inspected the back gate which was undamaged and closed but unlocked. 'Not much security on the gate. You could pop your arm over and open the lock. Or he might have just left it open. Took the bins out and forgot to lock it.'

'Any similarities to the break-in the other day?' Matt asked.

'In both incidents it would seem they probably entered in through the back. Benedict's basement and back doors were wide open when he woke up. This alleyway runs around the back of the whole square, separating them from the houses behind. The wall is fairly high, so I doubt you'd see anyone passing from the houses. It's not Chelsea. There are no mews.'

'Well, you'd know,' Matt said cheerily. 'Was anything taken?'

'The owner, the novelist Benedict Carr-Ridge, didn't think so.' Caius gave Matt the look. 'He said he was drunk so his statement isn't hugely reliable. He may just have been hallucinating.'

'The back door at the Institute was unlocked too. Digby's bike was out there. Do you think this is someone just trying their luck? They're breaking into houses in the area and accidentally stumbled on Digby after they'd searched the house. It would explain the set of partials.'

'No.' Caius opened the gate and popped into the alleyway. A high wall ran alongside the other side, blocking the squat two-storey houses behind from overlooking it. He walked down it as Matt followed. He stopped at the end of the path and looked out onto the main road. Buses were stopping and starting as they swallowed and vomited passengers, brave cyclists with and without helmets flying in between. 'Quite a few of the houses have cameras but they're all within the gardens and pointed at their gates. No one has a visual of the alley. Makes sense. You don't want to apply for planning permission, and all any would care about was someone breaking into their own house.'

'What are you thinking?'

'I don't know. Digby and Scott were definitely killed by the same person. Had to be. The PO Box connection cannot be a coincidence.' They walked back into Jimmy's garden. 'These two break-ins could be a coincidence. The murder happens at the same time someone else is targeting the area.'

'Jimmy's death really could have been accidental,' Matt said, walking over to the steps where he died. 'They were not well maintained. The whole house is less chic, more shabby.'

'Perhaps Benedict was saved by being three sheets to the wind?'

'What do you mean?'

'He was drunk. Couldn't identify his own reflection. Jimmy, on the other hand. We don't know what state he was in yet, but if he was livestreaming I bet he was sober. Plus however many witnesses were watching. You should check the livestream when we get back.' They re-entered the house, stepping around forensics.

Caius stopped in front of the door to the basement level. He went down the stairs. Unlike Benedict, Jimmy had renovated down there. No musty, abandoned books here. He'd removed the separate pantry and coal storage and turned the space into an open kitchen area with a large island right in the middle. The style was dated. He must have carried out the work during his heyday. Caius remembered Jimmy from Friday-night TV in his teens. He was a lager-swilling dilettante, or at least that was the personality he performed, and yet Jimmy had a pasta machine on the kitchen side. Caius stopped thinking of Jimmy in the abstract and started thinking about him making tortellini in his kitchen. That wouldn't do. He went back upstairs. Matt was in the living room, looking at Jimmy's recording set-up.

'You were on camera coming up the stairs then,' Matt said, turning around to Caius. 'He's got some nice lights and stuff. What time was the livestream?'

Caius checked the report on his phone. 'It was 1 a.m.'

'So the killer probably thought he'd be asleep.'

'They couldn't be following him on social media. They'd have seen that he was on a live. Another thing to suggest a random burglary. An unfortunate accident. "Fake Isolde" is clever; this doesn't feel clever. She stole real Isolde's life story somehow – I guess to slow us down. We spent a day searching for her. The PO Box purchased with a random card that they probably bought the details of on the dark web, using Scott to avoid being seen on the CCTV at the Post Office – all very smart, and yet Jimmy died because of a dodgy step.'

Matt picked up a pile of paper from a side table and started flicking through it.

'What's that?' Caius asked.

'It looks like Jimmy wrote a memoir,' Matt said, putting the papers back down.

'Another book. What a literary neighbourhood.'

'It might sell now he's dead.'

Matt and Caius went upstairs and searched the bedrooms. Nothing appeared to be missing. No empty spots in cabinets or dust disturbed. Nothing pulled out of drawers. The collection of ancient comedy awards in the loo was kind of sad, there was a bog roll balanced on top of a Perrier award, but Caius ignored them and checked in the medicine cabinet for any prescriptions. He found nothing other than half a packet of paracetamol and a pair of tweezers. They finished examining the lingering ephemera of Jimmy's existence and then met out the front while they waited for Jimmy's body to be carried out.

'It's a nice house. Needs a lick of paint. I'm not sure how he could afford to live in it,' Matt said, staring up at the house.

'He probably purchased it before the finance bros moved in when it was the early days of Kate Moss and Sienna Miller supermodel boho. Landfill indie Camden. Amy Winehouse. There were still plenty of squats around. Besides, Jimmy Jones would've been on big money at the BBC then. He did a travel show, right? About stag dos or something. And that late-night game show. It was a bit eurotrashy. I remember staying up to watch that when I was fourteen and thinking I was the absolute shit quoting it the next day in the back of maths.'

'When there were still goths in the market.'

'The good old days.'

'Yours or his?'

'His. Mine are yet to come,' Caius said, getting into the car. 'Or at least I bloody hope so.'

32

Priory Square

Eulalia was standing at her bedroom window on the second floor, watching the police carry another body out the front of one of the neighbouring houses. She'd been watching the scene unfold for the last hour. Eulalia had seen him again, perched on the car bonnet, dashing as he commanded his subordinate about. The corpse being carried away was the end of the scene. The curtains fell closed. She stepped away and put on the workout clothes that Mel had ordered last week for her online. A pair of mint-green leggings and a white crop top that left nothing to the imagination. She wondered if that was so Mel could see if she was sticking to the low-carb, high-protein chicken breast diet. Eulalia didn't want to do yoga. Not today anyway. Mel had turned on the guilt tap though, flooding her bedroom with 'I found the best teacher for you'; 'I had to bribe the receptionist at the yoga studio she teaches from to give me her number so I could book a private lesson'; 'I thought you'd love this. I really did'; 'she's actually fucking Indian'; 'I go above and beyond for you over and over again and you don't give a shit.' Eulalia looked at herself in the freestanding mirror. She turned to the side, running her hand down her concave stomach. There was a knock at the door. Silence. Another knock.

'May I come in?' Mel asked as a formality only.

'Piss off,' Eulalia whispered.

Mel opened the door but didn't step into the room. 'Sorry, what was that?'

'Nothing.' Eulalia shook her head, and then posed. If they were going to posture then she was going to thrust her hips out.

'The postman's been.' Mel dumped a pile of letters and other crap, old books and dried flowers, that her fans had sent on her sister's dressing table. The label had forwarded it on. Mel had of course opened and read through every single one and signed all the photos of 'Eulalia' performing live at Glastonbury to be sent back to the fans herself. She just thought that the pile of shred-able adoration went some way to placate her sister's ego and distract her from thinking too much about her girl crush on the posho hat girl.

'I'm sorry,' Mel said. She was wearing black leggings and a baggy white T-shirt.

'I find living with you stressful. I think perhaps—'

Mel cut Eulalia off with a raised finger and a louder voice. 'I said I was sorry.' She looked at the glass of water she was holding. 'I am under so much stress right now and snapped at you.'

Eulalia rolled her eyes.

'We both are.'

'Yeah.'

'I thought yoga would help us relax. It'll be fun.' Mel handed her sister the glass of water.

'Sure.'

Mel took two packets of tablets from her pocket and popped one each out of the packaging. Mel gave them to her to take, but instead she just stared at the tablets in the palm of her hand.

'I liked those couple of bars of lyrics you wrote yesterday,' Mel said brightly. Eulalia had scribbled a line or two down and left it outside Mel's door at 4 a.m., describing her bitterness at being rejected by Callie last night.

'They're OK.'

'I think they're better than that. They're perfect for a bridge.' Mel had been working away on a new tune secretly.

'Yeah.' Eulalia didn't want to look at Mel. She knew that Mel was placating her. That a keyword might make it into the final version. She hated that she couldn't hold a note.

'Amala's downstairs for our session.'

'Someone else has died,' Eulalia said, walking over to her desk. The tablets were still in her outstretched hand.

'Where?' Mel asked. She was annoyed at her sister's morbidity. It sold records but the *Guardian*-reading masses should try to live with it. 'People croak all the time. Someone probably dies every second or something. Take your medication.'

'On the square. The police are outside again. There were loads of flashing lights.' Eulalia watched Mel move to the window, concerned that her sister was imagining things. Eulalia put the tablets in her bra – not for the first time that week – and swallowed a huge gulp of water that made her cough. She could feel herself existing on the edge of two different states: her current misery and looming freedom. She didn't need the pills any more. She was doing just fine. 'These pills are too big.'

'Yeah, but you have to take them.' Mel turned to look at her.

'Do I?' For a moment Eulalia felt powerful while her sister looked briefly petrified at the prospect of her unravelling.

'Everything will be for nothing if you don't.' Mel, sensing the power imbalance, switched the topic of conversation to the real reason she'd come in. 'Mum and Dad had the police round at theirs because someone bought a dodgy fucking PO Box on Mum's card.'

'Wasn't me.'

'Are you sure? Mum said you'd told her some bullshit that I don't let you have your own money. So she gave you her card details.'

'You don't. You keep control of everything.'

'I give you cash whenever you want it.'

'You give me a couple of crumpled-up notes every now and then. I don't have access to my own bank card. I wanted to buy clothes on the internet. They won't take a manky twenty.'

'Did you buy a PO Box?'

'What's a PO Box?' Eulalia flared her nostrils.

'I'm not keeping your money. I'm not doing it to be mean. I'm investing it.'

Eulalia shook.

'When you're manic you buy random shit. You spend small fortunes on crap. I'm just protecting you.'

'Whatever.'

'How was dinner last night?'

'Fine.'

'Have you got the receipt? I can claim it as a business expense.'

'I don't think Callie likes me.'

'What makes you say that?'

'I'm too much.'

'What do you mean?' Mel was concerned. Had her sister done or said something? Thank God for the NDA.

'Never mind.'

'I hate to say it, love, but this is a business transaction for her.' Mel felt mean, but her sister had to learn. Besides, she didn't want an outsider gaining too much influence. Not now. Not when they were finally so close to having it all. 'Calliope is going to present to me, umm, you and the cosmetics people tomorrow and then that will be that. You'll never get invited round for cosy candlelit suppers or whatever posh bitches like her do for fun. You're not going to spend the weekend at her boyfriend's castle shooting pheasants and quaffing port. I know that's what you wanted, as soon as you saw that stupid TV clip I could see that you wanted to be her, but you won't be.'

'But why not?'

'It's not how the world works. Now come downstairs. Stretch your adductors, open a chakra and relax.'

★　★　★

Eulalia stepped out of her post-yoga shower. She'd enjoyed twisting herself into knots while Mel demonstrated the flexibility of a plank of rain-sodden wood behind her. Amala showered her with compliments on her form while Mel's Herculean effort was only politely noted. The pills had nearly fallen out of her cleavage during a downward dog and she had to feign cramp in her hamstrings to shove them back in. She should've flushed them before they started. Eulalia had lathered herself with a body wash that the cosmetics guys had sent over earlier that morning. They were so sure that the make-up line was going to sell well that they were already thinking about other health and beauty expansions. The scent was divine. She smelled like a ripe fig waiting to be plucked and split open between greedy fingers. She felt soft and promisingly sticky and sweet. She could be smashed into mere pulp any minute by a firm, grasping hand. Eulalia dropped the towel on the bathroom floor and opened the matching body lotion, rubbing it in over every inch of her body. She spritzed a brightening toner on her face that they'd also sent over, a peptide serum with raspberry enzymes and then their hyaluronic moisturiser with added SPF.

Eulalia sat on her floor naked. She opened her laptop up and started writing. The girls who followed her on the fanfic site were going to love this – although Issy9786 had not replied to a single one of her messages complimenting her last story. Eulalia was going to outdo herself with her next instalment.

She wrote furiously for half an hour. The heat from the shower had worn off and although it was warm outside, she was starting to feel a chill as she lolled around naked on the hardwood floor. She wasn't going to get dressed. Not when she was writing about a threesome. Mel was calling her down for lunch – more poached hunks of protein – but she didn't want it. She was going to skip lunch and instead parade her flat stomach around the house all afternoon, once she had finished.

<h1 style="text-align:center">33</h1>

The Police Station

'I spoke to David Glossop, Jimmy's fan, who called the police after the livestream never ended,' Amy told Caius. 'He said that he saw the intruder briefly but they were dressed in dark colours and it was poorly lit so he couldn't say who they were. They couldn't judge their height, but they thought the intruder was either white or Middle Eastern.'

'Figures. Amy, I need you to start reading Horatio Combe's journals. All twenty-one of them.' Caius hadn't shaken the idea that the crime had some sort of literary bend to it. Digby was planning on writing a book, Jimmy had penned an unpublished memoir and Benedict had written one controversial banger and then exploded into self-doubt after one scathing review.

'Oh God.'

'It's going to be like reading a Flashman novel without the comfort of knowing it's fiction.'

'What are you doing?' Amy wanted to know how she got the short straw.

'Reading the comments on Jimmy's most recent social media in case anyone appears to be a crazy fan,' Caius said with a finality that let Amy know not to push it.

Amy went off to find the journals.

★ ★ ★

'According to Jimmy's agent, he had "moved away from bombastic and shocking comedy to more nuanced political satire". Well, that's what I wrote down anyway,' Matt said.

'And the memoir?'

'His agent was going to try and shop it around once he'd done another draft. It was about his fall from primetime grace and into a rehab centre in leafy Surrey. It sounded pretty interesting, actually. I'd read it. Jimmy had done a lot of therapy.'

'You know the saying, are you funny or did you have a stable childhood?' Caius got his phone out and found Jimmy's YouTube channel. He clicked on the first video.

Jimmy Jones:

Tax evasion? It's a joke.

Caius paused the video. He scanned down the sidebar. 'OK, yeah. He really, really hates tax evasion. He despised it enough to do five videos in the last month. He got serious. No more minge flaps for him, only runaway inflation.'

'Surely, there's a happy medium?' Matt said. He found both ideas tedious.

Amy who had spent the last ten minutes trying to read the first paragraph of the first journal let out a frustrated yelp.

'You OK?' Caius asked.

'I can't read it. The letters are all the same. It's just squiggles.'

'Hang on.' Caius found the number he wanted and called it, putting her on speakerphone. 'Hi, Willow, it's DI Caius Beauchamp. I was wondering if you might help us? You mentioned before that you were typing up Horatio Combe's journals.'

'Did I?' She paused. She'd sounded unsure but then found a renewed enthusiasm for the topic from somewhere. 'Yes, I did. All twenty-two of the bloody things.'

'Did you do it on Digby's typewriter?' Caius watched Amy shoot up from her desk, unsure as to what had warranted such a reaction.

'Umm. No, my laptop. I kept making too many mistakes to type them up that way. It took me ages to get used to the hand-writing. I didn't finish typing it all up so Digby never saw it.'

'Have you still got the files for all the journals?'

'Yes, somewhere. Hang on.'

Caius looked up at Amy who shook her head, mouthing 'twenty-one'. She had them all in front of her, after all, and had just counted them.

'Are you sure there are twenty-two volumes?'

'Yes. I'm looking at the documents now on my laptop. Each journal is a separate Word doc.'

'There were only twenty-one in the library upstairs.'

'Oh yeah. That makes sense. One of Digby's forebears removed this one specific volume from the collection for being lewd. It was kept under lock and key in Digby's desk. Digby had been told by his grandfather not to read the twenty-second volume, but I had to. He had me start there, actually.'

'The malaria year?' Caius asked, remembering what Nathan had said.

'Yeah. It's weird. It's all gibberish about communing with the dead and orgies. There were diagrams. I didn't transcribe those. I did take a couple of pictures that I shared with the girls though. To be fair, Horatio died that year so he could very well have been malarial. I don't think Digby knew it was that kinky, otherwise I think he would've been too proper to get me to type them up.

Not that I care. We're all grown-ups.' Willow giggled and then resumed talking, this time slower. 'I do hope the journals will be of use to you. I spent so long typing them up.'

'Thanks, Willow,' Caius said, ready to end the conversation.

'Any luck with the weirdo who dressed up like me?'

'No, not yet,' Caius said, furrowing his brow. 'We'll let you know if we do.'

'Sure.' Willow gave a whimpering laugh. 'I've not been sleeping great. I keep thinking that I've got some creepy stalker.'

'Have you noticed anyone acting oddly around you?'

'No . . .' Willow tailed off. 'But still . . . What if there was someone who lived on the square who was watching my every move?'

Caius did everything he could to reassure her before hanging up.

'Was the twenty-second volume there, Amy?' Caius asked.

'No,' she said firmly. 'Me and Tiny Simm went through every inch of that building. Any paperwork in Digby's drawers was taken into evidence.'

'Missing? Or stolen?'

★ ★ ★

Caius, Matt and Amy were all crowding round Caius's computer looking at Horatio Combe's sex diagrams that Willow had sent over with the typed-up journals.

'Is that what straight sex is really like?' Amy asked, tilting her head. She was a gold-star lesbian. 'I've seen it in films. Men flopping about.'

'I'm not convinced that that's impossible, but I'm sure physics has to come into play here somewhere,' Matt said.

'I think you could do it if you had a winch and a really strong core,' Caius said. He closed the picture. 'Amy, are we really sure that we didn't miss the dirty journal at the crime scene?'

'For the last time, yes. I went through Digby's drawers myself. There was not another journal there.'

'Why steal it?' Matt asked.

'It has the family's famous damson jam recipe?' Caius shrugged. 'Regrettably, Amy, I'm going to need you to read through Willow's transcription.'

'I'll approach it with the detached humour I'm known for.'

'That's the spirit.'

★ ★ ★

Caius was reading through Scott's post-mortem and Matt was replaying the footage of Jimmy's livestream, when Amy called them both over.

'I started with the malaria year. I don't know why, but I thought it sounded more interesting and the day is almost over.'

'Right?' Matt asked. He peered over Amy's shoulder and started scanning through a chunk of text that Amy had high-lighted. 'What the hell am I reading?'

'Willow was right. It's weird. There's a lot of group sex described in mystical, penetrative terms. Horatio was holding seances in the basement of the Institute and other houses in the square too. Sometimes the two things seemed to merge.'

'Hmm.' Caius remembered what Benedict had told him about a previous inhabitant of his house.

'Horatio was part of a little group. It reads like some sort of sex cult, if I'm honest. He's the only guy and he's sleeping with all of them. The others all lived around the square so maybe the seances were just a cover for proto-swinging.'

'The others?' Caius asked.

'Yes, a widow and her daughter at number 7. Mary and Emmeline Plunkett.'

'That's Benedict's house.'

'A man who worked for the Foreign Office at number 21. Josiah Hargreaves. He'd been to the same boarding school as Horatio and seems to be sycophantic towards him. He just watches.'

'Jimmy Jones's house,' Matt said.

'And a woman artist who lived at number 35. Lavinia Caddington. She was banned from entering the Royal Academy for undressing during one of their summer exhibitions, apparently. I googled her. She was fashionable for a short period before spending a prolonged time at the seaside taking the air.'

'Nothing's been reported as of yet at number 35,' Caius said, going back to his computer and pulling up a map of the square. He pressed print. 'Benedict told me that there had been seances in his house in the Victorian era.'

'How did that come up?' Matt asked, raising an eyebrow. 'Was it an interesting titbit or a veiled boast?'

'Titbit. He was going to write about it at one point.' Caius picked up the map from the printer and sat back down with it. 'I noticed there was a marking on the wall in his basement kitchen level that looked like a pentagram. A layer of paint had peeled away. He stores books in his. The old lady he'd bought it from had lived her whole life in the house or something and knew its history.'

'Do you think it's connected to Digby's death?' Amy asked.

'The square as it is now or its history?' Caius took out two of his favourite Muji highlighters from his drawer and highlighted Digby's and Jimmy's houses in red and Benedict's in orange.

'Either,' Amy said.

'Yes. It's "fake Isolde's" hunting ground. Two victims whose workplaces were within five minutes' walk of each other. Then the break-ins happening in those two specific houses. We suspect that Digby's house had also been searched.'

'That's three out of four,' Matt said.

'Matt, call in at number 35 on your way home. See if they've had any trouble.' Caius highlighted the house in yellow. They made a cross over the square. 'Amy, start a crib sheet on the journal. Include anything you come across that talks about the square, anything valuable he nicked on his travels, anything that might have repercussions for our age. You know what I mean.'

'Sure,' Amy said.

Caius turned back to his computer. 'I'm going to have a little dig on the history of the square before we clock out.'

★　★　★

Caius had found a blog on Priory Square. It had footnotes to those books that fill up the local history stack at the library. Benedict had been roughly right.

Priory Square had been the site of St Agnes's Priory founded by Eleanor of Aquitaine in penance after a fight with her husband in 1188. The priory flourished, in part due to its proximity to London. Many nobles at court sent their young daughters there to be educated. The land that the priory controlled was vast and at one point in the fourteenth century it provided one-tenth of London's pork. Its immense wealth was coveted by many, including the nobles and yeomanry who farmed adjoining land.

The fall of the priory from grace, like all of its sister institutions, came during the Reformation. Henry VIII gave the land away to a loyal courtier, Sir Walter de Cressy. Sir Walter's descendants through a matrilineal line developed the houses as they are today and still own the leaseholds in the area.

The priory was thought to have been located on top of an Anglo-Saxon chapel which was built itself on top of a Roman ruin. Multiple ecclesiastical sources from the twelfth century cite the remains of a temple to Minerva as being located underneath the chapel. As is well documented many early Christian buildings were built on top of former pagan sites.

One of the priory's most infamous inhabitants was Alice de Burge. She was a young nun of possible aristocratic birth (although little is known about her family's circumstances) supposedly blessed with prophetic visions. She claimed that Henry VIII would die without a male heir and that the country would fall into chaos if he married Anne Boleyn. Alice de Burge was burnt at the stake for heresy in 1532. All known copies of 'Her Visions' were set alight with her. Professor Andrew Clifton of King's College London has surmised that Alice de Burge's sentencing was not in fact due to prophesising the demise of the Tudor line – although a serious enough offence – but instead for the radical preaching Alice did, inspiring a wave of young and otherwise incredibly eligible noblewomen to take the veil at an inordinately high rate, much to the horror of their parents and suitors who were keen on advantageous marriages.

In the 1860s, when the houses that now form Priory Square were constructed, there were rumours that the digging of the basements revealed a level of medieval masonry, but no known formal excavation has ever been attempted.

Caius clicked on the hyperlink for a page about Sir Walter de Cressy and scanned the page. Norman blah blah. Gentleman of bedchamber blah blah. Baronetcy went extinct blah blah. Heiress married . . .

'You all right?' Amy asked as Caius shot up from his chair.

'Yeah. I've got to make a personal call.' Caius left the incident room, ploughing down the corridor until he found an empty room. 'Hi, Dad.'

'You all right, kiddo?'

'Priory Square.'

'NW1?'

'Yeah.'

'Finally taking an interest, are we?'

'So we own it then?'

'The leasehold yes, and a third of the houses still. The ones we own were all converted into flats in the 1980s. Due a refurb. You want to manage that? I think a chunk got sold off at the time they were built. The price the sold houses fetched paid for the building of the others. Another wave went on the market in the 1950s to cover the death duty after your great-great-uncle died. It earns well. Prime location.'

'Fuck.' Caius took his glasses off and stabbed one of the arms into his forehead. 'There's been two murders, and one accident-but-looks-dodgy connected to the square.'

'Oh dear.' Marcus's chipper tone fell away.

'Look, I'll see you tomorrow, Dad.' Caius hung up and went back to Amy in the incident room. 'My dad owns it.'

'Owns what?'

'Priory Square. It's Beauchamp land.'

'Oh shit. What are you going to do?'

'I've got to tell the Chief Superintendent. I'll be taken off the case. It's a conflict.'

'What'll happen then?'

'You'll have another DI until it's over and I'll end up doing paperwork for a bit. Before I go, let's work out a plan. It depends on who you guys get and how much they think I'm an arse, but if you're busy already chasing down leads they'll probably leave you alone for a bit while they get up to speed.'

Caius quickly put in writing a request to Fenella Combe-Watson to gain access to the basement of the Horatio Combe Institute so they could see where the infamous seances took place, and chased up a CCTV request that had been bothering him. He called Matt on his mobile, explained the situation, and Amy then took out a pen and wrote Caius's strategy down in a notebook, before he trundled off to the Chief Superintendent's office with the map he had printed out of the square.

34

Priory Square

Matt banged on the door again. Harder this time. He'd pressed the bell twice but whoever was in hadn't heard him. There were lights on and he could hear a faint bassline coming from within. He opened the letterbox and yelled 'Hello' at someone's crotch. The door swung open so quick that he didn't have a chance to stand up.

'Yes?' A surly woman stared down imperiously at him. The chorus of Radiohead's 'Creep' slinked feebly down the stairs.

Matt straightened himself up and then fixed his tie, over-compensating for the ignoble position she had found him in. 'DS Matthew Cheung. Met Police.' He showed her his badge. 'Are you the homeowner?'

'I am.'

'We've had two break-ins on the square.'

'And a murder or two, right?'

'Yes, well. I just wanted to come in and talk to you about your security? We're worried that your house may be targeted in the future.'

'Security isn't a problem,' she said, gesturing to the camera above him pointed at the front door. 'There's one at the basement level and the back door as well. We have a fully functioning alarm system too.'

Matt looked down past the railings and saw the camera she was referring to. 'Is it possible for me to see your basement?'

'All right,' she said, letting Matt in. She didn't want to but it would be the quickest way to get rid of him. She walked down the hallway and gestured towards a set of steps leading down-wards. Matt went down first. The basement had been renovated recently. The plasterwork was too perfect. He came out in a small area with a sofa plonked against a wall. He opened the door off the space.

'You've got a recording studio down here,' Matt said, poking his head through. 'That's cool.'

'My sister's a musician,' she said. She smiled weakly. Matt didn't think she sounded totally pleased about that. 'We've done an extensive renovation down here.'

'I see.' Matt turned back upstairs. 'I'm so sorry, I didn't catch your name.'

'It's Mel.'

'Thanks for your time, Mel. If you think someone is trying to break in, please call 999. If you notice anything off going on, people in the square acting suspiciously, then please call,' he said, handing her his card.

'Thank you,' she glanced at the card, 'DS Matthew Cheung.'

Matt left the house. Mel bolted the front door. Then she climbed up the two flights of stairs to her sister's room. She shoved the door open without waiting to be admitted.

'Hey, my door was shut. What the hell, Mel?'

'We just had the police here.' Mel went over to Eulalia's record player and pulled the arm up, stopping the track dead.

'And?'

'They wanted to check that we had security.'

'We do, don't we?' Eulalia rolled her eyes, shaking her head at her sister as if asking why she was bothering her with this. 'What's your problem?'

Mel took the LP off the player and snapped it in half. She was sick of listening to Thom Yorke whinge. 'My problem is that the police officer who was just here has the same name as the one that visited Mum and Dad.'

'And?'

'What have you done?'

'Me? Nothing. I don't go anywhere.'

'I swear to God, if you blow this for us there will be hell to pay.'

'Piss off, Mel.'

'If you ruin this for me, I will never forgive you. We are so fucking close to everything we've ever wanted.'

'We're close to everything you've wanted, Mel. I'm just here for the ride. I'm just a lamb to be sacrificed, to be defiled. Pawed over.'

'It's not my fault you can't fucking sing.'

'It's not my fault you're ugly.'

'What comes out is a cat being strangled. You can't hit a single note correctly.'

'You have a flat arse and a flat nose.' Eulalia stopped, took a deep breath and turned away from her sister. 'I know, I know. Shhh.'

'What was that?'

'What?'

'Just then. You weren't talking to me, were you.' Her sister seemed a bit more screwy than normal, but she'd definitely given her her medication this morning. It must be the stress of the new album, or perhaps her dosage was off again. Mel would schedule an urgent appointment with her sister's private psychiatrist on Harley Street tomorrow.

'Get out of my room,' she said quietly. Mel would try to meddle with her now. She had that look. Eulalia turned back to her laptop to scroll obsessively as her sister left the room. She hadn't been surprised by a single thing Mel had said. She knew she was out to get her. She'd sent a spy to watch over her at dinner with Cal, after all. He'd offered them little cups of poison.

35

Caius and Callie's Flat

Callie opened the front door to her father.

'Hello, uh.' She went to call him Peter but he got funny when she did, despite that being the name she'd called him for 97 per cent of her life.

'I hope you don't mind me stopping by,' Peter said, peering over her shoulder to make sure she was home alone.

'Not at all,' Callie said, inviting him in with the wave of her arm. 'Would you like a cup of tea?'

'Yes, please.' Peter sat down on the sofa. 'His nibs not in?'

'Don't call him that.' Callie had a playful edge to her voice but she meant it. She filled the kettle.

'I'm only teasing,' Peter said, putting a file down on the coffee table. 'I like the bloke. Surprisingly down to earth.'

Callie wondered what he was doing here. Peter didn't like to pop in to her domestic sphere. He liked to take her out to dinner publicly and show her off – not that she readily accepted his invitations too frequently. Despite his professed fondness he was intimidated by Caius. This was partially due to how they had first met, but mostly due to Peter's snobbery. She found it rather amusing; she was certain Peter had had elocution lessons in the eighties when he was a petty bourgeois, Thatcherite social climber and yet here was Caius's family with their splashy vowels, glottal stops and accidental baronetcy.

'That Max has sent a formal apology in writing. Did you want to read it?'

'No.'

'Thought as much. The gist of it was: he's very sorry, won't happen again, would like to remain friends and he's always got an ear to lend you.'

'I can't believe I nearly married him.' Callie rolled her eyes. 'Was it just an ear he offered?'

'You're smarter than that, girl. You're on to a good thing here.'

'A good thing, eh?'

'You won't do better than Caius.'

'I couldn't want better. You know, I think Caius is the first man I've ever been with who actually likes women. So many men hate us. Many more than you'd think.' Callie noticed the file Peter had brought with him. 'What's that?'

'It's about the Simpson Foundation.'

'Cool.' She had pressed him on it earlier that week. 'Earl Grey? English breakfast? I've even got some oolong?'

'Breakfast will do.' Peter sat back on the sofa and watched her. 'The document is setting out the initial financial endowment. Do you still want to be on the board?'

'Yes.'

'It's a lot of boring numbers.'

'I bet.'

'A lot of tedious regulation stuff.'

'Are you trying to talk me out of it?'

'Perhaps.'

'Why?'

'You're not a Simpson, are you?'

'Not this again.' Peter had tried the other month to get Callie to change her surname to his now that their relationship had briefly been a tabloid headline.

'What? You're my only daughter, aren't you?'

'Am I?'

'Biologically speaking.'

'Sugar?' The kettle boiled. Callie poured the water into the cups. She didn't know how he took his tea.

'No, thank you. Splash of milk.'

'There's no point in me changing my name.' She regretted saying that as soon as it flew out of her mouth.

'Oh really?' Peter caught the subtext.

'What's the focus of the foundation going to be?' Callie tried to change the subject but she could see that Peter wanted confirmation. Callie stood tight-lipped.

'Undecided as of yet.' Peter let it go, retreating to the idea of the engagement party he'd throw them. It would be grander than Harriet's garden party. He'd use it as an opportunity, of course, to propel himself to the forefront again. Try and claw his way back up to the dizzying heights he'd fallen from.

'Maternity care in Bangladesh. Women's health clinics. Buy them some folic acid at least. It was a mostly female workforce that you exploited, after all.'

'All terrific ideas.' Peter didn't enjoy being called out directly, but in an odd way he liked that Callie took after him and said what the hell she was thinking with little care. 'Charities are rather technical. There is a lot of legal expectations around duty of care involved. Even I'm not sure what's possible and what's not.'

'A splash of milk.' Callie handed him the cup. 'Why don't you go on a fact-finding mission to all the places where your brands had factories working for them? Take a camera crew if you like.' She thought if it was broadcasted then he might actually stick to it. 'You're going to have to face up to it at some point. The tide will turn against a sea of cheaply made polyester blouses that fall apart after a machine wash or two. Better for it not to be on your deathbed or worse, posthumously. You'd have no right of reply then. The vultures would just be gleefully picking over your corpse.'

He didn't like that metaphor. 'A fact-finding mission. Not a bad idea that. You could come too if you fancied?' Peter could picture it now: earnest interviews in the Sunday papers; him wearing a rolled-up linen shirt boasting a tan from whatever third-world country he'd just jetted back from; Callie, who had the right bone structure for the camera, charming the pants off Middle England and making him look sympathetic.

'I don't feel inclined to travel much at the moment,' Callie said off-handedly. She opened a sketchbook that she'd left on the dining table and tore out a sheet. She started writing down a plan. 'I'm much too busy.'

'You come across wonderfully on screen. You're like me, nat-urally funny. You held it together tremendously when Max pulled his silly little stunt.'

Callie changed the subject. 'You'll need someone to be the face of the fundraisers though, right? Lunches. Galas and whatnot.'

'I will,' Peter conceded. He had been missing his ex-wife in this respect and had been considering replacing her with a kinder, gentler, younger model for such purposes. Not that he'd met anyone, yet.

'Well, if you don't want me anywhere near operations then I suppose all I'm good for is garden parties.'

'That's an important job. Fundraising is crucial.'

'Yes, and I do now have exclusive access to a very nice historic private house just outside London.' Callie sat in the armchair opposite him, placing her ginger tea on the side table. 'I really do need to introduce you to Marcus. You'd get on. I told you that he has all the sheep and no way to make money from the wool. I had the idea to make small artisanal batches of natural dyed yarn. I'm not sure on the execution yet though.'

'Do you want me to look into the machinery you'd need? I know a few manufacturers.'

'Yes, please. That would be really helpful.' Callie could picture herself stirring a vast vat of bubbling purple.

The door opened and Caius called out.

'We're in here,' Callie replied.

'Hello,' Caius said, coming into the room. 'Hello, Peter. How are you?' They shook hands.

'Not too shabby, not too shabby,' Peter said, standing up rather quickly.

'We were just talking about your dad's wool problem.'

'Oh God. I don't like sheep. It's their eyes,' Caius said, sitting down in the free armchair.

'I can't stop. I've got a thing,' Peter said.

'Lovely to see you, Peter, if only briefly,' Caius said, aware that it was his presence that had hastened his departure.

Callie stood up and followed Peter to the door. She handed him the notes she'd just scrawled. 'You know what you really should do?'

'What?' Peter said from the doorstep.

'Fuck setting up a charity. Write the Bangladeshi government a cheque. Sorry for exploiting your people. Here's some money. Do with it however you see best. Toodle-loo.'

'That's not a bad idea either. It would save a lot of time.' He could see the headlines calling him 'pragmatic' and lamenting his lack of Cabinet position.

'Saves you having to faff about with safeguarding or whatever not being an arsehole is called in corporate settings these days.'

'Very efficient.' Peter winked at her and left. He turned around and waved goodbye from the bottom of the path.

'Bye, Dad,' Callie called after him, shutting the door. She walked into the living room and sat back down in her chair. She took a sip of her ginger tea. It was still too hot to drink.

'He didn't touch his tea,' Caius said.

'He's intimidated by you.'

'Me? I'm a pussycat.'

'Meow.' Callie got up and sat in his lap.

'I've been taken off the case I was working on.'

'What happened?'

'The series of crimes happened on a square that my dad partially owns, something about leaseholds. I don't know. It's ours anyway.'

'Ah.'

'Plus side is that I was obliged to take a couple of days off as annual leave so we can head off to Frithsden as soon as you've done your pitch.'

'Well, the pitch is nice and early at 9 a.m., but then I'm meeting Tabs at eleven for coffee. How about I try to get back here for lunch at 1 p.m.?' Callie got off his lap and wandered over to the kitchen. She started loading the dishwasher.

'Parfait.' Caius picked up Peter's cup of tea and took it over to the sink, tipping it away. 'How was your midwife appointment?'

'All good,' Callie said, looking up from loading the cutlery tray. 'I'll get a hospital appointment in the post for the twelve-week scan.'

'Let me know when and I'll get time off.' He came over and kissed her on her forehead. 'And how are you feeling, darling girl?'

'Nauseous. But apparently that's a good thing so . . . Everything is ticking along.'

'We're going to have a baby.'

'They're going to have little toes.'

'And a little button nose.'

'They're the size of a blueberry.' Callie shut the dishwasher, looked pointedly around the flat and then up at Caius. 'Are we going to have to move?'

'Move? Why? This flat is big enough, right?'

'It's fine for us two, but fit a pram in the hallway, a cot in the bedroom, a playpen in here and it'll be cramped. It's only a one-bed.'

'We could always buy our own place? We'd probably have to move to the back end of Walthamstow though.' Caius didn't fancy it.

'We could.'

'But?'

'I was procrastinating earlier and read a report in the *British Medical Journal* on the effects of London pollution on tiny lungs.'

'Right?'

'And now I'm wondering if we should move out?'

'Move out to?'

'Near your parents. You can get the train into Euston from Hemel Hempstead. I could drop you off at the station in the morning. You'd be at your desk in forty-five minutes. Think about it. We could have a separate nursery. A proper garden and not a five-by-five-metre square. Plus I'm sure having your parents nearby will be super useful when we want a babysitter so we can go out for dinner.'

'I'll think about it.' Caius went over to the fridge, looking at the ingredients inside for possibilities. He couldn't fault her logic. He just wasn't sure that he was totally ready to leave London yet. He wasn't a transplant. He'd grown up here. Besides, if they did move out to Hertfordshire his dad would foist more and more on him. He wasn't done with the Met yet. 'Mushroom risotto?'

'Oh yes, please.' Callie came up behind him and looped her arms around his waist. He lifted his arm over her shoulder and held her. 'Have we got any more oranges?'

'Are you craving them?'

'I guess so. I've eaten two big ones today already.' Callie released herself. 'I also had three scrambled eggs for breakfast and I've never tasted anything so delicious.'

'Let me know if you crave anything else. I'll do an online shop for next week tomorrow. Berries? They're good for you.' Caius began dicing an onion and two cloves of garlic. 'Are those the flowers?'

'Yeah, the ones I texted you about. The flowers from Eulalia.'

'They are a lot, aren't they?' Caius couldn't quite believe the size of the bouquet. It looked more like a centrepiece for a state banquet than a posey for a coffee table.

'Exactly my point.' Callie went over and looked at the arrangement. 'Quite an unusual group of flowers. Asphodel, carnations and bay leaves aren't normally put together.'

'What do they mean?'

Callie glanced at her grandmother's copy of *Language of Flowers* on the shelf. She picked up the book and found the entries for each flower. 'Asphodel means "My regrets follow you to the grave".' She flicked through the book. 'Bay leaves mean "I change but in death", and red carnations mean "Alas for my poor heart!".'

'That's intense. Was it done on purpose? Or was the florist just wonky.' Caius put a knob of butter in the frying pan and turned the hob on.

'I think it's on purpose. She knows that I have a thing about floriography. She talked about it.' Callie stared at the flowers. 'On Monday I thought Eulalia was a bit eccentric. That's not unusual for creatives. Being an artist almost comes with a weirdo pass, but I thought there was something off with Eulalia at dinner. I don't know if she's OK, she was oddly hyper at one point and then really withdrawn. I feel bad for her. She's clearly lonely and trapped in a bubble.'

'Presentation tomorrow morning.' Caius wasn't sure what to think other than he didn't want Callie mixed up in a Britney situation. He put a stock cube in a measuring jug and boiled the kettle. 'Distance yourself afterwards unless it's in a professional capacity.'

'I think Eulalia is one of those people who wouldn't see the signs. You know. A bit oblivious to the social cues she doesn't want to see.'

'She'll get the message eventually. If she really doesn't and it gets extreme you can set Peter's very expensive lawyer on her.' Caius put the diced onions in the frying pan on a low heat. He walked away from the kitchen area for a moment and grabbed one of Callie's many sketchbooks. He flipped it to the back page and drew Horatio Combe's diagram from memory. It had burnt itself in there. He showed it to Callie. 'Humour me, please. Is this position possible?'

'Absolutely. You just need to put a chair against the bottom of the bed.'

'Right, yeah.' He turned the diagram around. 'I can see it now.'

'Where did you get that from?'

'From a one-hundred-odd-year-old document that we were looking at for this case.'

'Want to try it later? I might be up to it.'

'Abso-fucking-lutely.' Caius looked down at the pan. The onions were beginning to burn. 'Bugger.'

'I don't think I can call you Daddy any more. Not like that anyway.'

'I suppose not.' Caius finished pouring the arborio rice into the pan and followed it with the water from the boiled kettle. He'd forgotten the garlic and the stock cube was left waiting in the measuring jug. 'Can you stir this? I need to put a chair at the end of bed.'

FRIDAY

36

Priory Square

Callie knocked on Eulalia and Mel's front door. The meeting wasn't for another thirty minutes but she wanted to be early to get set up. The taxi driver was kind enough to carry her things to the door for her. She thanked him warmly and he blushed. Caius had offered to drive her over to wherever it was she needed to go but she'd said that she wanted the taxi ride over to clear her thoughts. She was, in truth, nervous about introducing Caius to Eulalia. Not that she thought he'd fall at Eulalia's probably perfectly manicured toes and profess his sudden and devasting undying love for her, but because Eulalia had been just a little too interested in him. Callie suspected that Eulalia, despite her ethereal beauty pushing her beyond the normal barriers, was potentially a bit of a 'Laura'.

Mel opened the door. She looked a little flushed. 'Good morning, Calliope,' she said. Mel looked Callie up and down, taking in every inch. Callie wasn't thin. She wasn't fat either, but still, she shouldn't have been this attractive. Mel thought Callie's make-up helped, she'd got a good hairdresser who'd given her a blow out, and besides, her dress was doing the heavy lifting. It was gorgeous. Mel was furious. Just the perfect mix of relaxed and chic. Why couldn't she be like that.

'Good morning. I hope you don't mind my being early. I should have everything set up ahead of the meeting. I emailed you, but I think perhaps you'd finished for the day as I didn't get a response.'

'It's not a problem,' Mel said. She admired Callie's work ethic and the mountains of props she'd brought with her, Mel felt she was getting her money's worth at least, but she didn't appreciate the confidence she had marched in with. Mel let it go. The quicker this was over, the quicker she could get her sister to Harley Street. The sleeker Callie's presentation, the easier it was going to be to placate her darling sister's precious sense of agency, and the quicker the commercial contracts got signed.

'Where shall I set up?' Callie asked. Mel still had her standing on the doorstep.

'Oh. This way. Follow me.' Mel, in a bid to get everything over and done with quickly, picked up a couple of the easels and went inside. She led Callie into the living room and stopped in front of the fireplace. 'Here works.'

'Perfect,' Callie said, taking in the room. It was plainer than she'd expected. There were fewer art works, fewer books, fewer textures, fewer colours than she thought an artist like Eulalia would surround herself with. It was less depressing, or morbid rather, than she had supposed too. 'What glorious weather we've been having.'

'Hmm.' Mel didn't want to make small talk.

Callie placed her handbag – a tan Mulberry Bayswater she'd had for years and years – on the floor next to the sofa. The top flopped open as the bag slouched over backwards and the ball of cotton wool that had been taped to her arm after the blood test yesterday rolled out. She didn't notice. Callie went back to the front door and grabbed the rest of her things. She set about arranging the five easels in front of the fireplace, taking each of the boards she'd prepared out of the case she'd carried them in.

Mel watched her from the doorway, taking in the work Callie had done. She hated to admit it but her sister had been right about her. 'Where's your eyeshadow from?' Mel begrudgingly asked. She was asking not as a compliment but more so that she had more information with which to be envious.

'Pat McGrath.' Callie stopped what she was doing and tilted her head. 'I love her. She's a genius. Her runway work. I mean . . . So gorgeous.'

'Cool.' Mel smiled, but Callie could see that something was off.

Mel opened the double doors that separated the living from the dining room. On the table arranged neatly were small bottles of mineral water, a jug of orange juice and five plates. A small woman came into the room and started setting teacups down.

'I hate having meetings here.'

'It's all very uncomfortable when the domestic clashes with the grubbiness of business, isn't it?' Callie said. She was trying her best to smooth things over.

'You talk like you were born a hundred years ago.'

Callie laughed. She didn't find the comment amusing but it was the only real defence she had. 'Do I?'

The doorbell rang, mercifully. Mel looked at her housekeeper, who silently dashed off to answer it this time. She returned moments later with a box of pastries from a nearby bakery.

'Those smell divine,' Callie said.

'Do they? Divine?'

'Yes.' For a second Callie thought Mel was soliciting her in conversation but then she caught the mocking undertone.

'When's Cal arriving?' Eulalia walked into the living room. She was wearing an oversized pair of jeans and a plain white T-shirt. She was stiff with tension, like she'd take flight after mistaking a car backfiring outside for a gunshot. 'Oh you're here already. Hey, sweetie. I love your dress. Where is it from?'

'This?' Callie looked down at herself. It was from her *Howards End* phase. 'I made it last year.'

'You're so pretty.' Eulalia started moving towards Callie, but then turned around and took in the boards that Callie had placed. 'Wow.'

Callie turned away from Eulalia's gaze and focused intensely on her own work instead.

'Mel, darling,' Callie began. She liked to call people she disliked darling. She knew it was bollocks, they knew it was bollocks. It was altogether thrilling. 'Where's your bog?'

'Bog? Don't you mean toilet?'

'No, darling, we never say toilet.'

'Up the stairs, first door on the right.' Mel chewed the inside of her cheek.

'Cheers.' Callie picked up her bag and left the room.

'Why are you being such a bitch?' Eulalia hissed.

'Me?' Mel whispered back with faux offence.

'Yes, you.'

'No, I'm not.' Mel affected sweetness.

'You don't like other women. You know that? It's such a manly quality of yours. So masculine. You don't like her because she's so pretty. Because she makes her own dresses. Because she's feminine and you look like a hog in lipstick.'

Mel ignored her sister and checked her phone. 'You've got an appointment with Dr Patel at 2 p.m.'

The housekeeper came back in with a glass bowl of bananas and set them down on the table.

'I'm going to get ready for the meeting.' Mel left the living room and went up the stairs, pausing outside the bathroom. The lock clicked and she scurried away into her room before Callie saw her.

Eulalia stared at the ground at the spot where Callie's bag had been and picked up a piece of rubbish. But it wasn't rubbish. It was a bloody treasure. Eulalia shoved it quickly into the pocket of her jeans.

Callie went back downstairs and into the living room to find Eulalia staring at the boards. 'What do you think?'

'I adore it. I adore you.' She grasped Callie's hand and held on to it tightly. 'You understand me so well.'

'I'm so glad you're pleased,' Callie said, tactfully freeing herself. She took out the five booklets with the concept's visuals in and gave one to Eulalia. She spread the other four out on the coffee table in a fan shape. Callie hadn't had time for anything too fancy but she'd had the pages printed yesterday afternoon at a copy shop in Archway. She'd then bound them herself Japanese-style with black velvet ribbon, and covered them with the few remaining scraps of a warm orange and chocolate brocade from a random couple of metres she had left over from a skirt she'd made two years prior.

Mel came into the room. She'd changed into her customary white shirt and black trousers. The same safe outfit she'd worn when Callie first laid eyes on her at Tate Britain. She had that pair of black stilettoes on and appeared to have shaken her attitude. She'd applied a lick of mascara and a red lip. It was obviously her armour. If Callie was being critical, which she was but only in her head, the shade was too warm for Mel's cool skin tone and was pulling a little orange. Callie smiled at her, nonetheless. Mel sailed past Callie and sprayed Eulalia with a bottle of perfume.

'I love a gourmand. That's practically edible,' Callie said, taking in the honeyed scent. 'Yummy.'

'I know, right?' Eulalia said, smirking at Callie. 'Devour me.'

'Are you all set?' Mel said, turning to Callie and interrupting whatever it was her sister was trying to do. 'A few minutes of pleasantries and pastries, present your idea and then we're done.'

'Fantastic,' Callie said. The end was in sight – as was the bank transfer. She was beginning to feel overwhelmed by the whip-lash between adoration and loathing she was receiving from the pair.

The doorbell rang. The housekeeper, it seemed, had disap-peared for good this time. Mel went and opened the door and in doing so found a whole new disposition.

The team from PCQV had arrived, impossibly chic and relaxed about it all. A man, whose no-nonsense, well-tailored suit made Callie think he was the business side, and a woman, a familiar face that Callie couldn't quite place.

'Callie? I thought it must be you. There aren't that many Calliopes in the world.'

'Hello, sweetheart.' Callie couldn't remember her name. She was certain she'd been at art school with her. Yes, they had a ceramics class together in first year. Her name was a city. Paris, maybe? Geneva? It would come to her. 'How on earth are you?'

'Fantastic.' The woman took her by both hands and held her in. 'I bumped into Dot the other day at Chiltern Firehouse. She's looking glorious.'

'Glowing, isn't she? They're coming to visit my boyfriend and I this weekend, actually.'

'I heard you've got a new beau.'

'I have, yes. I'm terribly smug, I'm afraid.'

'Be as smug as you like.'

Mel had lost control of the room and Eulalia was neither the centre of attention nor holding Callie's. Eulalia coughed.

'There she is,' the uni friend said. 'The woman of the hour. You smell heavenly. I knew you'd like the honeyed plum scent best out of the five.'

'The five?' Eulalia asked. No one really heard her, except for Callie who was confused by Eulalia's tone and by Mel's resulting undefinable smugness. Eulalia shot her sister a dirty look. Mel refused to look sheepish. Of course she'd gone through the samples first and whittled it down to the products she wanted Eulalia to pick and hidden the others.

'Would anyone like some refreshments before we begin?' Mel asked.

The suit picked up a bottle of water and a pistachio croissant, and Callie's uni acquaintance took a bottle of water only. Callie quite fancied the look of the croissants but stuck to water. Caius had made her another omelette for breakfast. She wasn't starving and she didn't want to get crumbs down her cleavage. It was bad enough having tits in front of fashion people let alone ones covered in carbohydrates.

'Shall we start?' Mel asked with a briskness that took everyone else by surprise.

'Yes, let's,' the uni friend said, smoothing it over by perching lightly on the sofa. Her little pet businessman sat down beside her.

'It appears that I don't need to introduce Calliope to you, Venetia,' Mel said.

'Oh no, we go way back,' Venetia said, winking at Calliope. 'But to make things clear, I'm in charge of brand and my colleague Adam is from business planning.'

'Wonderful,' Callie said, relieved she hadn't called her Florence.

'Shall we get on with it then?' Mel asked, plonking herself down in an armchair with a determined thud. Eulalia hovered by the window. She stared out of it. Venetia and Adam picked up the brocade-bound booklets, unfazed by Eulalia's nonchalance.

Callie stood in front of the boards, explaining the concept. The typography. The textures. The feelings. The glamour. Sword-wielding viragos. Joan of Arc. Armour. Pearls. Anne Boleyn's 'B' necklace. Appalling luxury. Oyster shells and pearls. Lancelot. Guinevere. Gawain. Tristan. Isolde. Marie de France. Heraldry. Chaucer. Heath Ledger. Courtly love. Burning. Yearning. Botticelli and Michelangelo and Leonardo da Vinci. Venus. A Renaissance woman. Rubies. Velvet. Doll heads. English gardens. Mazes. Saints. Finger bones in reliquaries. Pagans and their trees. The plague. Woodsmoke. Death is everywhere. The Nazis falling down into gaping pits after trying to leave with the Holy Grail in *Indiana Jones*. Julian of Norwich: 'All shall be well, and all shall be well, and all manner of thing shall be well.'

★   ★   ★

Mel saw Callie, who was relieved that the whole ordeal was over, Venetia and Adam out. Callie didn't mind that Mel was keeping hold of the boards. She'd paid her handsomely for them, after all. Callie's phone had vibrated in her pocket as soon as she stopped giving her presentation. Mel had made the payment as she was winding up. Adam was hailing a taxi as Venetia stood with Callie on the square.

'I've got to say, that was bloody fascinating. I love the booklet you made. So much more original than the usual shit I see. I'm going to take this one back with me to pass around the office,' Venetia said, staring at the magnolias overtaking the square. 'I wasn't sure how that was going to go. Well, those two. One is too present and the other not enough.'

'I know what you mean,' Callie said.

'Good business is still good business.' Venetia gave Callie a knowing smile. 'Are you doing much creative consultancy these days?'

'Yes,' Callie lied. 'I'm moving away from design to consultancy.'

'Darling, let's go for lunch soon. I have other projects that you might be able to help with.' Venetia gave her a business card.

'I'd love to.' Callie placed the card in her bag. She'd email her on Monday and invite her out the following week.

'Love the dress, by the way. Who's it by?'

'Me, of course.'

'It's darling. You're darling.'

Venetia and Adam's cab pulled up. The two women air kissed and then Venetia was gone. Callie was about to start off when she heard someone call her name. She turned.

'Hey, Eulalia,' Callie said, smiling at the girl. She looked heartbroken. 'Are you OK? You look, well, devastated.'

'Yeah.' Eulalia looked at her. Looked at her a little too hard. 'No.'

'Did Mel say something?' Callie had come to the conclusion that their relationship was not just a little strained.

Eulalia didn't say anything. She watched a bird land on the iron railing around the square with suspicion.

'Did you like the presentation?'

'I loved it.' Eulalia let out a sigh.

'Is something wrong?'

'No, umm. Did you want to go and get lunch?'

'Sorry, I've got a meeting with a stylist in half an hour.' Callie chose to say stylist rather than friend. She somehow thought it would make it easier for Eulalia to deal with.

'Oh. I see.' Eulalia teetered on the edge of the kerb. 'What are you doing this weekend?'

'I'm away this weekend.'

'With your boyfriend.'

'Yes.'

'At his parents' house? I'd love to see it.'

'One day . . . perhaps.' Callie performatively checked the time on her phone.

'They burnt her there,' Eulalia said, pointing at the garden in the middle of the square.

'Right.' Callie remembered her saying something about a mystic nun. She didn't want to get sucked into whatever implosion this swirling vortex of loneliness and disassociation was heading towards. She was going to be someone's mum. She needed to take care of herself. 'Got to dash, Eulalia, it's been an utter pleasure. Have a lovely weekend. Take care.' She sped off before Eulalia could invite herself along.

37

The Police Station

The Chief Superintendent stood in front of Matt and Amy with DI Robbie Eastley.

'Robbie here will be taking over as the active lead on this case as Caius has flagged with me that these crimes happened on property that his father owns the leasehold on. I'm sure Caius has told you that he will now take a period of annual leave and will resume desk duty next week until the case is closed.'

'Great to be working with you, Robbie,' Matt said, sticking out his hand. Robbie shook it but the gesture took him by surprise.

'Likewise,' Robbie said, releasing Matt's hand. He wasn't looking forward to the next few weeks with these two. At least Caius wasn't there. He found him intimidating at the best of times. 'Amy.'

'Please get Robbie up to speed as quickly as possible,' the Chief Superintendent said. He left the incident room to deal with the paperwork that he now had to fill in, all the while wondering how much the ownership of the leasehold of a whole postcode in NW1 was worth.

'Right,' Robbie said, sitting down on Caius's desk. 'Where had little DI Fauntleroy gotten to then?'

Matt stopped himself from rolling his eyes. He hated it when people called Caius 'DI Fauntleroy'.

Amy, who had briefly worked with Robbie on a case before, pointed to the whiteboards behind him. She gave him the broad gist of it all, making it very clear that they already knew what they were doing.

'Right, so let me get this straight: Digby Combe-Watson is killed by a poisoned salad by a woman supposedly called "Isolde" who was dressed as his intern. He met her through a lonely-hearts ad that she responded to. Those responses were delivered to a PO Box, which was paid for with stolen credit card details of a Yorkshire woman, and collected by an incel called Scott that this "fake Isolde", as you call her, had seduced in the nearby bakery that he worked in, where he hit on every other female customer who came in. There have also been two break-ins on the same square, one of which has resulted in the accidental death of former comedy enfant terrible Jimmy Jones.'

'You've pretty much got it,' Matt said. He'd been at his desk checking his emails. They'd received permission from Fenella to access the blocked basement of the Institute. 'If you look at the map there, with the highlighting—'

'What are the colours?' Robbie cut in.

Amy began. 'Red means a death, orange means a break-in, the yellow one—'

'They're evenly spaced,' Robbie said.

'Yes, so Caius thought—' Amy tried again.

'Is there any significance to that?' Robbie asked.

'I'm . . .' Amy let out an exasperated, guttural groan.

'What's wrong, Amy?' Robbie said.

'Amy's trying to tell you the answers to your questions because we've already asked them ourselves, but you keep cutting her off and she is now feeling frustrated,' Matt said. He thought Robbie might hear it if he said it.

'Ah. Well, talk louder then.' Robbie stared at Amy. She stared back. They reached a stalemate. Robbie broke the silence. 'Sorry, Amy. Do continue.'

'Caius interviewed Benedict Carr-Ridge, the novelist. He lives at number 7. It was a break-in, although—'

'Was anything taken?'

'—no,' Amy said, speaking loudly as he'd just instructed her to. 'I was about to tell you that, and that Benedict was drunk at the time.'

'Sorry, um.' He was more nervous than he'd realised.

Amy began again at a normal volume. 'Benedict told Caius that the house had been the site of seances in the Victorian era.' She saw Robbie have the impulse to stop her so she just started talking louder again and he stopped instantly. 'I began going through a transcript of Horatio Combe's diary yesterday. He's the guy the museum is about. He led a group of occultists that lived in these same four houses in the square. The square is built on top of the ruins of a medieval priory which in turn was sup-posedly built on top of a pagan temple. His diary said that these houses were rented, or purchased in Horatio's case, specifically because they are the cardinal points of a compass and form a nexus over the site. There were rumours when the modern square was built one hundred and sixty years ago that medieval ruins were discovered.' Amy stopped to check that Robbie was keeping up.

Robbie didn't know what she expected of him so he just slowly nodded.

Satisfied, Amy continued. 'Having considered motives revolv-ing around Digby's personal life, we are now considering the idea that whoever killed Digby did it so they could gain access to the journal documenting the occult stuff. The original, hand-written twenty-second journal is the only missing thing from the Institute. We've only got the transcript Digby's intern typed up.' Amy knew she had gone through every drawer in that building. 'According to Willow, the student intern, it was kept locked away because there's a lot of weird sex stuff in there. There was a partial print on the door to the basement which has been sealed up for decades that we've been unable to identify. Benedict Carr-Ridge thought the burglar had been in his basement but he's unreliable. The footage from Jimmy Jones's interrupted livestream shows a burglar, probably the same one, coming out of the area where the basement stairs are. Caius thought that wasn't a coincidence. Someone is searching the basements.'

'OK. Now we're getting somewhere. What was little DI Fauntleroy going to do next?'

'I went round to number 35, the yellow house on the map, last night. They've got really good security. State of the art. They've not been broken into but we could always ask to access it just in case anyone attempted to and aborted when they realised they'd be visible. It seems highly likely that they would try to get access to their basement too,' Matt said, wrinkling his nose. 'Caius requested permission for us to take the door down to the basement off in the Horatio Combe Institute. Digby's mother Fenella is the only other surviving trustee and she agreed this morning. I'm going to go over there now and will liaise with forensics.'

'Sure,' Robbie said, sitting down at Caius's desk. He'd been told. Amy scowled at him from across the desk. 'I tell you what, Matt, I'll come with you. Get a feel for the crime scene.'

'That's not a bad idea,' Amy said, failing to hide her relief.

★ ★ ★

Before they got in the car, Matt turned to Robbie. 'Don't call him that.'

'What, little DI Fauntleroy? It's funny.'

'It's only funny if the other person thinks it is. If not it becomes bullying. I wouldn't like to think you were as bad as Billy Fairweather.'

'Billy was a good lad. Not his fault little DI Fauntleroy socked him one and had the nerve to kick up a fuss about it.'

'Three things. Two of them are easily verifiable and the third you'll just have to take my word for. Firstly, Caius snapped and hit Billy because he used a slur to describe his grandfather because Billy didn't realise what Caius's background was. Secondly, he did get suspended for hitting him, but the thing about Caius is that he takes notes and he had a whole dossier on shit Billy had said and done. He'd already reported him twice and nothing had happened. Thirdly, on my first week working here I saw Billy doing a line of coke off his keys in his police car in the car park. He called me a "chink" when he realised I saw and said he'd ruin me if I told. So, yeah, no more of that DI Fauntleroy shit, and treat Amy with respect. Not because she's good at her job, but because she's a person.' Matt got in the car.

★　★　★

Matt called in on Mel at number 35, he needed a moment away from Robbie to collect himself, but she didn't answer the door. He put his card through again with a note on the back asking her to call. He thought there was an off-chance that their security cameras may have caught the burglar. He rejoined Robbie. The forensics team who met them at the Horatio Combe Institute were busy chipping away at the century's thick layer of paint over the door. Finally they managed to take it off its hinges. They took the door back with them as evidence. It had a partial print on it, after all. A member of forensics went down first. They had a hazmat suit on. The basement hadn't had fresh air since Lord knows when. Matt put his sleeve over his mouth and nose in a futile effort not to smell the staleness that had begun to waft up the staircase.

'There's a crystal ball,' their voice carried back up from the depths. 'And tarot cards on the table too. And – is that a hand?'

38

The Purple Toad Bakery

Callie was delighted to find that the pistachio croissants, which she had forsaken earlier, were from the bakery Tabs had picked. She ordered one and a cup of peppermint tea and settled down into a comfy armchair in the corner while she waited for Tabs to arrive. People entering the bakery kept eyeing up the empty seat. Callie took out her phone and texted Caius a quick summary of her triumph. He responded within five minutes. Such a novelty.

'Hullo, you,' Tabs said, dumping her bag on the spare chair opposite Callie. She gave her a quick one-armed hug and scampered off to order a flat white.

'How are you?' Callie asked as Tabs sat down with her coffee, slumping into the free chair like she owned it.

'I'm pretty good. Went on a date last night with a girl. She was cute and I think we really clicked. We'll see.'

'Cool.'

'I hear you've been working on a certain pop girlie's rebrand.'

'How did you hear that?'

'DJ Sonikk, also known as Cecil, is dating a girl who I went to school with. He's not very discreet.' Tabs theatrically sniffed.

'Oh dear. I'm sure he signed an NDA. He needs to be careful there.' Callie thought Mel would happily commit a war crime if she found out he'd been talking about them to anyone.

'He said it's really weird. Didn't go into too much detail but that there's something worrying going on with the sister.'

'Worrying? They're an odd pair.' Callie picked up her tea and took a sip, ending Tabs's line of questioning. She felt like she had

243

a duty somewhere but she wasn't sure what it was. She changed the subject. 'How's Arthur Hampton doing?'

'Surprisingly well, Mummy says. Throwing himself into his work.'

'I can't imagine losing your son, your brother and well, your husband all in a week.'

'Have you heard from him?' Tabs was really asking whether Caius had.

'No, I haven't.' Callie wondered whether she'd been sent as a scout. Either way she already knew this chat was somewhere between personal and professional.

They chatted for an hour. Tabs relayed her ex Joly's drama (moving to Dubai after getting a hair transplant in Turkey), her stylist business picking up after she signed two pseudo-posh reality stars that are scared of her and her brother's looming wedding.

'How do you like Frithsden?' Tabs asked.

'It's lovely.'

'Isn't it. I don't think Rupert ever really appreciated the place. The new Beauchamps? Do they appreciate it?'

'Yes, I should say so. Marcus is working very hard to get it into working order again.' Callie wasn't exactly sure what Tabs was getting at. She decided to be blunt about it, although with a knowing look in her eye and a quick and gentle tap of her hand on Tabs's. 'What do you want to ask me?'

Tabs looked a little flushed. 'What's he like? Caius? Rupert despised him, but that was because he thought he'd turned Nell against him, whereas Nell – who is rather aloof at the best of times – has never mentioned him, apart from once when she was incredibly drunk and she cried, saying he saved her life.'

'He was just doing his job.' Callie had almost forgotten about seeing Nell last weekend. 'Is she all right? I have friends in common. She looked a little . . . when I saw her at a distance on the weekend.'

'Yes. She's all right. I suppose. The wedding's next month. Weddings are so stressful, aren't they?'

'I do love a June wedding. I hope your mother is wearing my hat.'

'Of course she is. She told me to tell you that she needs a wide-brimmed something or other, if you're still making them, that is. She said she'd pay you double and you can have our box at the Albert Hall for a night during the Proms.'

'I don't know right now.' Callie was vaguely tempted by the Proms. 'Things are rather in a state of flux. She will of course be the first person I tell if I get back to making.'

★ ★ ★

'I brought some bread back with me from the bakery,' Callie called out as she walked into the flat. She picked up a package from the hallway floor that Caius had ordered. 'I grabbed a baguette for lunch and a couple of sourdough loaves for the weekend.'

'That's my girl,' Caius called from the garden. He'd been doing a strength workout. He was carrying the judgy garden gnome. It was time for it to go. He shoved it into a black bin bag of clothes that he was going to drop off at the charity shop on their way to his parents'. 'I bought some steaks. How about that with a little salad and a little bread.'

Callie gave him the package and he kissed her on the cheek.

'Steak for lunch?' Callie was, she hated to admit, a little more affected by diet culture than she liked to admit and she tried to keep her lunches small. It was something she'd started doing as a teenager. That and eating pudding with a teaspoon. Now though, she felt she had a duty to fill up.

'You need the iron and the protein.' Caius took the steaks out of the fridge. 'I want a full blow by blow.'

'Really? A full blow by blow? Before lunch.'

'Of the presentation,' he said, putting the steaks down. 'But if you're offering?'

'That's the only meat I want right now,' Callie said, picking up the packet of steaks and giving it back to him.

'Fair enough,' Caius said, opening the packet. His hamstrings felt tight after last night's Victorian chair escapade.

Callie told Caius about how Venetia from Ceramics 101 was working for PCQV now and how well the handmade brocade-backed booklets had gone down. 'You know, for such an amazing opportunity, I'm relieved my work for Eulalia is over.'

'It was a quick turnaround. You've pulled a lot of late nights.'

'That's not it. I like having a time pressure. It makes me work smarter.' Callie caught her reflection in the kitchen window and remembered Mel being weird about her eyeshadow. 'Her sister, Mel the manager, was being a bitch to me. She was never friendly but this was overt, and then Eulalia followed me outside and did this whole sad puppy dog act and tried to invite herself along this weekend.'

'Yikes.' Caius's phone rang. He took the call, wandering into the garden and leaving Callie to start making the salad.

'Caius, it's Amy.'

'How's it going?'

'It's got weirder. There's a skeletal hand in the basement of the Horatio Combe Institute. It was on a table set up for a seance.'

'A hand? I don't know what I was expecting but not that.'

'Yeah, Robbie has got Matt down there now. Forensics are having a field day.'

'Robbie Eastley?'

'Yeah, could be worse.'

'He's a dick, but he's good at his job. Human remains will keep him up to his eyeballs in paperwork. He'll have to leave you alone to get on with it.' Caius stared at the grass. 'Keep going through the malaria-year diary. I know it's tempting to try to work out who the hand could be but that killer is probably long gone, whereas whoever killed Digby and Scott, possibly Jimmy too, is walking around out there.'

'Sure.'

'There's something that just doesn't add up, Amy.' He looked into the flat. Callie was pretending not to be paying attention to him. 'It's Isolde. The real Isolde. Why did they copy her life story and not just make something up? It feels really personal. That has been the hole in the middle of this case all along. Isolde will be the key to this.'

'I'll have another look at Isolde Burrell then. Maybe we've missed something.'

'Call me again if you need me.' Caius hung up.

'Everything all right?' Callie asked. She was slicing tomatoes, juice squirting everywhere.

'Yeah,' Caius said, staring at her. The light through the kitchen window hit her as if she were in a Vermeer. 'I have never seen any woman look as beautiful as you do right now.'

'Shut up, you,' she said, putting the knife down. 'I love you.'

Caius picked up the baguette she'd bought. 'The Purple Toad.'

'Yeah, I went there with Tabs. It keeps going viral online. The croissant I had was stunning.'

Caius resisted the urge to tell her that one of the victims in his case had worked there. They'd agreed that he wasn't going to talk about details like that. 'Not as stunning as you.'

He kissed her.

Callie returned to the tomatoes.

Caius sat down on the sofa, watching how utterly perfect she was. He looked down at the rug, imaging a toddler crawling across it and then at the bright red hat of the judgy gnome sticking out of the bin bag. All of a sudden the flat felt too small. Like it was cramped with the memories of his previous lives, and loves. He didn't want to move to the arse-end of Walthamstow. Perhaps being near his parents wasn't a bad thing. The air was cleaner. His mum loved children. Callie wouldn't be stuck in the flat on her own with a newborn while he chased down drug dealers.

'We need to move, don't we?' Caius broke the end of the baguette off and ate it. It wasn't bad considering it had been baked in England.

'Yes, my love. I think you're right.'

★ ★ ★

'This isn't the route we normally take,' Callie said, peering out at the fields from the passenger seat.

'We're taking a quick detour,' Caius said.

The satnav told him to take the next left. He waited at the crossroads while a tractor pulled out in front of him and they crawled behind it for half a mile before turning off again along the side of an ancient woodland. Caius pulled down the drive of a farmhouse. His father was already waiting outside for them in a battered Land Rover that had come with the estate.

'Afternoon,' Marcus said as they both got out of the car. It annoyed Caius that he was so bloody jolly, but then he was getting exactly what he wanted. 'Welcome to Meadowview. As you can see, it's a Georgian farmhouse. Let's take a look, shall we.'

'Why are you talking like an estate agent?' Caius asked. He wasn't sure why he was being so surly. Callie took his hand and squeezed it.

'Because it's my estate. Honestly, Caius.' Marcus shook his head. 'Callie, love, ignore him. It's a beautiful house. The plumbing and electrics have just been done. The plasterers are coming in a week or two. The kitchen will be sorted soon. You just need to pick out the cabinets.'

Marcus took the keys out of his pocket and opened the front door. He held it open for Callie who walked into the entrance hall while Marcus and Caius lingered outside. Marcus turned and gave Caius that look that fathers have when they suspect you've disappointed them.

'What?' Caius asked, returning his father's gaze.

'What have you done?' Marcus asked quietly. 'You're acting like a moody fifteen-year-old, which means you've fucked up. You were adamant you weren't going to move up here and now here we are, surprising Callie with a charming little country bolthole. Did you cheat on her? Moving out of London to get away from some side piece? Is that it? A fresh start away from temptation?'

'No!' Caius was genuinely upset that his father's mind had wandered to infidelity first. You cheat on one girlfriend when you were nineteen and it tars you for the rest of your life.

'Good, because you won't do better.'

'Jesus, Dad.'

'What is it?' Marcus opened the front door. 'Your mother will get it out of you.'

Callie, who had wandered into the living room, came back out. 'Marcus, this is such a sympathetic renovation.'

'Thank you,' he said, smiling at her and following her off into the kitchen. 'We could put an island in if you want one. There's plenty of room.'

'If you don't mind me asking, how many bedrooms does it have?'

'Of course I don't mind. It's got four and a delightful, flat garden out back. There's even an orchard.' He opened the back door and Callie wandered out onto the patio.

Caius had followed them both into the kitchen. His father, having made sure that Callie was out of earshot, turned around to him and said, 'Bedrooms, hmm?'

Caius knew he knew.

'I won't tell your mother.'

'Of course you will.'

Callie came in from the garden. She seemed happy. They toured the upstairs bedrooms, marvelling at the light coming in through the bay windows. Even Caius had to admit the light was different than at home in London. Sharper almost – there was less haze from pollution. Tiny lungs. Caius stared out over the fields from the master bedroom and then walked into the room opposite. He supposed that this would be the nursery. It overlooked the woodland that ran around the back of Frithsden's parkland. Callie flitted between rooms, approving of how Marcus had managed to save the original floorboards. Marcus showed off the bath with clawed feet. Caius could see that Callie was decorating the house in her head and Marcus was lining up administrative tasks that he could push onto him. Velvet cushions and emails. Wallpaper and sheep farming. Paint swatches and agronomics.

They finished and went out front.

'Well, let me know.' Marcus stood in front of them both. 'Like I said, once the kitchen is fitted it'll be all yours. If you want it.'

'I'm going to swing by and speak to Paul about the almshouses.' Callie squeezed Caius's hand. 'Dad, would you mind taking Callie to that farm shop nearby. We need supplies for the weekend.'

'Let's go scout out the competition. I'm thinking of opening a farm shop myself in the village. I'll cut out the middleman,' Marcus said, unlocking the Land Rover and holding the door open for Callie. He shut the door on her, took out a second set of keys for the house and chucked them at Caius. It was a done deal. 'You won't miss London when you leave. There comes a point where it just becomes too much, you know?'

'I do.'

39

The Police Station

'I left Robbie to deal with forensics at the scene,' Matt said, opening his drawer and taking out a packet of digestive biscuits. He offered Amy one.

'Good idea,' Amy said, taking a bite. She was printing off the notes she'd made of Horatio's malaria-year journal.

'I saw the hand.' Matt checked to see if he had a message from Mel from number 35. 'There were candlesticks on a big round table and all sorts of weird markings everywhere. It was eerie. It was sealed like a creepy time capsule.' He took a second biscuit. 'Fascinating stuff. Communing with the dead. It's a universal human drive. Being Chinese, I bloody love a good ghost. We do ancestor worship, you know. I wonder where the hand came from? Grave robbing? Highgate Cemetery isn't too far from there.'

'Caius said to focus on the twenty-first-century crime.' Amy collected the last page and stapled them together, then put them on Caius's/Robbie's desk.

'Absolutely. Robbie can get bogged down in the Victorian shit.' Matt looked at the strategy that Caius had given Amy yesterday evening. 'You said you'd look into real Isolde again, right? Try and find as much as you can about her as if you were Joe Public. We need to work out how "fake Isolde" knew that much about her. I'm going to call Fenella and let her know that human remains have been found on the property.'

She handed a copy of her notes over to Matt. 'Have a read of this after.'

'OK.'

'The missing journal is really bugging me. I'm going to go back to the Institute and see if I can find it first. It doesn't seem like stealing it is a good enough motive for killing Digby but I think it's important that it's missing. Is that OK? I'll do some more digging on Isolde when I get back.'

'Try Digby's house too.' Matt knew well enough to go with Amy's instincts.

★ ★ ★

'Hi there, Ms Combe-Watson, it's DS Matthew Cheung,' Matt said, sitting down opposite her in the interview room. 'You were dealing with my colleague DI Caius Beauchamp previously.'

'Has there been progress made?' Fenella Combe-Watson asked. She gripped the table.

'Yes, of a sort,' Matt said, furrowing his brow. 'Thank you for granting us permission to enter the basement of the Horatio Combe Institute. Have you ever been down there yourself?'

'No, it's always been sealed off.'

'Do you know when that happened?'

'No. As I understand it the conditions of my great-great-grandfather's will clearly state that the house is not to be altered in any way.'

'Right, Horatio's will.'

'That was what was holding Digby back from returning the mokomokai. He was going to seek legal advice to see if he could send them back to New Zealand.'

'Do you think that the basement was sealed up by Horatio himself?'

'Yes.' She gave the question a little more thought. 'One has to assume that he left it that way. I suppose my great-grandfather or any of my ancestors may well have altered the house without anyone knowing. We've never had any outsiders involved with the trust, you see.'

'And just to be clear, you are a direct descendant of Horatio's.'

'Yes, my father was his great-grandson. My great-great grandmother died when my great-grandfather was nine. Tuberculosis, I think.'

'Do you know where she's buried?' Matt wondered if the hand could be hers. Perhaps Horatio was perversely romantic and his seances were an attempt to contact his late, much-loved wife. Although the sheer number of orgies seemed to point in the opposite direction.

'Highgate Cemetery. We have a family crypt there.' Fenella fell silent. She was awaiting the imminent release of Digby's body. She had begun trying to organise his funeral.

Matt gave her a moment. 'Is there any family lore that never made it into the guidebook?'

'No, not that I know of. I don't think Horatio was a great man, despite how he insisted we portray him, merely a well-travelled egotist with a grim collection. My great-grandfather was either away at school or staying with his mother's relatives while Horatio was off galivanting across the globe. My father said they didn't have much of a relationship. Horatio died while Aloysius, my great-grandfather, was in his last year at school, I think.'

'Thanks, Fenella, that's really helpful.' Matt stopped as he tried to find the most appropriate phrase. 'Fenella, human remains have been found in the Institute's basement. There's a hand laid out in the middle of a table set up for what appears to have been a seance. We're not sure how old the remains are or where they're from. We've enlisted the help of a team of specialists.'

'Oh my God.'

Matt thought she looked genuinely shocked. 'We will be running quite a few tests. It's not likely to be resolved quickly.'

'What?' Fenella looked utterly bewildered as she looked down at her hands. Matt was surprised that she was so composed, but then what else was the poor woman supposed to do. Her only child was already dead.

'This must be awful for you.'

'What has this got to do with Digby?' Fenella's hands shook. She clasped them together to steady herself.

'We're not entirely sure yet.'

'I opened this yesterday. He sent it while I was away. I've been in such a state that I hadn't opened any post until this morning.' She took an envelope out of her bag and pushed it across the table to Matt. 'I almost didn't give it to you. It was the last thing he wrote to me, you see. I'd put so many of his letters in the recycling already. But then that feels rather karmic, doesn't it?'

'What does it say?' Matt didn't have any gloves on him.

'He wanted to arrange to go for lunch to discuss an offer for the Institute he'd received, which he also enclosed. He thought they were lowballing him and he'd wanted to tell them in no uncertain terms to piss off. He talks about returning the shrunken heads here too. He wrote about all the things we could do with our lives with the money once the millstone of the Institute was gone. It was glorious. He was going to really live.'

40

Frithsden Old Hall

Caius and Callie were sitting on the terrace overlooking the rose garden. Caius was reading his book and Callie was content with viewing the parkland, taking pleasure in the gentle breeze brushing over her. It was cooler here than in London. She wished she'd brought a sketchbook with her. A butterfly landed in front of her on the stone balustrade. Callie wished that she had a gentle enough touch to pick up the creature and inspect its orange and black wings – nearly the same shades as the fabric she'd used for Eulalia's presentation booklets. She shook thoughts of Eulalia off as she watched the butterfly go.

Bridget brought out a Victoria sponge that their freelance cook had made the day before. She cut a generous slice and placed it on a plate. 'Callie, love, would you like a cup of tea? I'll put a pot on.'

'Have you got anything herbal?' Callie asked, taking the cake from Bridget. 'Thank you, this smells delicious.'

'Would you like peppermint, camomile or lemon and ginger?'

'Lemon and ginger would be lovely, thank you so much, Bridget.'

Bridget looked at her watch. 'It's four in the afternoon on a Friday. Something stronger perhaps?'

'No, thank you.' Callie tried to be as blasé as possible.

'I'll have a beer, Mum, please.' Caius put down the history book that had arrived that morning. He thought non-fiction would help get him out of a reading slump. He was still working through the Digby Combe-Watson case at the back of his head even though he wasn't allowed in the incident room and was finding it hard to concentrate on the book. The fault might lie with the author's dry prose rather than Caius's agitated mind.

'Get it yourself,' Bridget said, giving Caius a look that said come with me. He got up and followed her back into the house while Callie sunned herself on the terrace. She picked up a delicious morsel of cake, before flicking through a copy of *Vogue*.

Marcus was waiting for them both in the kitchen.

'More bedrooms, Bridge,' Marcus said.

'More bedrooms, Marcus?' Bridget peered down her nose at Caius. 'Callie loves a strong cup of tea. She quite likes a gin in the afternoon too. Ginger?'

'I'm not saying anything,' Caius said staunchly, but then relented easily at his parents' united, imperious gaze. 'Well, not for another six weeks anyway.'

'You can have the wedding here,' Marcus said.

'If we pull our finger out you could have it in August. Caterer. Marquee. Someone to do the flowers. Callie knows people who could do her dress on a short turnaround,' Bridget said.

'Whoa.'

'What?' Bridget said, giving him a look. 'Out of wedlock?'

'Calm down, it's the twenty-first century and the law's been changed.'

'Have you got a ring yet? We've got family ones. No point in buying something new,' Marcus said, hoping to defuse the situation. 'Callie likes old stuff anyway.'

'Calm down,' Caius said again, but then he smiled. 'But good to know. Where's the beer, Mum?'

'Where do you think it is?' Bridget asked.

'In the fridge?' Caius answered.

'Well done. You're almost sensible enough to be a father,' Bridget said.

'You two are going off tonight, aren't you?' Caius took a beer from the fridge. He didn't feel like being treated like a fifteen-year-old in front of Georgie.

'Oh yes, we're off to Margate for the weekend, aren't we, Bridge?' Marcus said, before humming 'Oh I Do Like to Be Beside the Seaside' to himself.

'We're taking the sea air,' Bridget said, removing a teacup from the cupboard. 'It's much fancier now than when I was a girl. There's not a donkey in sight.'

'They're going to do an exhibit based on the Turner we donated to the nation at the Tate there next year. They're commissioning a group of artists to riff off it. They've invited us down for some sort of donor dinner thing.'

'I've bought a lovely new dress,' Bridget said, putting the kettle on. She couldn't pretend everything came out of the back of the wardrobe. 'Callie told me about this place that does second-hand designer stuff off the King's Road. It's very chic. It's that Japanese designer who does pleats. I look arty.'

'Georgie, the guy coming tonight. He's a painter and sculptor. He's phenomenally talented,' Caius said, but his parents weren't really listening. Bridget left the kitchen in search of her phone. She'd put it down somewhere and it would take an age to find it again but she was desperate to have a look at baby clothes online.

'I'm going to be a fun granddad. I'm going to crawl through every ball pit in every soft play,' Marcus said, patting Caius on the back. 'Mum's the word.'

Caius looked around the kitchen. 'Dad, do we have anything creepy in the house?'

'What do you mean?'

'Shrunken heads? Anything like that?'

'No, nothing that morbid. Although with this family you have to wonder how some of the antiques were acquired. Never mind the antiques, actually. I'm pretty sure someone enclosed the common. I wouldn't mention it in the village. I don't know whether they're still angry about it. I've joined the cricket team, and written them a nice cheque to renovate the pavilion so I'm popular right now. Well, until they see me play.'

'Tax break?' Caius asked.

Marcus gave him a look. 'It doesn't hurt to be in favour with the yokels. Or HMRC.'

'All right.'

'Funny you should ask actually about the art and things. I had a historian email the family office asking questions the other day.'

'Oh yeah?'

'About the priest holes. I don't think we've found them all, you know. My builder's brain thinks there's some negative space that's not accounted for.'

'That makes me uncomfortable.'

'I'll forward you the email. You can liaise with him. I'm not averse to some swot poking around and writing about the place.'

'And so it begins.'

'What does?'

'Nothing. What if we've got sculptures from Benin, or a bit of Greek temple? Something from the Forbidden City that we shouldn't have? You know? I have no idea what's in this building.'

'We don't need the bad vibes.' Marcus nodded along. He wasn't emotionally attached to any of that stuff. 'You find someone who knows about old stuff and see how much they'll cost. See if you can get them to write a leaflet about the house while you're at it, and you can give tours on Saturdays. Charge people £10 a pop.'

'I'm not doing tours.' Caius shook his head, and went back out to the terrace, cracking open the can as he went.

Callie looked up from her magazine.

'Did you like the farmhouse?' Caius asked, sitting beside her and taking her hand. He liked the house. More than he was willing to admit. He'd never imagined himself having that much space.

'Loved it.'

'We need to pick a kitchen first.'

'They know, don't they?'

'There was absolutely no chance we were going to keep the baby a secret. The crime rate would plummet if the Met would only hire those two.' Caius stroked her on the arm and took his book up again. He looked at the cover covered in cartoon portraits of Elizabeth I, Winston Churchill and all the other usual offenders of England's past glories. He didn't read much history. He preferred fiction. It was less upsetting.

Bridget appeared a minute or two later with a tray carrying a pot of lemon and ginger tea and two teacups. 'Your little friends have just arrived, Caius.'

'I'm not six, Mum,' Caius said, getting up from his seat. 'It's not a playdate.'

'Sure, you're not. Imagine a six-year-old as tall as you.' Bridget turned to Callie. 'Your friend, she's pregnant, isn't she? I thought she might like a cup of ginger tea too. So good for morning sickness.'

'Thanks, Bridget,' Callie said, getting out of the chair. 'That's very kind of you.' It was odd to watch someone else turn into a teenager around their parents. She had thought that was just her, but perhaps it was a universal phenomenon.

'Has your ex gone away?' Bridget asked Callie as they all walked back towards the house together.

'Oh yes, my father's solicitor sent a very strongly worded letter.'

'Glad it's done the trick,' Bridget said as they entered the house, traversing the worn black and white tiles. 'I've got to say, Caius, all of my friends have been sending me these little funny pictures with your face on.'

'Memes, Mum. I've become a meme.'

'Whatever they're called, they all agreed how handsome you looked.'

'Well, that's nice, isn't it?' Callie said, pinching Caius's cheek.

Dotty and Georgie were waiting in the hall. It was an old house so it was more of a great hall than a thoroughfare. Dotty had perched herself on a wooden bench and was holding her side. People were introduced. Callie showed Georgie and Dotty back through to the terrace, grabbing Georgie a beer from the fridge as they went, while Caius gladly drove his parents to the station.

SATURDAY

41

The Police Station

'I've found the company that made the offer to Digby for the house,' Matt said.

'What's that?' Robbie asked, looking up from the mountain of paperwork that he needed to complete for the skeletal hand.

'Fenella Combe-Watson, Digby's mother, brought in a letter yesterday that Digby sent to her while she was away.'

'He sent letters to his mum? Where does she live?'

'Out Oxford way. He was a character. He was purposefully anachronistic.' Matt took a deep breath. Robbie's questioning was reasonable. 'He sent her a copy of the deal he'd been offered.'

'Right. And you've found the company that made the offer?'

'Yes, on Companies House. Interestingly, the contact address is a PO Box.' He gave Robbie the context before he could ask. 'Digby sent letters to "fake Isolde", the killer, via a PO Box. The two registered directors are a Mr Gerard Bourne and a Mrs Margot Bourne. They live next door.'

'Has—' Robbie began.

'Amy spoke to Mrs Bourne already,' Matt said, picturing the woman in the matchy-matchy workout gear with a little dog who was fawning over Caius. 'I'm guessing she didn't tell Amy that she'd offered Digby less than a third of what the estate agent had advised.' Matt remembered the estimate they had found early amongst Digby's papers from his office.

'Great work, Matt,' Robbie said, standing up from his desk. 'Let's get this Margot Bourne in for questioning. Property is a fantastic motive for murder.'

★　★　★

'Miss Bourne,' Matt began. He remembered that it had worked for Caius last time.

'Margot, please,' she interrupted. She liked this policeman too. Less than the other one, he was a dish, but still.

'Margot, did you make an offer to Digby Combe-Watson for the Institute?'

'Yes, why?'

'We're asking the questions here, Margot,' Robbie said. He stared her dead in the eye before picking up Amy's notes of her interaction with her and silently reading them, leaving Margot to wonder what the hell was going on.

'Where's the other detective?' She stroked her dog. She had claimed it was an emotional support animal and neither Matt nor Robbie wanted to argue with her. It was the size of a shoe and barely moved in her arms anyway.

'He's not here,' Robbie said.

'Margot, we've got a copy of the proposition that your and your husband's company proposed to Digby.' Matt placed the offer that Digby had sent to his mother on the table in its plastic evidence bag. 'It was well under the market value.'

'And? There's nothing wrong with going in low on an opening gambit.'

'The thing is, Margot,' Robbie began.

'Mrs Bourne.'

'Mrs Bourne,' Robbie tried again. 'We have to wonder whether you forgot or if you hid the fact from DC Noakes that you'd offered the deceased a really low amount for his property shortly before he died. It looks like the beginning of a motive, doesn't it?'

'Does it?' She stroked the dog. It sprung to life, bearing its little teeth. 'No, Halloumi. The nasty men aren't attacking Mummy. I want a solicitor.'

'Of course,' Robbie said, getting up from the table. Matt followed.

Amy was waiting outside the room.

'I'll speak to her again once the lawyer is present,' Robbie said, holding his hand out for the folder Matt had picked up from the table. Matt gave it to him while hiding his annoyance with how poorly Robbie had handled the interview. 'Are you all right, Amy?'

'I just wanted to grab Matt for a second. I can see you're really busy, Robbie.'

'Sure,' Robbie said. He already started going through the folder while Matt returned with Amy to her desk in the incident room.

★　★　★

'Is this about the missing volume of Horatio's journal?'

'No, but there's no trace of it and I still think it's odd,' Amy said, looking up at Matt. 'I sent Tiny Simm over to Dollis Hill and he didn't find anything either.'

'Was there anything in Willow's transcript so far that might lend itself to murder?' Matt went over to the whiteboard and wrote '22nd volume' as a possible motive.

'It's mostly sex and occult stuff. Frequently they're the same thing,' Amy said. 'I think I might have found something else though. It's like Caius said, "fake Isolde" is the problem, so I started simple and searched for Isolde Burrell on Google. I found an article on her as a sixth-former winning a poetry contest in

Dorchester in 2011. I've read through her whole Twitter account which was so dull. She didn't post a single thing about her personal life. I went through every platform I could think of. I trawled her LinkedIn, nothing. She doesn't post on there. You can just see that she left her job at a primary school in East Ham a couple of months ago. Her Instagram is set to private. She has one of those usernames that's got numbers in and it's hard to identify as hers without prior knowledge. She told Caius what it was when he interviewed her.'

'OK, so those are all dead ends. What did you find then?'

'This time I searched the random number name she has on Instagram and it threw up an account on a fanfic site?'

'Fanfic?'

'It's an online community where people share stories they have made up about characters from other works. Dramione is popular. It's Draco and Hermione from Harry Potter. I understand from Fi some of them are spectacularly good and eventually get published properly. There are so many different fandoms. A lot of the stories people post are smutty. There's some weird shit on there. I found a whole series of kinky stories about Richard Nixon. Waterplaygate.'

'And Isolde is on there?'

'Yeah, and what's more, she wrote a little introduction post last month to one of the forums. She mentioned a couple of the things that "fake Isolde" told Digby in that post, but she has been writing stories where she's clearly using bits of info from her life. Including all of the remaining details that were told to Digby.'

'OK, so let me get this straight. Isolde is writing dirty stories, sharing them online and using her own biography as material.'

'Exactly. She has been really active in this one group. Isolde's got a thing, probably nominative determinism, about medieval knights and shit.'

'So the killer could be one of her readers.'

42

Frithsden Old Hall

Breakfast for once was in the breakfast room. Caius and his family were still not used to eating anywhere other than the kitchen. They had eaten in the dining room a few weeks ago, but they thought it was silly. Callie, however, had suggested that Caius try and use the house as intended that weekend. He'd made bacon and egg sandwiches with the provisions Callie had purchased from the farm shop. Dotty's veganism had faltered as soon as she started craving pork chops. Georgie had been delighted that he no longer had to secretly snaffle burgers when out of the house.

'Dotty, we'll let you set today's agenda,' Callie said.

'Hmm. We passed through the village on the way in,' Dotty said, putting her cup of lemon and ginger tea down. 'How about a little wander around the duck pond?'

'There aren't any shops, only the Post Office, but there's a dreadful tearoom that Bridget wants to take over. Apparently, it hasn't changed since the 1970s.' Callie had yet to see it for herself and was desperate to go.

'Don't encourage my mother,' Caius said. He loved his mother but she was not much of a cook.

'Well, I for one love experiencing ghastly tearooms,' Dotty said, turning to Georgie. 'En plein air?'

'Oh yes,' Georgie said, eyeing up a second bacon and egg butty. 'I liked the look of the woodland at the bottom of the park.'

Caius had escorted Dotty and Callie around the duck pond in the glorious sunshine. They had balked at the tearoom when presented with the reality. Instead they stopped in at the pub and had a glass of lemonade each. They hadn't lasted there long. The pub was empty, the lunchtime rush hadn't begun, and the barmaid was a little too interested in them for Caius's liking. They had decided to have lunch back at the house via the enemy farm shop a few miles away. More bacon, a few wedges of cheese, someone's granny's secret recipe green tomato chutney and a delightful-looking tea loaf had been purchased.

Caius was in the kitchen knocking up a quick walnut and blue cheese (pasteurised) salad. His parents had retained the cook after his grandfather's death – she still came in for one day every two weeks and froze everything – and he had put one of her quiches in the oven to warm through to have along with the remaining half of a sourdough loaf. He then found an ancient wooden board and placed the cheese, the chutney and the bread on it.

Dotty thought Georgie would forget to eat if he wasn't reminded. She had summoned him to the terrace by text message and was expecting him to surface from the bracken at any moment. She was peering over the balustrade eagerly as the baby kicked her in the ribs.

'I think I'm going to pop,' Dotty said, rearranging herself in the chair. 'I thought pregnancy would be spiritually fulfilling and connecting with my foremothers but then I remembered that my grandmother was a harridan. No one warned me about pelvic girdle pain. I've still got three months to go.'

'What's pelvic girdle pain?'

'I get these random shooting pains because something is stretching or something. Lightning crotch.'

'That sounds fun.'

'The hormones are crazy. I'm really horny all the time this trimester but I just feel exhausted constantly too.'

'Really selling it to me, Dot.'

'Do you guys plan on reproducing?' Dotty looked at Callie. Callie looked back. 'Callie . . .'

'Don't tell anyone. It's the size of a blueberry or something right now.'

'Oh my God, mate!' Dotty grabbed her hand.

'Shush.' Callie looked back at the house, but Caius wasn't in sight. Not that she thought he would mind, but they had agreed to keep it quiet for now. 'It's still in the "don't tell anyone in case" phase. It was an accident. My implant ran out and I hadn't realised.'

'I had two miscarriages before . . .' Dotty rubbed her bump. 'I regretted not telling anyone other than Georgie.'

'I'm so sorry.' Callie squeezed her hand. 'I can't imagine how that felt.'

'It was pretty shit, but I went to boarding school. I can detach from anything.'

'Dot . . .' Callie wished she'd known. Not that she'd have been much help. She'd have gone round and made cups of tea and rubbed Dotty's back. She'd have cursed whichever god Dotty had felt like. 'It's OK. Now, it's OK. I had counselling. It's so common. We just don't talk about it. There are so many women just walking around with that grief like it's nothing.'

'Love you.'

'Love you too.'

Georgie appeared from behind a bush, waving as he walked

along the rose-lined path, sketchbook under his arm and a ruddiness to his cheeks. 'My gorgeous girls,' he said, climbing up the steps, kissing Dotty and plonking himself down next to her.

'Darling, go help Caius carry lunch out.' Georgie did as he was told and Dotty picked up her romance novel. 'Our babies will be best friends.'

Callie put her hand on Dotty's arm. Callie's phone rang. It was Eulalia. She ignored it. It rang again. She started scrolling through her Instagram feed. 'Oh no!'

'What is it?' Dotty asked.

'Eulalia's identity has been revealed.'

'Thank God, I've been desperate to ask but we thought you'd probably signed an NDA or something.'

'I did. It was around her identity and not revealing anything about the process until the new album and look have dropped.' Callie scrolled through the article that was linked to the picture of Eulalia moseying around Primrose Hill in the baggiest clothes that she could find. 'DJ Sonikk let it slip.'

'I've never met a DJ that wasn't either a moron or a coke-fiend. Send me a link.'

'He's in for a rough ride.' Callie sent her the article. 'There's something about her sister that I don't like. I think she could be quite nasty if crossed.'

'Her sister?'

'Yeah Mel, she's her manager.' Callie scrolled through the article. 'Mel was fine the first time I met her but she was really off with me when I presented yesterday. It was at their house so I guess it was some sort of dislike of having to do business at home. Venetia from Ceramics 101 was there though. She works for PCQV now.'

'Vennie? Oh really. She's a sweetie.'

'Mel didn't like that I knew her. Actually, neither of them did.'

'Is Mel plain? She sounds it.'

'Yes. I suppose. Eulalia and Mel are quite clearly sisters but one of them, as you can see, looks like a goddess and the other looks like a Picasso. Same features but wrong proportions.'

'What was Eulalia like?'

'I think she's a bit of a "Laura".'

'Oh, really?'

'She was a bit too interested in Caius.' Callie tucked her hair behind her ears. She carried on scrolling through the article.

'You've got to be careful now you're together. There are more "Lauras" out there than you'd think. People who you've never met will loathe or adore you because of what you represent. You've either got your foot on their neck or they want to hang off yours. "Class warfare" either way.'

'In hindsight, she must have seen the clip from Chelsea and the little puff pieces in the press. I think that's why she contacted me.'

'Even if she is a bit of a "Laura" – and cares about who you make hats for, who your dad is and who you love – she ultimately contacted you because you're talented. If she did see the clip, she saw you talking passionately about your aesthetic philosophy.'

'I nailed the presentation yesterday.'

'You see. No room for impostor syndrome here.'

'I think Eulalia fancies me a bit.' Callie leaned in. 'I went for dinner with her in the week, and it sort of felt as if I was on date. I can't explain it. Eulalia had an expectation of me. She lost it when this guy tried to buy us drinks. Then she tried to get me to go back to hers to listen to music. If she was a man . . .'

'She sounds lonely.'

'Oh for sure. The poor thing.' Callie still had that sinking feeling that she needed to do something about Eulalia, or for her. 'But still, it was intense.'

Caius and Georgie approached the table carrying lunch and Eulalia was forgotten for a moment. Once everyone was seated, the quiche portioned out and the sourdough smothered in butter the gossip resumed.

'Is she hot?' Georgie asked.

'Georgie.' Dotty couldn't be bothered to hit him. 'But is she?'

'Freakishly hot,' Callie said.

'I assumed she'd be a bit, well you know . . .' Caius said. He didn't want to say 'ugly' – it felt cruel to describe someone that way. Callie had been very restrained in her descriptions with him.

'Why?' Callie asked.

'The heads she wears when she performs.' Caius put his cutlery down. 'Realistically, no label is going to hide a pretty face. So there are two options: she's either Quasimodo, or she can't sing and they're using the head to hide the fact that she's lip-syncing.'

Georgie pulled up the footage of her from the Mercury awards ceremony on YouTube and played it. 'Sounds live to me.'

'All right, then the real voice is stood offstage singing live?' Caius asked. He was still aggrieved that he'd had to walk away from the Priory Square case and was trying to get his fix elsewhere. 'What do you know about her, Callie?'

Georgie leaned in. He could see Caius was going into detective mode and was utterly thrilled.

'Not a huge amount.'

'Any life details?' Caius asked.

'Want me to write all this down?' Georgie asked, getting his sketchbook out. 'Jolly Yeoman?'

'No,' Caius said, laughing. 'Sorry, overactive imagination.'

'She studied at the Royal College of Music.' Callie was intrigued now. She needed to know why the vibe was off with them.

'Royal College of Music. Do you know the year or discipline?' Caius asked.

'You're really getting into it,' Dotty said, unsure as to what was going on.

'I don't know, she's not that old though. Mid-twenties.' Callie got up and walked over to him, standing over his shoulder as she watched him scroll through the graduates of their Vocal & Opera course.

'Wait, that's her,' Callie said, pointing at a young woman who had graduated five years ago.

'That's Eulalia?' Caius asked, surprised.

'No, that's Mel, her sister.' Callie looked up at Dotty and Georgie. 'You're right, it's a scam. That's why Mel was so weird. Mel's the voice. Eulalia is the face. That's why they resent each other.'

'But Eulalia, the face, walks around acting like she's the star, right?'

'She talks the talk,' Callie said. She vividly remembered Eulalia waxing lyrical about her creative process and performing. Had she really been lying? 'I guess she has to, to pull it off, but maybe she's a bit delusional.'

Caius turned to Callie. 'She's paid you, right?'

'As soon as I closed my mouth.'

Caius sat back in his chair and took a bite from a slice of bread. He stared at it. The crumb was perfect. Angus must have been really anxious that day.

43

The Police Station

Amy and Matt had been going through the stories in the forum that Isolde was active on. Isolde had written quite a dull Arthurian retelling that somehow included Harry Styles and a well-endowed dragon. Amy had suffered through it. She'd never be able to listen to his songs again.

'This whole forum is what? Inserting real contemporary people into a medieval story where they get it on with whoever or whatever,' Matt said.

'Insert is not the right word to use here,' Amy said. She didn't need to know anything about the imagined reproductive anatomy of mythical creatures and yet she did.

'Well, that's what happened to a cucumber in the one I just read. I'll never look at a salad the same way again. It was one of my favourite veggies. Not any more. I used to love a crushed cucumber with chilli oil. Nope, nope, nope.'

'Shush.' Amy put her finger to her lips. 'People can get their freak on however they want. I am not judging. But I also don't want to read about it.'

'In my one, skipping the salad sex, Isolde talks about being allergic to strawberries. There was a lot of rubbing up against various fruit. Her allergy was one of your facts from Digby's letters, right?'

'Yeah,' Amy said, finding the list she wrote. 'She quoted Dickens in mine. Somehow. Not sure how she squeezed *Little Dorrit* in between the giant dragon penis and poor Harry Styles, but she did.'

Matt refreshed the group page. 'Another story just dropped. It's not from Isolde's handle though. Just someone who likes all of hers and is always commenting.'

'I'll make you a cup of tea if you read it.'

'Only if you let me have some custard creams from your desk drawer.'

'What custard creams?' Amy had been sneaky with replenishing her secret biscuit supply.

'You can read whatever this is then.'

'Fine. Earl grey? Black.'

'Slice of lemon if you can find it.'

'I doubt it.' Amy got up and went to make the tea.

Matt started reading the story. Amy returned a few minutes later with the tea. She was grateful so she hadn't left the teabag in to stew like she normally would in an effort to deter Matt from asking for another one ever again.

'Amy, listen to this.' Matt began reading the story aloud. 'Let me set the scene. A squire, not yet a knight, is learning his trade in rescuing fair damsels.'

'So far so normal. They've got style. There's flair there.'

'Who's the only knight-in-training we know?'

'Caius.' Amy shrugged initially but then recoiled at the possibilities. 'Oh boy.'

'Yep. A youngling butchered by a troll, left in a sacred well. The nymphs wept for her. He brought the troll to justice.' Matt looked up at her. 'I remember that case, it was one of the first ones he worked on as a DS.'

Amy stood over his shoulder. ''Neath a laurel, the gaudy lady spoke not truth. Days sat in a temple of lustful delight. Misadventure, her dark knight an ignoble lover. He loved all over town.' She looked at Matt. 'Clemmie O'Hara, found dead

278

under a bush after having an affair with her boss in that dodgy art gallery.'

'Caius worked on both of these. That poor kid whose dad . . . Her Barbies were all lined up on the side of the bath.'

'That's grim.'

'And referenced here. This story is all about Caius and Callie. There's a bit here about a buxom fair maiden with enchanted fingers who is celebrated for making garments for princesses. That's Callie's hats. She's got a very fancy clientele. Caius said that most of her sales for the year come from Ascot.' Matt scrolled down the story.

Amy read over his shoulder. 'That bit there with the monster kidnapping girls, that sounds like the Eliza Chapel case.'

'So we're agreed that the preamble is about Caius and Callie then.'

'Agreed.' Amy would definitely describe Callie as buxom.

Matt continued scrolling. 'The writer has put themselves into an erotically charged love triangle.'

'Oh, it's just a bog-standard threesome. Phew. Got worried for a second. I don't think you'd call it a love triangle. They're not competing for each other's attention.'

'There are too many tongues and too much licking. This is so explicit. I feel weird reading this.' He kept reading, holding his breath as he did so. 'It's mercifully short.'

'Click out of the story.' Amy peered over Matt's shoulder as he took her back to the summary. 'All of these stories have been published online after the whole Monty Don ex fiasco at the flower show. You have to explain this to Robbie,' Amy said.

'You go wait for him downstairs. He's probably nearly fin-ished giving Margot Bourne a hard time.' Matt swivelled on his chair. 'I'll call Caius.'

44

Frithsden Old Hall

Georgie had convinced Caius to play him at tennis. Caius, who was only vaguely aware that there was a tennis court on the property, was at a disadvantage. Georgie, it turned out, had once been considered a prodigy before he discovered WKDs, smoking and girls at fifteen. Tim Henman's former coach had tried to train him and he'd been tipped as a potential Wimbledon hopeful. Georgie looked wistfully misty-eyed when he talked about turning down sponsorship by those squash people so he could spend time with Delilah his first girlfriend who dumped him three weeks later anyway. Caius successfully returned only three of Georgie's shots. He never stood a chance against his serve. While he was being annihilated the girls were relaxing on the terrace. They'd barely moved all weekend. Dotty was halfway through her romance and Callie was still mulling over the never-ending conclusion of her encounter with Eulalia while attempting to flick through Caius's copy of the satirical magazine *The Cutter*.

'She's rung again,' Callie said, checking her phone and then turning it upside down.

'Turn your phone off,' Dotty said without looking up. She was getting to a good bit. She loved the fake-dating trope.

The table vibrated. Callie picked up her phone to finally turn it off, but put it back down again. It was Caius's phone. Matt was calling.

'Hi, Matt, it's Callie.'

'Hey, is Caius there? It's super urgent.'

'Sure, hang on.' Callie made small talk with Matt about his new flat, recommending a sustainable paint company, as she walked round the side of the house and past the walled garden. 'Caius, it's Matt.'

Caius, relieved to be released from Georgie's merciless backhand, jogged over. Callie handed him his phone and he walked off, keen for her not to hear. Georgie ambled after him slowly.

'Hey, mate, all fine? Ah . . . What? Are you fucking kidding? No . . . About us . . . And they're in the same group. Right . . . It's medieval? The bread. Hang on, I'm putting you on speakerphone.' Caius walked back over to Callie and put his phone on speaker. 'OK, Matt, Callie's here.'

'Hi again, Callie, I was just wondering whether you'd noticed anyone being a bit stalkery with you recently?'

'What?' She turned to look up at Caius who was grimacing.

'Maybe not that far,' Matt continued. 'They may not be following you to your car or anything but they are trying really hard to get to know you. For example, asking lots of questions about Caius and your relationship? Personal stuff.'

'Yeah, actually. I've just completed a design consult for Eulalia. The singer with the bobbleheads. She was asking quite a lot of personal stuff for a week-long consulting gig. She was pretty cool the first time we met but she's always been a little too interested in Caius. She started to feel off by the end of the week.'

Caius chimed in, 'We think actually that Eulalia isn't a singular popstar, if that makes sense. They're sisters.'

'Mel is the brains and the voice,' Callie added. 'While her prettier sister is making the appearances and going by Eulalia. Hence the heads being used to hide the fact that she's lip-syncing.'

'Hang on a minute,' Amy said. She'd been silently listening before. 'Eulalia as in, "My heart bleeds, it spurts, it gushes. My love it needs, this hurts, my blushes. Wailing screaming throwing up. I hate you. Make me come." That Eulalia. Her identity just leaked, didn't it? She's cute. I thought she'd be cute. She sounds cute.'

'That's the one,' Callie said, rolling her eyes. Eulalia's music had taken on a new feeling the more she knew her.

'Did you say Mel?' Matt asked, taking control.

'Yes. There's something going on there for sure. Has something happened to Eulalia? I knew there was something dodgy going on. You could try DJ Sonikk. He's been working with them. He went to the press yesterday.'

'Cal, she's into medieval stuff, right?' Caius asked, knowing full well that she was. Their living room had been taken over by the period's florid iconography for the last week.

'Yeah big time. That was the whole vibe of the consultancy work I did for her. Joan of Arc, you know.'

'Romances? Arthurian and whatnot?' Matt asked.

'Mad for them. She's really into courtly love.'

'You bought that bread from The Purple Toad Bakery, didn't you?' Caius asked.

'Yeah. I'm confused. What's wrong with the bread?' Callie looked confused, and then worried that she'd poisoned everyone with an arsenic-laced sourdough or something stupid.

Georgie had come over now.

'The bread's great.' Caius looked up at Callie. 'Where does Eulalia live?'

'Priory Square.' Callie thought back to their dinner earlier in the week. 'She said she moved there because she liked the history, something about a nun.'

'Does she live at number 35, by any chance?' Matt asked.

'She does. How did you know that? What's going on?'

Caius took Matt off speakerphone and walked away from them. Callie could pick out words like 'stalker' and 'restraining order'.

'Everything all right?' Georgie asked Caius as he came back over.

'Yeah,' Caius said, a little too brightly to convince either of them.

'Best go check on my beloved,' Georgie said, tactfully walking back towards the terrace, leaving them alone.

Caius turned to Callie once Georgie was out of earshot. 'The case I was working on. Eulalia might be involved. Someone has stolen another woman's identity. It's complicated.'

'What?'

'Matt's on it. I'm not allowed near it because of the potential conflict so it won't come up again.' He put his arm around her shoulder. 'Let's just have a lovely weekend. Look how sunny it is.'

'Matt shouldn't have called you. You're off.'

'Special circumstances.'

'Oh come on.' Callie gave him the look that told him she had gone straight from laid-back to overwrought and there was little he could do to bring her back down bar telling the absolute truth.

'I don't want to go into it right now,' he tried.

'Well, I do. How will this work with a baby?'

'Whoa, what are you talking about?'

'You can't even be officially removed from a case. They still call you about it. Where's the work–life balance? I can't care for a newborn on my own.'

'I'm not quitting. I'm not done with the police. Not yet. I can't do it forever, but I'm not ready to stop. Am I happy to move out of London? Yes. Will I have a think about what my career is going to look like? Also yes. Do I love you? More than anything in the world.'

'Fine. That will do for now.'

'Look.' Caius hadn't been going to tell her this bit, at least not until Eulalia was in custody, but he didn't think he was going to get away with hiding it. 'The reason Matt called is because Eulalia has been writing slightly disturbing erotic fiction on the internet.'

'Sure, why not. Whatever floats your boat.' Callie looked confused. 'Why did Matt have to call you about it?'

'The dirty stories are about us.'

'What?' Callie wasn't sure what to think. 'Us?'

'About inserting herself into our relationship.'

'Are you trying to say a threesome?'

'Sort of. It sounds more like an angsty throuple.'

'That makes so much sense. She was asking me about our relationship. She was really interested in you and Frithsden.' Callie tilted her head. She'd gone from mad to bewildered to curious. 'Can I read it?'

'Matt said it was poorly written. The grammar is a bit . . .' Caius had hoped that would be enough of a deterrent but he ended up handing Callie his phone so she could read the link Matt had just sent. He looked out across the grounds as she read. It was a beautiful day. The sky was clear and there was a gentle hum from the bees flitting from dandelion to dandelion. Caius looked through the open gate and into the walled garden. His mother had been busy trying to restore the kitchen garden to working glory. A red kite soared above them, diving down into the grassy parkland after a rabbit.

'Atrocious use of similes,' Callie said, handing Caius his phone back.

'You'd expect someone who writes really explicit pop music to be better at smutty stories.'

'It's not that smutty.'

'Do you think?' Caius wasn't so sure.

'Seems pretty suburban to me.' Callie had read much filthier things in a book with a pastel-pink cartoon cover that Dotty had loaned her when she was trying to get her mojo back post-Max. She noted the name of the website. She might have a look on there later if she got bored. 'I'll get Peter's lawyer on it though. He keeps him on a retainer.'

45

Priory Square

Robbie, closely followed by Tiny Simm who had been standing outside the Horatio Combe Institute while forensics trooped in and out all morning, was traipsing up the steps to 35 Priory Square. Robbie knocked on the door, and then harder a second time. He had to bring in this pervy girl that Matt and Amy had got their knickers in a twist about.

'This is a wild goose chase,' Robbie said, turning to the young constable. He banged again a third time to no avail. 'I don't know how little DI Fauntleroy gets these ridiculous cases.'

'Caius is all right.' Tiny Simm, all six feet five of him, crouched down and peered through the letterbox. 'Sir, there's someone unconscious on the floor.' He stepped out of the way for Robbie to see and called for back-up.

'Police, can you hear me?' Robbie called through the letter-box, but there was no response. The pool of fresh blood under the body was glistening.

Tiny Simm tried and failed to break open the door, wedging his broad shoulders against it, and then Robbie felt like he needed to have a go too for appearance's sake. It wouldn't budge for either of them. Robbie sent Tiny Simm down the servants' steps to the basement level but that wouldn't move either, and neither would the back gate give, even with his prop shoulders. They had to wait for an officer with an enforcer to appear and batter down the front door. An ambulance arrived, and not long after so did Matt and Amy.

★ ★ ★

'Who is she?' Robbie asked Matt. They were standing over the spot where she had lain only five minutes before. A rather aggressively boring formless statue with an unfortunately sharp-cornered base sat in the middle of the puddle ready to be collected by forensics.

'Melissa Parkin,' Matt said, picking up an electricity bill from a side table in the hallway. He remembered the graduation photograph on the mantlepiece. 'Daughter of Beverley and Nigel Parkin of Harrogate.'

'What?' Robbie asked.

'The PO Box that "fake Isolde" wrote to Digby from was purchased using Beverley's credit card. She told me she'd lost it in M&S Food and had stupidly left the PIN with it on a piece of paper.'

'Eulalia used her mum's card to buy the PO Box? That's so dumb,' Amy said, staring around the hallway. The house was beautiful, but it was decorated in such a way that screamed 'I've just got money for the first time, I need to buy art' – faux Andy Warhols and novelty sofas. 'I refuse to think that someone who was calculating enough to steal someone's identity, dress up as Digby's intern to enter the building and use a PO Box would be stupid enough to get their mum to pay for it.'

'What would the alternative be?' Robbie asked.

Matt was yet to catch Robbie up. 'Callie, Caius's girlfriend—'

'The posh bird he brought down the pub for Janet's sixtieth the other month?' Robbie interjected.

'Yes,' Amy said quickly, hoping that would be the end of it.

'Callie was hired by Eulalia to do some creative consulting over the last week. Mel, her sister, is her manager. Eulalia was apparently desperate to work with Callie.'

'It was probably the memes,' Amy said.

'Possibly. Caius and Callie think that Mel was actually the one with the musical talent and that's why Eulalia performs in those bobbleheads,' Matt said.

'So Eulalia, this dodgy popstar, is our little fanfic perv who stole that Isolde woman's identity?' Robbie asked.

'I think so.' Matt looked around the hallway. 'Is she still here?'

'No, the house was empty,' Robbie said.

'The latest story was posted, what an hour ago, Amy?'

'Yeah.'

'How long was Mel down here like that?'

'The medics weren't sure, but none of the blood had congealed,' Robbie said, staring at the floor. 'She was just about breathing when we broke the door down. Her sister did this then.'

'Jennifer,' Amy said, picking up another piece of post from the side table. 'Jennifer Parkin.'

'Let's spread out. See if we can find something that tells us where she might be right now,' Robbie said, before heading down the stairs to the recording studio.

Amy searched through what they thought was probably Mel's room. Matt found what he thought was Eulalia's room – the walls were covered in a collage of Blu-Tacked pictures of female saints, queens and general feminine medieval bumf on display. There was a bloody cotton wool ball in an open silver jewellery box in pride of place on her bookshelf which he couldn't work out, but it looked like it had been placed there especially. She'd left her MacBook on the bed and it didn't have a password. Matt unlocked it. She was still logged in to the forum with her account. He then checked her emails. He found a confirmation for the PO Box buried amongst the thousands of unopened emails. There was also a booking – please pay £60 in cash on arrival – from a taxi firm that she'd ordered forty-five minutes ago.

'I found these in a drawer in Mel's room.' Amy walked in holding two packets of medication. 'Olanzapine and lithium. All prescribed to Jennifer Parkin.'

Matt looked up. 'That's a lot. An antipsychotic and a mood stabiliser.' He remembered a module he'd taken during his degree. 'I'd say she's bipolar or possibly schizoaffective.'

'Mel had control of her medication.'

'Mel's either really controlling or Jennifer sometimes comes off it when she shouldn't.'

'So her sister keeps hold of it and makes sure she takes it.'

'If Caius and Callie are right, and Mel's the talent and Jennifer is the face, then Mel needs Jennifer to keep it together. Her coming off some quite heavy antipsychotics whenever she fancied without a psychiatrist being involved would make her a massive liability. Mel's dependent on her. Well, they're codependent. That could make Mel feel the need to control her. Her career is reliant on her sister acting as the physical embodiment of her musical talent. The resentment between the two of them must have been unbearable.' Matt checked his phone and clicked on the link from the Royal College of Music that Caius had sent over. He played it.

'It's opera, but it's still clearly "Eulalia",' Amy said. She was quietly devastated. She'd been a fan. Fi was going to book tickets for her next tour.

Matt went over to Jennifer's desk. There was a scrapbook sat in pride of place. He flicked it open. There were press cuttings she'd found on the internet of Caius, organised chronologically, and a screenshot of the infamous meme. She'd even found an article about Lydia's case: 'Her younger brother Caius made an appeal last night.' He showed the scrapbook to Amy.

'It feels inevitable, really, that he'd attract a stalker. If you like men, I could understand fancying him. He isn't terrible to look at. He rushes about, doing minor heroics.'

'Plus the whole Cinderella thing. Grew up thinking he was a normie, but turns out he's Norman.'

Amy opened Jennifer's closet. She peered at the clothes. Most of them were drab and probably too large for her – lots of baggy jeans, oversized T-shirts and hoodies. Jennifer would've been lost in them. Her body would've been lost in them. No one could lust after you if they couldn't see you, Amy supposed. One item of clothing caught her eye.

'Matt,' Amy said, holding a hanger with the bright red cardigan up. 'It's just like one of Willow's.'

Matt took out his phone and found Willow's Instagram. 'It's the same brand she buys.'

'Jennifer was stalking Willow too?' Amy put the cardigan in an evidence bag. 'Willow did mention being friendly with a girl who lived nearby.'

A jumble of scarves, brightly coloured party wigs and handbags fell off the shelf at the top of the wardrobe. Matt bent down and picked up a tote from The Purple Toad Bakery and a cheap brunette wig cut into a bob.

'She has to be "fake Isolde",' Matt said, taking a couple of evidence bags from Amy.

'Is the missing volume of Horatio's journal here?' Amy sealed the cardigan up and began looking through Jennifer's bookshelf. There was a lot of poetry; Arthurian legends; retellings of women from Greek myths; piles of scribbled-in notebooks that she knew she'd have to read through later. She turned to a huge pile of letters on the dressing table. They were from fans. She flicked through, merely glancing at their adoration for the hybrid popstar. She moved a drawing of Eulalia wearing a mermaid bobblehead straddling a very suggestive dolphin and found it. 'Matt, it's here. The missing volume.'

46

Frithsden Old Hall

Caius looked up at the terrace from the rose garden. Georgie, Dotty and Callie were chatting. Callie threw her head back at something Dotty said, while Georgie shook his head in faux displeasure. He breathed out. And in. And out. He had decided on the course of action. Up the steps and he was in front of them.

'Callie wants us to hide in the priest holes later. You'll have to come and find us,' Dotty said, shaking her head. 'Although, I don't think I'll fit.'

'They were meant for sixteenth-century hobbits,' Caius said, standing behind Callie's chair and putting his hand on her shoulder. She grasped it reassuringly. 'Did Callie tell you we're moving out of London?'

'No,' Dotty said, raising an eyebrow. 'Out here?'

'Yes, the great smog doesn't excite me any more,' Callie said, putting down her glass of water. 'I've had it with London. It's so dirty and noisy.'

'So true,' Dotty said, reaching over and squeezing Callie's arm. 'And it's got so busy. You can't go to the V&A any more without a mob of tourists blocking every single exhibit. I understand why the people in Barcelona get so pissed off.'

'Callie, why don't you show Dotty and Georgie the farmhouse,' Caius said, rather firmly.

'Huh?' Callie looked up at him, bemused. They'd just settled in with a new pot of lemon and ginger tea and thick slices of the tea loaf.

'It's just down the lane for a mile, skirting the bottom of

the woods that Georgie was drawing in this morning,' Caius said.

'You've got some spectacular ancient oaks, you know,' Georgie said, taking a slice of tea loaf from the plate in the middle of the table.

'My dad gave me the keys yesterday. I'll grab them while you guys get ready to go. Georgie can drive you down.'

'Sure,' Georgie said, looking at Caius. None of the others knew what to make of him.

Caius turned to Georgie and said, 'Jolly Yeoman.'

Georgie sprang into action. 'Calliope, I'm desperate to see your new gaffe. Let's go right now.' He helped a bemused Dotty out of her chair.

Callie, who by now had realised that she was being put out of harm's way, felt a curious mix of fear, anger and amusement. No, not amusement. It was surreal.

★ ★ ★

There was a wooden bench outside the front of the house. Caius's father had put it there on the gravel so his grandfather could sit and watch the birds. Having seen the others off, Caius sat there now waiting for Eulalia with cash in his pocket. He'd have to remember to expense it. A minicab pulled in past the gatehouse – the gardener was thankfully in Tenerife for a week with his wife. Caius texted Matt as it wound up the gravel drive. He held the door open for Eulalia, who had come with a small suitcase. He handed the driver the £60 – and a generous tip all wrapped around a note, asking him to call Robbie at the station immediately – and waved him off.

Caius sat back down on the bench, her bag at his feet. She sat down next to him, peering across like he was a zoo creature. Her energy was hectic. So much movement, but she held his gaze steady – the eye of the storm. He understood how people had believed in possession in the past.

He turned and asked her, 'Do you mind if I record this?' He was already recording.

'Record what?'

'Our conversation.'

'Why would I mind?'

'Do you?'

'No.'

'What's your name?'

'Eulalia.'

'What's your real name?'

'Jennifer Parkin.'

He placed his phone down on the bench between them. 'DI Caius Beauchamp,' he said. She held out her hand but he didn't take it. 'But you know that already, don't you, Jennifer?'

'Thank you so much for inviting me this weekend.' She stopped suddenly and turned her head as if she heard something, before turning back to Caius. 'What a pretty view. So many birds. Do you sit out here a lot?'

'Sometimes.' He felt it was best to respond to her questions with as little detail as possible. 'We've met before, haven't we?'

'It was fate.'

'I bumped into you outside the Horatio Combe Institute the morning after the murder of Digby Combe-Watson. Did you do it on purpose? Were you following me? Or were you watching the crime scene?'

Jennifer stared into the mid-distance. If she had heard what Caius had asked, she failed to respond.

'Did you know Digby at all?'

'Is he dead?'

'Yes. Digby was the curator of the museum. Had you ever spoken to him? You live across the way.'

'Willow.' She said the intern's name as if the breeze was meant to carry it.

'Willow?'

'His assistant.' Jennifer snapped her attention back to Caius. No longer absent, she began to talk quickly, giggling to herself intermittently. 'She's so charming. She eats her lunch in the square. We chat. I've not seen her in a week. I keep trying to get hold of her. There's no more writing. She won't answer. I've sent her so many DMs. I like her new cardigan. She has all these brooches on them. So shiny. She buys them all from charity shops. I like her. She understood. I told her about Mel and Eulalia. She hung out in my room. Mel kicked her out. No outsiders. I think it's the fairies who are blocking my messages. They're stopping my messages getting through. They tied my hair up in knots this morning. They're so naughty.' She put her hand on his knee.

'Jennifer, please remove your hand from my person.'

She did as she was told but she laughed as she did so, as if Caius was flirting with her. 'Where's my darling Cal?'

'She's popped out to the shops.'

'T'shops. What for?'

'For some strawberries.'

'I love strawberries. I have a friend who's allergic to them.'

'A friend?'

'Yes.' Jennifer started to become agitated at Caius's sceptical tone. 'Why do you look shocked. Of course I have friends.'

'I don't doubt that you do.' Caius spoke slowly and evenly, as he tried to calm her down. 'Are they an online friend or an in-person friend?'

'Oh, online.' She relaxed but still kept on talking at a pace. 'Her name is Isolde. Isn't that gorgeous. I wish that was my name. There were three Jennifers in my year in school. Mel doesn't like me having friends. She thinks they're going to distract me or sell our secrets to the press. Mel doesn't like Cal, but I think that's because she's pretty. Mel sent a creepy man from the label to watch us when we went out for dinner. He sent limoncello to our table.'

'From your music label?'

'Yes, they work for her. She wants to control me. She has spies everywhere. The crows work for her. They tell her where I've been.'

'Oh dear. It sounds like Mel is quite domineering.'

'She is, she is! I have to ask her for money. I don't have a bank account. Well I do, but she won't let me have my card. She just gives me £20 notes every now and then. My mum gave me her card details for emergencies and sometimes I use it to buy clothes or flowers. I love flowers. I love what they mean. That's why I love Cal. She understands that.'

'Did you hurt your sister, Jen?'

'No.'

'Did you have a fight?'

'No.'

'Are you sure?'

'Yes. No.' A crow flew past and Jennifer stopped to watch it, not speaking until it had disappeared out of sight. 'I said I was leaving to come here and she flipped out. I ran past her, opened the front door and jumped in the taxi. There wasn't much she could do about it. She'll probably have the label send some goon after me, but you'll turn him away, won't you?' Jennifer squinted at the car coming through the gates. 'When's Callie back? Is that her?'

'No,' Caius said. He felt so sorry for her. 'Jennifer is the modern form of Guinevere, isn't it?'

'Yes it is! I knew you'd understand.'

'Is that why you like medieval stuff?'

'What is in a name?'

'Why did you move to Priory Square?'

'Because of Alice de Burge. She's like me. I used to hear God all the time when I was younger. It makes me sad that She doesn't speak to me any more though. Although I can always feel her trying to whisper. God whispers to me. She says I'm in danger. I told Mel I wanted to live on the square and she agreed. Mel never bothered asking why. It's charming. The magnolias. Do you know what magnolia stands for?'

'When did God stop talking to you?'

'I miss Her. I want to hear Her again. Soon.'

The police car pulled up and two uniformed officers stepped out.

'My colleagues here are going to take you with them, Jennifer. They're going to look after you.'

'Oh, but I thought I was staying here?'

Caius sat still as they put her in the back of the car. She went without any real fuss. He handed one of them her weekend bag. The car drove off and he sent the recording to Matt's work email. He then texted Georgie 'All clear'. He took the handcuffs he had out of his back pocket. He was glad he hadn't had to use them; Jennifer was clearly manic but he himself, possibly naively, hadn't felt like he was in danger. His relief did partially stem from the fact the handcuffs weren't from work. He put them safely back in his pocket as Georgie's car pulled up the drive.

'What did you think?' Caius asked Dotty, holding the door open for her.

'Adorable, so adorable.' Dotty started waddling towards the house. 'And it's so close to London. It takes an hour and a half to get from one side to the other anyway, so you may as well have a lovely view and birdsong.'

'Great light.' Georgie winked at him. He followed Dotty in, leaving Callie and Caius outside.

'She came here, didn't she?' Callie asked, perching herself down on the bench.

'Yeah. She wasn't doing so great, but don't worry, she's been taken to hospital.' Caius sat down next to her and put his arm around her shoulder. 'Her name's Jennifer, by the way.'

'Far more grounded than Eulalia.'

'Cal, I'm sorry to tell you this but Mel was attacked.'

'She was killed by Eu . . . Jennifer?'

'I don't know what state she's in. Matt will let me know at some point if there's an update on her condition.'

'How dreadful.'

'Yeah.'

'I mean, what? I saw her yesterday morning.'

'That's the way it goes sometimes.'

'And it was Eu . . . Jennifer? I mean, she's obviously not well. Looking back, she's deteriorated over the week I've known her but I really can't see her trying to kill someone.'

A blackbird sailed past and into a nearby horse chestnut, warbling as it went. Caius turned back to look at Callie, taking her hand. 'I can't do this forever.'

'Your job?'

'Yeah. You were right earlier by the tennis court. How the hell do I keep doing this shit and whatever my dad's going to chuck at me and have a kid? Something has to give somewhere.'

'You're probably right,' Callie said, giving his knee a squeeze. She was relieved. She hated giving ultimatums, although this one had knocked her up so it probably wouldn't go as badly as it had with past boyfriends.

'That something is having part of a popstar who's likely just had a psychotic break after attacking their sibling dropping by unannounced with a weekend bag.'

'She had a bag?'

'Yeah, she was convinced she'd been invited to stay. She thanked me and everything.'

'Wow, the poor girl.' Callie stared at the wrought-iron gates she'd just passed through. 'Your dad should get some cameras.'

'Absolutely.' Caius stood up and Callie followed. He put his head on hers. 'Your gut was right about them. You thought there was something up. Don't ignore that.'

'Good old intuition.' Callie reached into his pocket and pulled out the handcuffs. 'Hullo, I don't think these were issued by the Met.'

'They were all I had at such short notice.'

'Short notice?'

Callie handed them back and Caius shoved them back into his pocket just in time. Georgie appeared at the door.

'How about a game of hide-and-seek but you two hide in these infamous priest holes and we'll have to come and find you?'

'I'll hide and the three of you have to find me, but I'm going to grab a beer first,' Caius said, going back into the house.

Caius took a torch and a set of keys from a kitchen drawer, grabbed a cold one out of the fridge and told the others, who were waiting for him in the hall, to close their eyes and count to thirty. He walked into the library and pushed the panel that led down to the tunnel. He walked down the steps and along the six hundred or so metres it took before he reached the hatch that opened up into the Temple of Venus folly that overlooked the lake. He shut the hatch, unlocked the padlock his dad had put on the temple gates and sat on the sandstone steps, drinking his beer and watching the sky turn orange. Callie called his phone after an hour. They wanted to give up but were worried he was stuck in a hole without any oxygen. He could see them on the terrace now. He waved as he walked back. Callie yelled down that they were ordering a curry because it was her turn to cook and she couldn't be arsed. Caius yelled back that he wanted a lamb rogan josh, and for a moment it felt like everything was almost well with the world.

47

The Whittington Hospital

Matt met Amy in the canteen. It was closed for the night, but there were staff members on breaks sitting at the tables, scrolling through their phones and disassociating. He'd bought her a can of Sprite and a packet of Skips from the vending machine.

'Mel is out of surgery. The doctor I spoke to thinks it's fifty-fifty. She'd lost a lot of blood. If she recovers she may never get the use of her right arm again.' Amy opened the can and took a sip. 'How's Jen?'

'They've taken her onto the ward,' Matt said. Despite getting into the car quite calmly for Caius, Jennifer had a rough ride down from Hertfordshire. 'They've sedated her. Poor thing.'

'Their parents are here, you know. We should speak to them.'

'They drove all the way down to London.'

'Hmm?'

'They were complaining about our fair capital city when I spoke to them.' Matt scrunched up his Snickers wrapper. 'We should speak to the Parkins tomorrow morning. They won't be in a fit state tonight.'

'Heard from Robbie?'

Matt checked his phone. 'Nope. He's probably up to his eyeballs in paperwork.'

'Do you think Jennifer killed Digby?'

'Digby had been to Harrogate. Perhaps it was her and Mel that they met in the Wetherspoon's and she carried around a cancerous resentment because he'd fawned over her and then forgot about her. Nathan's description fits.' Matt took a sip from his can of Coke Zero. 'I dunno. People have been killed for less, I suppose.'

'Perhaps if they had met that weekend in Harrogate he was the one to first tell her about the square, about its history. She's obsessed with medieval things, right? She broke into the Institute to steal the final volume of Horatio's journal . . .'

'But why? What's in that book other than orgies?'

'A lot of dodgy metaphors.' Amy shrugged. 'To be fair, she likes reading about orgies.'

'And cucumber sex.' Matt watched a tired-looking nurse get up from a nearby table. 'Snickers only for me from now on.'

MONDAY

48

The Police Station

'I listened to Caius's little chat with Jennifer.' Robbie looked down at his shoes. 'I'm not sure if it's admissible as evidence.'

'Depends on the judge,' Matt said.

'Quick thinking of him to get the taxi driver to call the station. I'll give him that.' Robbie had spoken to the driver the day before. He'd confirmed that she'd been erratic on the journey, talking to herself in the back seat. 'Where's Amy? Has she met Willow before? "Eulalia" said they're friends.'

'She's already on it.' Amy had asked her to come in already.

'I see.' Robbie paused, staring at a spot of water damage on the ceiling. 'I think we got off on the wrong foot. I get it, you're loyal to your DI and I didn't help matters with my attitude.'

'You asked around about Billy's coke habit, didn't you?'

'Perhaps.' Robbie had been caught. He held his hand out. Matt took it. 'I know you fobbed me off with the hand in the basement.'

Matt shrugged. 'A corpse is a corpse. Doesn't matter how long ago they died.'

'I guess you guys came up with a plan for the next few days after Caius was taken off in case I turned out to be a useless old duffer.'

'It's an unruly case.' Matt thought being frank with Robbie would be easiest. Everything could get swept under the same proverbial carpet. 'You were never going to catch up in time so we just pushed on regardless.'

Robbie had had enough of that conversation. 'In the

recording, Caius doubled back on the strawberry comment. What was that about?'

'Both fake and real Isolde are allergic to strawberries. It's in the letters to Digby, Caius asked Isolde about it when she was interviewed, and she mentions it in her stories on the fanfic forum. I think Caius was trying to work out whether she had met Isolde in real life, or if she was referring to what appears to be a somewhat nebulous reference by a fellow forum user that she had escalated as a deeper relationship in her mind.'

'Which came first?'

'What do you mean?'

'The letters or the fanfic forum?'

'That's a really good question,' Matt said, opening the fanfic site up. 'The first story was written a couple of days after the first letter from Isolde to Digby was dated.'

'That's interesting,' Robbie said, going up to the whiteboards that Amy was tracking the case on. He flipped one over and began writing on the back. 'All right, tell me what I'm missing.'

'OK.' Matt looked up from his computer. 'Jen steals, con-sciously or unconsciously, the identity of a fellow forum user, Isolde, and uses it to populate letters that she sends to Digby. Jen potentially met Digby a couple of years ago in Harrogate and is stalking him. She uses her mum's credit card to pay for the PO Box. Her mum lied to me and said she'd just lost her card and didn't recognise the transaction – they're coming in today. Jen writes to Digby after seeing his lonely-hearts ad in the *London Review of Books* – possibly finding out about it from Willow, his intern, who she has befriended on her lunchbreaks. Jen then dresses up as Willow while pretending to be Isolde in the letters.'

'So Jen goes to the museum for the date she's set up and kills Digby via a hemlock-laced salad,' Robbie began.

'Institute.' Matt was being pedantic for the sake of it. He took a breath. He needed to let it go.

'Goes to the Institute,' Robbie continues. He saw what Matt had been getting at earlier. It was annoying. 'Steals Horatio's pervy diary, presumably for kicks. Then Jen systematically breaks into another two houses on the square all perfectly aligned in a cross.'

'Yes,' Matt said, staring at Caius's printout of the square on the whiteboard. 'But why?'

'I don't know.'

Matt shrugged. 'I don't see it. This poor girl is in the middle of psychotic episode. I can understand her attacking her controlling sister in that state but anyone else?'

'It makes no sense. The way Digby's murder has been planned out is meticulous. The PO Box thing is clever. Like Amy said, messing up by using her mum's card is just silly.'

'No prints on the letters themselves. The envelopes have been fondled by everyone at the sorting office but not licked by the sender.'

'Picking that little incel to be her dogsbody was a stroke of genius. His mates are online not in-person. People lie online all the time. No one would believe him, and no one would miss him immediately other than his job and his mum, who probably struggles to be around her misogynistic son. Even then they didn't report him as missing.'

'Don't get me wrong, Jen's not, she's not well . . . She saw Callie on the television being made a fool of by her ex. Callie's quick on her feet, she's charming and turns it around, but Caius is in the shot. The press write a few puff pieces. She saw all of that and then said to her sister, "I want you to hire her." Then she wrote an iffy two-thousand word fantasy about them. Jen's not OK. This whole plan is a lot. Too much for most people, especially someone away with the fairies.'

Robbie nodded. Janet on the front desk called to let him know that DJ Sonikk had arrived.

★ ★ ★

Caius and Callie were sat waiting to be interviewed by Robbie and Matt. The rest of the weekend had been salvaged. They'd driven to another village nearby on Sunday, had a roast at a pub with a Michelin star and wandered around an antique shop-cum-warehouse full of Callie's favourite sorts of tat. Georgie claimed it had been one of the most thrilling weekends of his life, and Dotty had got through two novels by authors with pod-casts and divine haircuts so she'd had a grand old time.

Callie was on her phone, fielding emails from her work account. The Met had released a statement earlier that day and the gutter press had got a sniff – probably through the verbose DJ Sonikk – that she had been involved with the whole debacle.

'Calliope Foster will not be commenting on an ongoing police investigation. Yours, Amelia,' Callie said. Caius looked up from his book and nodded his approval at the short but firm reply. 'Poor fictional Amelia. She really has to deal with so much shit from people.'

'She's a real trooper. You should give her a raise,' Caius said, putting his book down and putting his arm around Callie. 'You look pale.'

'Just not a fan of it in here.' Callie smiled politely at the officer on the desk in front of them.

'Imagine how I feel coming in here every day.'

She turned to Caius and whispered, 'Why is that policewoman staring at us?'

'It's Janet. You came along to her birthday drinks.'

'Oh her.' Callie smiled and waved at her. Janet half-heartedly waved back.

'She sort of hates me, but is nice sometimes too,' Caius whispered back. He pulled back. 'You know the usual effect I have on people.'

'You charmer.'

'You feeling OK?'

'I still feel a bit sick. Same as half an hour ago. Stop asking.'

'All right. Crikey. I'll read my book in silence then.' Callie squeezed his arm as Caius resumed his place reading about the Tudor dynasty and the rise of the English nation state. He'd studied Henry VIII in Year 7, he could do the rhyme, but he didn't know much beyond that and the sinking of the *Mary Rose*.

'Calliope?' asked a lean man with sandy hair.

'Yes,' Callie said, looking up.

Caius put his book down. The young man wasn't police; his accent was far too heightened for a real job. 'And you are?'

'Cecil.' He leaned in and mouthed the words 'DJ Sonikk'. 'We've met before, haven't we? I'm sure we have.'

'We're both friends of Tabs.' Callie didn't think they'd met but knowing Tabs was close enough.

'Yes. Tabs, of course. God, she's fun.' He flopped down next to them. He didn't care that there were others around to overhear. 'There are Eulalia fans camped out in the garden in the square holding a vigil, you know. It's dreadful, isn't it?'

'Isn't it just,' Callie said.

'What a fucked-up family.'

'I take it you knew all along about who was doing what?' Caius cryptically asked in a low voice. No one was paying attention to them.

'Oh yes, but I wasn't given the full picture until after I'd signed everything, otherwise I wouldn't have touched it.' Cecil/DJ Sonikk stretched out on the chair next to Callie. 'I saw Mel really lose it once. The poor kid had had a friend over. Some girl with a bob. Mel went nuts. It was awful. Some choreographer had tried to sell pictures of Jennifer a few weeks before. They were both under so much stress. They're from a really normal family and just weren't prepared for the work, you know.' Cecil/DJ Sonikk leaned back in his chair, smug with his own 'accurate' assessment of the situation. 'I nearly rang the police, actually. As it transpires I should have.' His phone vibrated in his pocket. 'Anyway, got to dash.' And with that he left.

'I'm so glad you speak posh,' Caius said, sitting up straight in his chair. He'd seen Janet pick up her phone. She proceeded to nod sagely at him. 'I only understood a third of what he said.'

Robbie appeared and took them both through. Matt was waiting for Callie, and Robbie would speak to Caius.

★ ★ ★

Robbie stopped the tape. Caius had recalled the events of Saturday as well as he could.

'What are you reading?' Robbie asked. Caius had placed the tome on the table when he had sat down. Robbie wasn't sure if it was a power play or not, 'look how knowledgeable I am', or if Caius was just trying to detach and was losing himself in a book. Books were better than bottles, he supposed.

'Oh, um it's a history book. *Ten Figures Who Shaped Britain.* I don't really know much about history. Not my normal thing.'

'Me neither.' Robbie decided to believe that he was being genuine. 'I don't get to read as much as I'd like. I pick up a big thick thriller in the airport before lying on a sunbed for a week, but that's it for me.'

'You can't beat a good bit of escapism,' Caius said, picking up the book. The author's picture was on the back. He glanced at it and then at Robbie. 'It's by the real Isolde's ex-boyfriend, actually. He mentioned it when I checked her alibi so I ordered it online . . .' Caius petered out and stared at the picture.

'What?' Robbie asked.

'It says he's a lecturer at King's College.' Caius lost himself for a moment. 'I've asked my dad to get in touch in case our family office knows something about the site. I'll pass your details on in case anyone knows anything.' Caius stood up and offered Robbie his hand. He took it.

★ ★ ★

Matt escorted Caius and Callie out of the building and they walked down the road and off onto a quieter side street. Matt had asked Callie how she was, expressing his sympathy that she'd been dragged into yet another case. Callie pretended it was fine, and then walked off to have 'Amelia' field a few more press emails, leaving Matt and Caius alone.

'Get the real Isolde in,' Caius said.

'Sure.'

'Those stories. I read the ones written by Isolde. I just can't help but think an English teacher who likes Dickens . . . It wasn't well written.' Caius would never be able to look at poor Harry

Styles again. '"Fake Isolde" is nothing but an aggressive opportunist. I think I know who did it but I'm not entirely sure why.' Caius turned to Matt and began giving him instructions. He could see Callie in the distance getting really pissed off with him. 'It's the square that's important. Not Digby. He was collateral damage. They all are.'

★ ★ ★

Amy had returned to Willow's transcript of Horatio Combe's malaria-year journal. She'd made it about a third of the way through. 'Listen to this:

'What poetry.'
'The first bit is clearly sex. The second bit though?' Matt asked, looking up from the CCTV footage from 35 Priory Square. He'd watched the fight erupt between the sisters. Jen had tried to push past Mel who blocked her. Mel had been rough with Jen, trying to restrain her. Jen wrestled free and picked up a statuette from the sideboard and rammed the pointy end into her sister's shoulder before fleeing. Mel pulled it out and then the blood began to pour. She must have nicked an artery or something. It

was unfortunate. 'Who's the holy lady if not the Virgin Mary? But then she must be "Our Lady".'

'It could be Alice de Burge? The nun who was burnt for heresy during the Reformation. The one with the blob statue in the middle of the square. His little cult is "feeding" off the ancient site's energy.' Amy looked up at Robbie. He seemed to be following.

'Actually, Callie said the same thing about Jen. That she moved there because a woman was burnt as a heretic on the site,' Matt said.

'What does he say after the bit about ladies being sexy fruit?' Robbie asked.

'There's a few weeks' break between the next entry. That's barely coherent, and it's not in full sentences. It starts to get a bit gobbledegooky from here on. He keeps writing about tunnels.'

'Tunnels?' Robbie asked.

'Yeah, metaphorical tunnels, I guess, but he's also talking about hearts with worms. I don't know. He's a lunatic.'

'That history article Caius found.' Matt searched through his emails for the link Caius had sent him. He'd read it at the time. 'There's a reference to Victorian builders finding medieval stuff when digging out the basements, right?'

'Yeah, Caius read that bit out loud to me,' Amy said.

Matt forwarded the email to Robbie with the link. 'Is it possible that someone knocked through a basement wall and into any subterranean ruins? I mean, it sounds crazy.'

'You say that but they found that Temple of Mithras under a building after the Blitz, right?' Robbie said. He remembered seeing the opening of the ancient temple under the Bloomberg building on the news the other year.

Matt checked his phone. Caius had forwarded him an email from his account at his family's property company. Matt read it again. Caius did know who the killer was. He got up the CCTV from Whipps Cross A&E. Caius had requested it a while ago but there hadn't been a need to watch it before. 'Isolde and Andy sit down at 9.37 p.m. They don't move until 1.01 a.m.'

'The real Isolde? I thought we'd established that she has nothing to do with it and she was a red herring?' Robbie asked, looking up from the article. 'Have you got doubts about Jen? It all ties up perfectly. The cardigan, the wig, the journal, the pervy forum.'

'Yeah, I have.'

'Isolde was alibied by a friend called Keisha Jones who she was out running with in Walthamstow. Keisha helped her home at approximately 6.30 p.m. There is time unaccounted for,' Amy said, looking up at Matt. He knew something she didn't.

'We took her prints when she was formally interviewed and she didn't match the partials,' Matt said.

'What are you getting at, Matt?' Amy looked at him. He gave her a look as if to say go along with it.

'Are we sure she didn't do it?' Robbie asked.

'The fanfic forum has brought the real Isolde back under suspicion,' Amy agreed. She turned to Robbie. 'We should eliminate her beyond any reasonable doubt. What do you think? We should check her laptop at least. Should we get a warrant to search her place for evidence or just get her in for you to interview her? You might spot something we missed.'

'Let's do both,' Robbie said, nodding to himself. He might spot something indeed. 'Amy, when's this Willow girl coming in again? Make sure she actually knows Jen and that Jen wasn't stalking her too like she was Caius and his girlfriend.'

49

The Police Station

Amy had Willow in front of her. The poor girl had been in and out of the station all week. She was still wearing her 'uniform', although the weather had forced her to abandon her signature cardigan and she had indeed added a miniskirt to her rotation. Amy had gone to another floor to fetch her a claggy hot chocolate from the machine in the break room. She thought that she was the type of girl to drink that sort of cloying powdery thing rather than something heavily caffeinated. After all that effort Willow wasn't even drinking it.

'Willow, have you met this girl?' Amy slid her a picture of Jennifer that they'd taken from the house.

'Yes, oh her. Jen lives on the square. Bless her.'

'Bless her?'

'I think she's lonely. She used to *happen to walk by* when I was on my lunchbreak. I sit in the square if it's sunny and read while I eat.'

'What did you think of Jen?' Amy wrote down that Willow knew her by her actual first name and not 'Eulalia'.

'What did I think? She's nice. Friendly. Northerners are always friendly. How many Londoners will actually speak to a stranger?'

'What did you talk about?'

'All sorts. Jen's really into music. She kept trying to get me to come round and listen to her vinyl collection with her.' Willow tapped the table and shook her head. She started talking rapidly. 'And whatever I was reading. I love a romance novel and I get

through two a week normally. I like enemies to lovers and anything with a werewolf alpha situation.'

'Fanfic too?'

'What?'

'You know, people writing stories about celebrities or characters from books or shows they like.'

'No, sorry.' Willow wrinkled her nose. She was a snob. 'That's
not my sort of thing.'

'When was the last time you saw Jen?'

'Oh, the week before I found . . . The week before poor Digby
died. I was sitting outside in the square eating my lunch. She came
over to talk. Jen liked my cardigan. She wanted to know where it
was from so she could buy one. We started chatting but then her
sister came and collected her. Her sister was sort of intense.'

'Collected her?'

'Yeah, she said they had to go out somewhere so she took her
back to the house. It was a bit weird, to be honest.'

'And you've not seen her since?'

'No, although I think I saw her from a window the other week.
I waved but she didn't come out. Busy, I guess. Or maybe I said
something wrong? I don't know.'

'Why didn't you go round and listen to her vinyl collection?'

'I don't know.' Willow played with the tarot card pendant
round her neck. 'A vibe.'

'Too friendly? Or the sister?'

'Both, maybe. It's quite a bold thing to ask someone you only
know in passing round to your house. Stranger danger. I've only
been able to sit outside on my lunchbreak for the last five weeks
once the weather turned. She appeared every time. Like she
maybe was waiting for me.' Willow leaned in and spoke quietly
as if she was taking Amy into her confidence. 'If I'm being

honest, she creeped me out a bit. She was too beautiful. Why was she bothering me? If she'd have been a bloke I would've been worried.'

'Have you ever been to The Purple Toad Bakery?'

'I used to go there every week on my lunchbreak when the weather was colder. I didn't want to sit in the Institute longer than I ever really needed to. It was *meant* to be a little treat, you know? Their mortadella sandwiches are literal heaven.'

'Meant to be a treat. What do you mean?' Amy asked.

'There's a guy who works there who writes his number on your cup. It's vaguely cute, I guess. Well, is it? I don't know. It could be if you'd chatted before and hit it off.' Willow sighed and wrinkled her nose in disgust again. 'He gave me the ick. He used to watch me drinking from those cups he wrote on. Longingly. I started to wonder whether he'd done something gross to my chai, you know. Like spat in it or put one of his hairs in. Something weirdly sexual. Yuck! He'd done it to Jen too. She told me all about him propositioning her.'

'He wrote his number on Jen's cup?' Amy knew Matt was quietly looking at it from another angle but the more she spoke to Willow the more Jen looked like the killer. She sounded like she'd been more lucid when the plan was begun.

'Yes, I think he'd followed her on the street once too. She was so creeped out. Jen really is very pretty. I told her she could be a model if she wanted but she laughed.' Willow sighed. She looked up at Amy and gave her the old puppy dog eyes. 'Has there been an update on my crazy fan?'

'Huh?'

'Well the other policeman, he said something about me maybe having a disturbed fan who dressed up as me? So terrifying!'

'Nothing to report as yet,' Amy said.

50

The Police Station

Robbie's phone rang just as he and Matt were about to collect Isolde from reception.

'Robbie Eastley.' He listened carefully to the forensics person on the other end. He grimaced as he ended the call. 'I've got to go to the Institute, Matt. That nutter wasn't talking about metaphorical tunnels. Forensics have bloody found one.'

'What? Really? I'd give Caius's dad a call in that case. It's his land.'

'Why doesn't he get assigned to gang stabbings? Why is it always weird?'

Matt shrugged. 'I'll speak to Isolde then.'

'Sure. I hope I don't have to go down any bloody tunnels. I hate small spaces.'

★　★　★

'Thanks for coming in, Isolde,' Matt said, sitting opposite her. Matt introduced himself for the recording. 'My colleague DI Caius Beauchamp spoke to you before about someone using your details to catfish men.'

'Yes, have you caught them?' Isolde looked up at Matt. Her large green eyes were full of earnestness. 'I feel so freaked out by this whole ordeal.'

'We believe we have.'

'Thank God. I've been petrified all week. It's so grim. Stealing parts of my life to seduce and murder a man. I've been suspecting everyone I've ever met. Can you imagine? Someone fleeting. Someone you shared a lift with once. I've got the heebie-jeebies. I bought one of those doorbell cameras for my house.'

'About that . . .' Matt started to blush. He thought she was far too hot to be sat at home writing things like salad sex. Surely, girls like her were just out there getting laid rather than just imagining it. 'We think that they follow you on your fanfic account.'

'My what?' Isolde looked confused.

'Your fanfic account.'

'What? I don't have an account like that.'

'Do you not write medieval sexual fantasies online?'

'Absolutely not.' Isolde was offended.

'There's no need to be embarrassed—'

'I do not write dirty stories for strangers on the internet.'

'Are you sure?'

'Of course I'm bloody sure.' Isolde took her laptop out of her bag. 'Have a look for yourself. I was going to go to a cafe after and apply for English language teaching jobs in Italy.'

'May I?' Matt took her laptop – it saved them having to get a warrant to search her place and get it. He logged on to the station's guest Wi-Fi and opened up a new tab. He put the address for the fanfic site in and it popped up. 'You're still logged in.' He spun the laptop around.

'What the actual fuck?' Isolde stared at her homepage on the site. 'I didn't write any of this.'

'Look, you—'

'I didn't.' She clicked on the last story. 'Two things: firstly, I'm an English lead – the grammar is appalling. Secondly, I was at work when this was published. That's right in the middle of a school day. I was substituting in a school in Stratford. I didn't have my laptop, it was at home. I never use my own devices when I'm at work. I even turn my phone off. What sort of example would I be setting?'

Matt nodded, and turned the laptop back round to face him. He went back to the dashboard and the summary of the stories posted. 'Where were you on these dates?'

★　★　★

Matt escorted her out of the building. She was walking unevenly with her moon boot. They entered the lift.

'I feel so violated.' She turned to Matt. 'Why me?'

'We'll find out soon enough,' he said as the lift door opened. He walked her back to reception. Andy, her ex, was waiting for her.

'Everything OK?' he asked, placing his hand on her back.

'I need a strong drink,' Isolde said, shaking her head as if to hold back the tears that had been forming. 'Someone's writing dirty stories about me online.'

'Oh God, that's awful.'

Matt watched Andy. He briefly looked disturbed, and then angry. Andy handed Isolde his car keys. 'I'll be out in a second.'

Isolde took the keys and hobbled off.

'I didn't want her travelling all the way here on public transport. Her foot.'

'They have seats on the overground,' Matt said, smiling at Andy. 'That's very courteous of you. It's nice that you can have a grown-up relationship with your ex.'

'Well yes,' Andy agreed and gave Matt a smug glance. 'Look, am I to understand it that your boss, I guess, DI Beauchamp. The guy I met before. He's not on the case any more?'

'No, it was a conflict of interest. He just discovered that his family own the leaseholds in the area where the crimes have been concentrated.'

'I see. It's probably hard for them to keep track of all their property.' Andy nodded, quickly smiling to himself. 'Their house in Hertfordshire has lots of priest holes. It's an interesting site. And Priory Square has a fascinating history. Did you know that?'

'No, I didn't,' Matt replied. He wasn't sure why Andy looked so pleased.

'Your colleague's ancestors . . .' Andy sagely drifted off.

'Yes?'

'Well.' Andy moved closer to Matt. 'When the current houses were built in the Victorian era and the priory was exposed for the first time in three hundred years, the Beauchamps already knew what was down there. They chose to seal it up again, like their ancestors had in the sixteenth century. They knocked the priory down, you know. Left the crypt and basement levels only. Whether your colleague and his family have an idea now is a different question. I appreciate that there has been a change in precedence. I wouldn't be surprised if old Horatio knocked through. He was a Boy's Own psychopath, after all. He wouldn't have been able to help himself if he thought there was something valuable underneath.'

'Oh.'

Andy's mouth quivered. He wanted to ask Matt something else but backed off it. 'Anyway, I best drive Princess Isolde back home.'

Matt watched Andy leave. He returned to his desk in the incident room and started watching the footage from the security cameras at number 35.

'Amy,' Matt called over. 'Have you still got access to that program you used for the Post Office that scans footage?'

'Yep,' she said and sent him a link.

51

A Park Near the Police Station

Caius was wearing a pair of shorts. He'd popped out for a light jog while Callie rested at home. He'd left her sitting on the sofa browsing the internet for home decor. They'd be going from a one-bed flat with an open-plan living area to a whole house, after all, and she had her work cut out getting the place to her exacting standards before the baby was born.

'I've missed your little running outfits,' Matt said, walking around him. 'You're not skipping leg day any more.'

'Be serious, Matt,' Caius said, rolling his eyes but secretly chuffed. He was nailing his kettlebell squats.

'Fine. I won't use your skinny calves as a little light relief on a long hard day.'

Caius knew his calves weren't skinny. He looked at Matt. Matt smirked back. 'Callie's being a bit funny about work following me home. Now everything has sunk in, Eulalia turning up like that has made her feel vulnerable.'

'I get that, especially with her history.'

'How's the case going?'

Matt caught him up to speed and Caius told him what Cecil/ DJ Sonikk had told him in the waiting area.

'Andy brought Isolde to the station. He stopped me after I'd finished with her to talk about your ancestors.'

'My ancestors?'

'He essentially said that two different generations hundreds of years apart had both decided to seal up what was under the priory. That at some point your family knew what was down there but hid it.'

'Hid what?'

'He didn't say, but Robbie just got a call from forensics at the site. They've discovered a tunnel.'

'I knew it.' Caius took out his phone to call his dad – he'd need him to pull off the next stage – but his father was calling him instead. 'Hey, old man.' He listened for a moment. 'Hang on, Dad, I'm with Matt. He'll want to hear this too. I'm putting you on speakerphone. Matt's here but not here, if you know what I mean.'

'I do. Matt, how are you doing?' Marcus asked.

'All right,' Matt said.

'What a case,' Marcus said.

'Dad, can you repeat what you just said for Matt?'

'Well according to my legal bloke, technically the Beauchamps own the land, so anything down that tunnel is ours unless it's a jewel or something over a certain value, and then it becomes the queen's.'

'What do you think is down there?' Matt asked. He wondered if Marcus knew more than he was letting on. 'Any rumours?'

'No idea, but Caius's replacement called yesterday about a skeletal human hand that had been locked in a basement for a hundred-odd years, so I'm guessing as it's an old priory that the tunnel probably leads to a crypt and a load of dead nuns.' Marcus took a breath. 'Your mum doesn't like this business.'

'I can't imagine she does. She's low-key terrified of nuns,' Caius said. It was typical of Bridget who also sort of loved nuns at the same time.

'My legal chap is talking to English Heritage. If it is a load of dead nuns, quite frankly I don't want the bother.'

'That's fair,' Matt said. He wouldn't want the hassle either. 'They'll get a team of archaeologists and stuff in, won't they? It'll be a documentary on BBC Four.'

'I'll gift the dead nuns to the nation,' Marcus said. 'Oh hang on, boys. I'm in the study and I've had an email. Where are my damn glasses. Old age is no fun, you two. Oh it's from your Robbie fella. He's asking me to come down to the site tomorrow at 10 a.m. They're going to use a little robot with a camera.'

Caius looked at Matt. 'I'll meet you there, Dad.'

'I'm glad you're taking an interest.'

Caius rolled his eyes. 'Dad, I need you to call that academic who emailed us about the priest holes and whatnot. Invite him down for his expert opinion.'

'Right, well I best do that now then.'

'Great.'

'How's Callie?'

'She's fine,' Caius said quickly. 'Bye.'

Once Caius had ended the call he turned to Matt. 'We're moving house.'

'I like your place but it's a bit of a bachelor pad. You moving into another of your dad's places?'

'Yeah, in Hertfordshire.'

'Hertfordshire?' Matt was taken aback. He thought it would take longer than that to convince Caius to go. 'Are you quitting?'

'No, not yet. I'm not quite finished with the police yet. The commute will be only an hour. That's not bad. Well, when everything's running on time.'

'You're such a grown-up.'

TUESDAY

52

Priory Square

Caius and Marcus were sitting in front of the feminist blob statue in memory of the mystic nun burnt at the stake.

'But why is it a blob?' Marcus asked.

'I don't know,' Caius said.

'What does a blob commemorate? Other blobs?'

'Coffee?' Caius handed his father a cup he'd purchased minutes before from The Purple Toad. They hadn't recognised him without a shirt and tie. 'Pistachio croissant?'

'Don't mind if I do,' Marcus said, helping himself to a pastry. 'Don't tell your mother. I'm supposed to be watching my sugar intake.'

'I wouldn't dare.'

'I found out about the engagement rings, by the way.'

'Oh yeah?'

Marcus showed him the pictures he'd been sent from someone in the family office. 'A few are valued too highly to actually wear.'

'I don't want Callie walking around with something too expensive. Women get mugged for their engagement rings more often than you'd think.'

'There's a nice ruby. Not too flashy but not embarrassingly small either. Your mother counsels against the emeralds because they're not strong enough for everyday wear, apparently.'

'The ruby is pretty. I think Callie would want something a bit more original than a diamond. The sapphire is more her style though. It's more ornate.'

'All right, let me know when with a week in advance and I'll get hold of it for you.'

'What are those?' Caius asked, looking at the three packets next to Marcus on the bench.

'Full face masks. They can cope with everything, including asbestos. One each for you, me and Matt in case they want us to crawl past any dead nuns.'

'You're really hung up on the nun thing, aren't you, Dad?'

'There's a bloody hand down there, Caius.'

'Ahem.' Caius and Marcus turned around to see Andy approaching their bench. His shirtsleeves were rolled up ready for action. He was wearing all-sandy-coloured clothing. Caius wondered if he'd been trying to channel Indiana Jones or if he was just boring.

Caius and Marcus both stood up. 'Andy, nice to see you again,' Caius said, shaking his hand. 'This is my father—'

'Sir Marcus. A pleasure,' Andy said.

'This is Professor Andrew Clifton,' Caius said to his father.

'The expert historian. You wanted to have a look at our priest holes, didn't you? Nice to meet you.'

'Yes, I suppose I am rather the expert on the Tudor era. I've written six articles about the history of these hundred acres as well, did you know?'

'Have you really? Tell me,' Marcus said, suppressing a smile. He still found it amusing to be called Sir Marcus and whenever it happened he wanted to laugh in the person's face. 'Is it going to be a lot of dead nuns down there?'

'Quite possibly.' Andy nodded his head in a measured fashion. 'Did I just overhear you say that human remains had already been recovered from the site?'

'Yes, a hand,' Caius said.

'Fascinating. Where was it?' Andy asked.

'It appears that Horatio Combe and his followers were using it during seances,' Caius said.

'How bizarre,' Andy said, shaking his head in disgust.

'That's the Victorians for you. Morbid people,' Marcus said, mildly appalled. 'I've never understood why they were so keen on taxidermy. Gives me the creeps. I once saw a load of dead kittens wearing bloomers having a tea party.'

'The kangaroo in the Institute is cross-eyed,' Caius said. He looked at Andy, seeing if he was going to react.

'Oh, really?' Andy asked nonchalantly.

Marcus's phone rang. 'Hello. Yes, we'll be there in just a moment.' He turned to Caius and Andy. 'That was that Robbie. They're ready for us.'

The three of them walked through the square and out in front of the Horatio Combe Institute.

Marcus looked up at it. 'It's letting the square down.'

'My thoughts exactly,' said a female voice from behind them.

'Miss Bourne,' Caius said, turning around and meeting her gaze. 'Good morning.'

'Hello, detective.' She sidled up to him and clutched him by the arm, turning him away from the others. 'Call me Margot. How's everything going?'

'I can't comment,' Caius said. She still had his arm, although she was no longer clutching it, rather patting his bicep.

'I guess that's the end of the museum then.'

'Perhaps,' Caius said. He gently removed her from his arm.

Andy coughed, trying to remind Caius that they had somewhere to be. He barely hid his contempt for Margot Bourne.

'Please excuse me, Margot,' Caius said, taking a step away from her. 'We have a prior engagement.'

'Of course,' she said, smiling sweetly as she walked back up the steps and into her house.

'Who was that?' Marcus asked, watching her go.

'The neighbour. She wanted to buy the Institute so she could extend.'

Andy let out an exasperated sound. 'Imagine what we could've lost.'

'Like what, professor?' Caius asked. Andy didn't reply, just let out another exaggerated sigh.

Matt and Amy came out of the Institute. They kept it cool and expressed all the expected pleasantries.

'Dad, have you met Amy before?'

'I have not, but I have heard good things about you. It's a pleasure.'

'Hi,' she said back. She waved at him with both hands.

'Good news, I guess,' Matt said, in front of them. 'Forensics are down there setting up the robot and another flagstone looked dodgy. There's a second tunnel.'

'A second choir of dead nuns?' Marcus asked.

'Maybe, but the little robot's really cool. There's not been any air down there for centuries so they don't want to suffocate anyone.'

'You were looking forward to crawling through there, weren't you, Dad?'

'I've got my crawling jeans on,' Marcus said.

'Marcus, Dr Clifton, do you want to follow me?' Amy said, taking them over to a van parked up on the kerb.

'Mel's pulled through,' Matt said quietly. 'She will need to go through a fair bit of rehab to get moving again. Jen's been sectioned. I've checked the security footage from their house – as expected.'

'Right,' Caius said, glad that it hadn't ended as badly as it could have. 'Have you seen that the label has been taking a lot of flak in the press? DJ Sonikk did another interview.'

'All good?' Matt looked over at Marcus who was standing with Amy and Andy staring at a screen in the back of a van.

'Yeah, the plan's working so far.'

'Kid, they've found nuns,' Marcus yelled across at them. 'Dead ones.'

Caius and Matt came over and they watched as the little robot shone a light on the crypt. It was cavernous. Skeletal remains were piled high on stone shelves. Body on top of body on top of body. Every turn the little robot took, another skull came into view.

'Wow, just wow,' Andy said. He was ecstatic. 'They're recording this footage, right? It's a time capsule of late-medieval English ecclesiastical burial practices.'

'That's a mouthful, isn't it, Amy?' Marcus said, smiling at her. Marcus turned to look at Caius and shivered, mouthing the words 'too many nuns'.

The little robot was brought back out the tunnel. Caius and Marcus finished their coffees. Robbie came out and chatted to Andy who had practically melted into an incoherent puddle of enthusiasm. The little robot entered the second tunnel. It was longer than the first one. They all watched on screen.

'What is all that?' Amy asked, peering at a painting. 'The worms. That drawing is, what, a snake?'

'It's the snake in the Garden of Eden. That's what Horatio meant in his journal,' Andy said. He looked at Marcus.

'Right,' Caius said, giving Matt the look.

'Your family were Recusants.' Andy was hitting his stride. He'd clearly been working on a pitch to present to Marcus when the time was right. 'Your house is riddled with priest hides. They essentially buried all the religious artefacts from the priory before it could be destroyed by Puritan bullyboys and knocked down the priory to protect them.'

'That's a statue of Saint Agnes. She's got a lamb,' Caius said. Everyone looked at him. 'Catholic school.'

'They saved a treasure trove,' Andy said, watching the screen. 'There are books. God, there are books. What if there's a copy of Alice de Burge's text. We've only got snippets quoted by others. This is a major find. Major. The British Library are going to go insane.'

Marcus looked at Caius. 'The bloody queen is going to swoop in, isn't she?'

'Does it matter? There was no way Mum would've let any of this be kept,' Caius said.

'All right, I'll call English Heritage. I'll sign whatever paperwork. I don't want the bad juju. This belongs to the nation. We can deal with it as a collective. Spread it around like the national debt. We won't notice it that way. One stubbed toe for each of us.'

Amy's phone rang. She stepped aside. Matt and Caius were watching her as everyone else continued watching the screen. She ended the call. 'Robbie, can I borrow you for a second?'

'Sure.' Robbie stepped away and Matt followed him. Caius held back, still listening, of course, but he didn't want to upset Robbie. It was his investigation now, after all.

'Hi,' Willow said, behind Caius.

'Hello,' Caius said, turning around. Her timing was immaculate.

'I got a call from DC Noakes that they'd found a brooch of mine in the Institute. It must have fallen off when I was working. She said I should come and retrieve it?'

'Robbie,' Caius said, looking at Willow. She was blushing as she talked to him. 'You'll have to speak to DI Eastley over there.'

'Oh, um. Good morning, Willow,' Andy said. Caius watched him fumble.

'Hi, professor,' she said over her shoulder as she approached the three detectives. They all watched her as she innocently approached Robbie. 'You called me about my brooch? Can I get it?'

'Yes,' Amy said.

'What's your dissertation on, Willow?' Matt asked.

She stood looking at him, frozen on the spot. 'The Hundred Years War.'

'Is it?' Amy asked. 'I thought it was a feminist history of herbal remedies used in England between 1300 and 1500? That's what you said on an Instagram post three months ago.'

'What's going on?' Marcus asked.

'They're sleeping together,' Caius said, pointing at Willow and Andy.

'What?' Andy said, shocked.

'Runner,' Amy yelled as she shot after Willow who had turned away ready to sprint. She didn't get far.

'Willow Bell, I am arresting you for the murders of Digby Combe-Watson and Scott Brown.' Robbie stood over the twenty-year-old. 'You do not have to say anything . . .'

'I think you'd better come to the station with me,' Matt said, directing Andy towards a police car.

Amy watched from the kerb as Andy and Willow were led away. She turned to Caius once Robbie and Willow's car had left.

'Forensics found the paper cup late last night with Scott's address on from the rubbish we collected from the bakery. It had Willow's prints on it,' Amy said. She patted Caius on the shoulder. 'I'm sure she'll say she did it for love.'

'Undoubtedly,' Caius said.

'Bye, Caius's dad,' Amy said to Marcus.

'You're quick, aren't you?' Marcus was impressed.

'I am,' Amy said.

'Girl power.' Marcus pulled a 'peace' sign. 'See you later, love.'

Amy jumped into the front of Matt's police car.

Caius and his father were left watching the little robot on the pavement outside the Institute with forensics. Marcus quickly called his legal team and told them to call English Heritage and promise that whatever was down there was the nation's problem and not his. Father and son walked slowly towards the tube together.

'Is that a normal day for you?' Marcus asked as they turned down a leafy road towards the high road.

'No. There's a lot more paperwork usually.'

'You are your mother's son. You really are. Asking the rudest questions.'

'I caught a murderer or two.'

'Amy technically caught her. She was bloody fast,' Marcus said, dodging dog shit on the pavement. 'This city. It's cow pats I have to avoid now.'

'Callie was looking at kitchens online when I left this morning.'

'Tell her to let me know what she wants.' Marcus stopped under a London plane. He couldn't get over what had just happened or how blasé his son was being about it. 'What was that all about?'

Caius looked over his shoulder – no one was on the street. 'That historian, he's seeing the girl.'

'The young one.'

'Yeah, his student. He left his girlfriend of ten years for her. I suppose he feels bad about it so he's still on friendly terms with his ex. Pet sitting. Spare keys for emergencies. Probably didn't tell her he was shagging his tutee when he broke it off.'

'Right.'

'Willow, the kid, interns at the Institute and she knows a few things. Willow knows about the history of the site because her historian boyfriend is the authority on it and has told her about the rumours that our ancestors covered something up down there. Willow knows Digby her boss is going to sell the Institute, possibly to his neighbour Margot Bourne – the woman who grabbed my arm. Margot made a formal offer for the property but I bet she popped in first to talk about it. Willow knows that Margot wants to dig into the basement which might destroy anything of historical significance that her lover would die to see. He might be desperate enough that he'll forget his perfect ex who he keeps slipping in little details about into conversation. Willow is transcribing the crazed diaries of her boss's ancestor who describes going into tunnels and doing seances in the basement, so she knows there's something of historical importance down there. My guess is that the night he died he tried to talk Digby out of selling the Institute but he wouldn't listen. He wanted the cash from the sale and his own life.'

'What a stupid reason to kill someone.' Caius stopped walking. Two grannies were talking further along the pavement and he didn't want them to overhear. He shouldn't be telling his dad anyway.

'It was a complicated method too. My guess is that Willow spiked his salad before his 'date' that she'd set up. She had popped in early that afternoon to pick up a book she'd "forgotten". I think Andy went to the Institute to try and talk to Digby who'd ignored his letter previously via the back garden that night. There are no cameras down the alleyway and Digby leaves his bike out there so it's unlocked. He would've removed the poisoned salad if Digby had agreed to having the site excavated. Digby was supposed to be on a date with a woman with the same name and many of the same attributes as the historian's sainted ex who wasn't ever going to show. Willow knew that her boss was putting a lonely-hearts ad in the *LRB* so she responded. She probably proofread the ad for the poor guy. Willow's worried Andy will go back to her so she frames Isolde almost as a warning.'

'How you get them is how you lose them.'

'She knows Andy has Isolde's house key still and I bet their calendars on their phones were still synced, so she pops over when she knows Isolde is out. Willow created a fake profile for Isolde on the fanfic site and uploads all these smutty and info-laden stories. Two birds, one stone.'

'All of that effort over that historian? He wasn't even that good-looking.'

'One of them killed a guy who worked at a coffee shop who she used to deliver the letters to her boss. Stabbed him in the hallway and fled. Matt will have to get a confession out of them.'

'That's callous.'

'They're on a roll.' Caius was in love, deeply, but he still couldn't fathom the steps that Willow went through to keep a mediocre academic. 'They start searching the basements of the other cult members in case the tunnels lead from their basements. If that's not enough, Willow also had us looking at a vulnerable young woman, after befriending her to search her basement, who also lived on the square, after introducing her to the fake fanfic account. I think Andy was really pissed off with Willow that she roped Isolde into the whole mess, hence why she had to start incriminating Jen. Willow used Jen's laptop when she visited once to buy the PO Box too, probably while she was in the loo or something.

She posted a missing diary, a vital piece of evidence, to her disguised as a fan letter so we'd find it at her house.'

'Just come work for me, OK?'

'One day.'

'One day soon. I'm going into the office now for meetings, if you want to shadow me.'

'I'm going to go back to Callie.'

'Good idea.'

'I didn't tell you any of that.'

'It doesn't matter; I didn't understand half of what you said. See you later, son. Be safe.' Marcus patted him on the back before dashing into the tube station.

★ ★ ★

'I killed the creepy boy,' Andy said. Robbie and Matt just looked at him. Andy was a blubbering mess and willing to give it all up. 'I had to. He was a liability. Willow gave me his address and I stabbed him.'

'Where?'

'In the neck.'

'Right,' Robbie said.

'Issy had nothing to do with any of this. Nothing at all.' He stopped, and corrected his posture. He stared imperiously down his nose at the dilettante policeman in front of him. 'It was worth it. Imagine if what we saw today had been destroyed.'

'The break-ins?' Matt asked.

'That was me.'

'The guy who fell and impaled himself on the fence post?'

Andy paused. 'He chased me out. My presence spooked him and he fell. It was an accident.'

'And the salad?' Robbie asked.

'I-I—' Andy fell silent. There was no logical way for him to lie that he'd poisoned it.

'Or did Willow spike it when she popped in that afternoon? She knew that "Isolde" wasn't turning up. She also knew that Digby would eat it anyway rather than throw it out because he's tight.' Robbie looked at Andy. Andy looked at the table.

'That made you angry, didn't it? That Willow had used your ex as inspiration for a red herring. Did she include all the stuff you used to mention about Isolde? What I want to know is, were you always going to kill Digby? Was that the plan all along? Or did Willow take inspiration from her studies when Digby refused to listen to you that evening? We have the letter you sent, asking for an interview. I take it he ignored you, so she took matters into her own hands to get you access to the Institute. She probably thought you'd be as persuasive with Digby as you had been to get into her student knickers.'

★   ★   ★

'Willow's refusing to talk,' Amy said to Matt and Robbie as they stood outside the rooms they were being interviewed in separately.

'Not surprising,' Robbie said.

'She did it all,' Matt said. 'Andy's confessed to Scott's death and to being there for Jimmy's out of guilt, but none of the causes of death were accurate. He knew about the deaths though. He's trying to take the blame for her.'

'He thinks he's being noble,' Amy said.

'He's a historian. He thinks he's above the fray,' Matt said.

'Doesn't matter really, now we've confirmed that the partial fingerprints at the Institute are his,' Robbie said, shrugging. 'The CPS will decide what to charge him with, but she is definitely getting two accounts of murder and one of manslaughter. She won't see daylight until she's in her sixties.'

53

Caius and Callie's Flat

Caius had gone back to The Purple Toad Bakery and bought six more pistachio croissants. Callie had been craving them. He thought the extras might survive the freezer.

'Hullo,' he called as he entered the flat. Caius could hear her throwing up in the bathroom. He boiled the kettle and got a fresh cup out of the cupboard, placing a lemon and ginger teabag in it. He put a croissant on a plate, setting it down on the coffee table next to some fabric swatches. He wasn't sure if they were a remnant of the defunct Eulalia project or were for the new house.

Callie came out of the bathroom and flopped onto the sofa. 'I was finally sick.'

'I heard, you poor thing.' The kettle boiled and he poured the water into the cup.

'You look really hot. You need to know that.'

'Thanks, babe.' Caius placed the tea on the coffee table and sat down next to her. Callie fell into his lap and he stroked her hair. 'How's my girl doing?'

'Meh, but thank you for the croissant.' Callie didn't quite feel like eating it yet – she was just going to stare at it longingly for a while, or until that made her feel nauseous too.

'Anything for you,' Caius said. Callie sat up and he put his arm around her. 'I've got an update on Jen. Do you want to know?'

'No. Yes. No.' Callie reached for the fabric on the table. She rubbed it between her fingers. 'I heard from Venetia, the girl I was at uni with who was there at that meeting. We're going to go for a survivors' lunch next week. The deal's off with PCQV, obviously. Everyone at the record label is panicking because they're not sure how much they knew, if that makes sense.'

'They're definitely morally culpable if not legally. They're going to get crucified in the press when it all fully comes out. Talking about crucifixions.' Caius took his phone out and showed Callie some of the stills from the footage of the little robot's second journey. 'My ancestors hid all these religious artefacts during the Reformation. Dad's giving it to the nation if he can.'

'Were there any skeletons in the end?'

'Yeah, hundreds of them. I've never heard the words "dead nun" spoken so many times.'

'I really would've been a terrible nun.'

'You're too earthly.'

'Earthly?'

'You like pleasure too much. Pinot Grigio, pistachio croissants and getting railed.'

'None of that. That's what got us into this mess.' Callie stuck her tongue out.

'What can I say.' For a second Caius wondered if she was having second thoughts.

'You smell really good.' Callie picked a letter up off the coffee table. 'We've had the date for the twelve-week scan come through.'

'I'll book time off,' Caius said, kissing her on the forehead. He got up off the sofa and went to peg the washing out on the line.

SIX WEEKS LATER

54

The Whittington Hospital

Their appointment for their twelve-week scan was ten minutes ago, and Caius was watching the waiting room clock anxiously. He reached into his pocket and started playing with the ring box he had there. He had booked dinner for later that evening at the Italian restaurant they'd tried to go to on their first date. Caius pulled his hand out of his pocket. He didn't want to lose the ring or break it or something stupid. Callie was looking at a sofa on her phone. The new living room was much larger than their old one, and Caius's old utilitarian, grey IKEA sofa with storage under the chaise end would have looked odd in a Georgian house.

'Blue or green stripes?'

'Blue,' Caius said.

'Really?' She sounded mystified as to why he chose that colourway.

'Green then.'

'I think I like the green more.'

'All right.' Caius laughed. He wasn't sure why she had bothered to ask him. She could pick any sofa she wanted as long as it wasn't woven out of gold. Although at the moment he might be persuaded to buy her anything she damn well wanted.

'Is that a bit cliché though? You know, the millennial green sofa.'

'Who cares? It's us who has to look at it, and more importantly sit on it.'

'Fair point.' Callie put her phone away. She squeezed Caius's free hand. 'Is it stupid to have a theme for the nursery?'

'No.' Caius didn't think it was stupid at all. 'What are you thinking?'

'Woodland animals. That room looks out over the woods and I thought it would be cute to have squirrels and acorns and little foxes, because we'll probably see them all the time when we go for walks.'

'Oh squirrels. That's adorable.'

'Foster, Callie-o-pe, Cal-e-op?' asked a nurse.

'That's me,' Callie said, standing up. She shot Caius a look. No one ever knew how to pronounce her name.

They followed the nurse into a room, where the consultant greeted them both. He got Callie to lie down and applied jelly to her stomach. Callie made small talk with the nurse, who had admired her hand-embroidered trench coat while the consultant moved the ultrasound wand across her abdomen. The room went silent. Caius, who had delivered enough bad news himself, knew what the consultant's sharp intake of breath meant. The bottom fell out of his stomach as he braced himself.

The consultant tried a different angle. Another breath.

'I'm very sorry, Miss Foster. There's no heartbeat.'

Callie nodded. She wanted to cry but there was nothing. The void where a tiny possibility had been a moment before had hollowed her out. Caius squeezed her hand.

'You've had what's called a missed miscarriage. The foetus stopped growing at nine weeks but your body still thinks you're pregnant.' He waited a moment for those details to sink in. 'You have a few different options: wait for the pregnancy hormones to drop and let nature take its course; we can give you medication to speed up the process; or there's the surgical option.'

'I . . .' Callie began to cry at last.

'You don't need to decide right now.'

Caius took a leaflet from the nurse.

'Why?' Callie whispered.

The consultant slowly shook his head. 'I don't know. Usually there's a genetic problem with the foetus which makes it incompatible with life. Sometimes it just happens.'

★　★　★

They'd sat in the back of the taxi in silence. Caius had wanted to talk but Callie hadn't. She'd just stared out of the window as they drove through Archway. They were at home now. Callie had changed into a nighty and was curled up on the sofa under a blanket watching some reality TV show about estate agents. Caius was staring down at his phone. He needed to feel that the world was going to Hell and not just him so he'd opened the *Guardian* app. He was reading about yet another school shooting in the US when his scrolling was interrupted by an ad for baby clothes. He'd been browsing online the other day. He put the phone down. Disassociating was only going to make this worse.

'Cup of tea?' Caius put the kettle on and went over to the fridge.

'Yes, please.' Callie sat up. 'I'm sorry.'

Caius put the milk down on the counter and went over to her on the sofa.

'There's nothing to be sorry about.' He grasped her hand. 'You haven't done anything wrong.'

'But . . .' Callie couldn't look at him. She stared at her hands instead. She'd placed them on her tummy instinctively but now recoiled at the action.

'No, it's not your fault.' He put his arm around her as she cried. 'It just is what it is.'

'What if we can't, what if I can't . . .'

'That leaflet the doctor gave us says that it can happen to any woman. They're really common.' Caius thought it was awful to take refuge in statistics. 'Ten to twenty per cent of pregnancies. Most are a one-off.'

'But what if it's not a one-off. What if I can't have children.'

'That doesn't matter.' It really didn't.

'But it does. Your family . . .'

'I want to be with you whether we ever have children or not. I don't care whether I have an heir. The National Trust can have the lot.'

'Do you want to try again?'

'At some point. But not right now. You need to recover, and we need to move into our dream house first.'

'You've got a lot of painting to do.'

'Exactly. I'll be too tired to do anything else. You'll have me up and down a ladder.'

'I love you.'

'I love you too.' Caius picked up the remote and put on *A Knight's Tale*. It was one of Callie's favourites and they needed something to distract them. They lay on the sofa together watching the film.

'Is it based on Chaucer?' Caius asked. He'd never seen it.

'Yeah, I guess. It's fun though.'

'There's no Old English in it?' Caius had a copy of *The Canterbury Tales*, but it was in the original and there were so many stray vowels he couldn't understand it.

'No, but there's Queen.'

'Which queen?'

'Freddie Mercury.'

★　★　★

Caius ordered a pizza. He went to collect it to get a bit of fresh air. He didn't want to look too disappointed in front of Callie lest it make her feel guilty again. He phoned his mum.

'How was the hospital?' Bridget asked. She knew something was up. He'd have sent her pictures of the scan otherwise.

'Callie's had what they call a missed miscarriage,' Caius said. He'd been dreading calling her.

'Oh, the poor thing. That must have been a terrible shock.'

'Yeah.' It was devastating. He hadn't even considered it as a possibility before. He wanted to cry but there was a group of teenagers across the road. 'Mum, I feel really shit. I was so excited. The day I met Callie I was like, you're the one. You're it. And everything has progressed exactly as I would've wanted it to, and yeah the baby was unplanned but it would have been perfect.'

'I know, honey. You were both so excited.' Bridget paused. 'I had a miscarriage after I had you.'

'Did you?' Caius wished he'd known that before.

'Yeah. It was awful. I was in bits for months afterwards.'

'How did you get over it?'

'Time helps.'

'I'm not going to propose tonight.'

'That's for the best. You can take your time a bit more now.'

'I've got to go, Mum. I'm collecting a pizza.'

'Take care, love. Call me if you need to talk or anything else. Callie too. Tell her she can call me. I understand.'

'Thanks.' Caius ended the call. He had reached the bottom of their road when a car with blacked-out windows pulled up beside him.

The window wound down. 'Jump in,' came a familiar voice.

'No,' Caius said to Arthur Hampton – former Cabinet minister, the late Rupert's father and patrician schemer who liked to manipulate Caius into investigating politically expedient cases. Caius walked away towards the high street. He wanted to run – his fight or flight response had kicked in.

The car pulled over next to him.

'I don't want to have this conversation with you on the street for anyone to hear.'

'I don't want to have a conversation.'

'Yes you do.'

'No. I do not want to spend my life being manipulated into aiding whatever shadowy plot to take down the government you've come up with this time.'

'How about being the government instead.'

'What?' Caius froze.

Hampton stepped out of the car. 'The post-World War II order is about to collapse. We're in the dawn of a new age. You follow the news – you can see what's going on with Russia, with America. China in the wings. AI. You're meant for more and this is our only chance.'

'Chance for what?'

'For England to survive.'

'Are you high?'

'I've not touched a thing since 1997.' Hampton sighed. 'Call Hunderby. There's a safe seat for you.'

'No.'

'Look, my old mob somehow look like they've made it through their leadership change and are clinging on. This Parliament has only two more years left and then real change can be made.'

'Real change? You were in that government until very recently.'

'I'm a pragmatist. I have no loyalty to party, only my country. I put the things I needed to in place.'

'Out for yourself more like it. How much money have you made from Help For Hippos? How much ecstasy did you legally sell because you changed the law?'

'That was necessary, and practical. Drug deaths have plummeted. Tourism is up. Who cares if I made a little from it? It's taxed quite heavily. Taxation and regulation.' Hampton smiled; he was enjoying this debate. 'You're too bright to be a policeman forever – politics seems like a natural fit for you. You studied it at university. You interned in Brussels. If it wasn't for what happened to your sister—'

'A tragedy that you exploited. You gave me hope that I'd be able to find out what happened with that stupid special unit.'

'I can see that you're angry.'

'Yes, I fucking am. I've had one of the worst days of my life, and then you showed up and made it worse.'

'I'm sorry that you're having a bad day.'

Caius stared at the ground. 'A bad day' was one way to describe what had happened. 'I don't want to hear about whatever Anglo-Norman paternalistic revival you're planning because you think that the US is on the verge of tyrannical collapse and Russia and China are howling at the gate. I don't care if you think you can save the country from the inevitable post-capitalist, fascist, climate-emergency, AI-driven, neo-feudalistic world. This is the *Mad Max* timeline. It keeps me up at night, but you know why I don't want to hear about it any more? Because I don't think you can do anything. No one even wants to build windfarms. They don't even think climate change is real. We're all just fucked.' Caius stared at Hampton who nodded. 'Excuse me, I have a pizza to collect.'

'We're not fucked. You know that. There's always one last hope,' Hampton called after him. Caius fought every fibre of his being not to flip him the bird over his shoulder. Hampton got back into the car.

'That's your chap, is it?' asked the woman next to him.

'He's very good. He'll come around.' Hampton pushed a little bile that had risen up his throat back down to his stomach. 'We need people like him. He's the right sort.'